TRIPWIRE

A SAINT SQUAD NOVEL

OTHER BOOKS AND AUDIO BOOKS
BY TRACI HUNTER ABRAMSON

UNDERCURRENTS SERIES

Undercurrents

Ripple Effect

The Deep End

ROYAL SERIES

Royal Target

Royal Secrets

Royal Brides

SAINT SQUAD SERIES

Freefall

Lockdown

Crossfire

Backlash

Smoke Screen

Code Word

Lock and Key

Drop Zone

Spotlight

Tripwire

GUARDIAN SERIES

Failsafe

Safe House

STAND-ALONES

Obsession

Deep Cover

Chances Are

Chance for Home

Kept Secrets

Twisted Fate

TRIPWIRE

A SAINT SQUAD NOVEL

TRACI HUNTER
ABRAMSON

Covenant Communications, Inc.

Covenant

Cover image: *Beautiful White Modern Yachts at Sea Port in Montenegro* © Elen11. *Woman Profile* © lekcej. *Programming Code Abstract Technology Background of Software Deve* © monsitj. *Bearded Man Portrait Close-Up Blue Eyes* © cloverphoto.

Cover design copyright © 2018 by Covenant Communications, Inc.

Published by Covenant Communications, Inc.
American Fork, Utah

Printed in the United States of America
First Printing: April 2018

24 23 22 21 20 19 18   10 9 8 7 6 5 4 3 2 1

ISBN: 978-52440-535-9

For Lara

SEAL TEAM 8

COMMANDING OFFICER

KEL BENNETT

& Marilyn
Backlash

SAINT SQUAD COMMANDING OFFICER

BRENT MILLER

& Amy Whitmore
Freefall

TRISTAN CROWTHER	SETH JOHNSON	QUINN LAMBERT

& Riley Palmetta   & Vanessa Lauton   & Taylor Palmetta
Lockdown   *Crossfire*   *Smoke Screen*

JAY WELLMAN	DAMIAN SCHMITT	CRAIG SIMMONS

& Carina Channing   & Paige Vickers   & Sienna Blake
Lock and Key   *Drop Zone*   *Spotlight*
                                                Tripwire

ACKNOWLEDGMENTS

Thank you to my amazing editor, Samantha Millburn, for your insight and support as you navigate each project through the publication process. I also want to thank the rest of the Covenant family for the many milestones you've helped me reach, especially Kathy Jenkins and Stephanie Lacey.

Thanks to Paige Edwards, Kanani Cox, and Tiffany Hunter for your proofing and editing abilities, and my continued appreciation to my critique group: Ellie Whitney, Paige Edwards, Jen Leigh, and Valerie Burgoyne for helping me find the story.

Also, thanks to Rosie and Miguel Bella for giving me the inspiration for gifting frozen tamales. Yum!

Thank you to my family for your continued support, especially Jon, Gabe, and Luke, who are so adept at fending for themselves when I disappear into my fictional world, and Diana, Christina and Lara for helping me name my characters.. I also want to express my appreciation to the Central Intelligence Agency Publication Review Board for taking sometimes challenging deadlines and making them work.

Finally, thanks to the readers who have helped the Saint Squad come to life and for expressing your desire that they not retire anytime soon.

1

CRAIG GRIPPED HIS WEAPON AND made his way silently forward through the woods surrounding the target area. He and his teammates had arrived on board the aircraft carrier USS *Ronald Reagan* only six hours before they had taken a helicopter to the Turkish border of Abolstan.

Though desert landscape made up most of this country known for harboring anti-American extremists, the area near the ocean boasted several thousand acres of thick forest. The trees gave the seven-man squad of Navy SEALs the perfect cover to infiltrate the enemy camp without being seen. Unfortunately, it would offer their enemies similar protection.

Craig's eyes swept the landscape, his ears in tune for anything out of place as they made their way on foot toward the suspected terrorist hideout. Ahead of him, Tristan's hand came up signaling everyone to stop. When Tristan leaned down, the movement confirmed his teammate had found a booby trap.

They started forward again. Craig took only a half dozen steps before he noticed a faint impression of human presence, the remnant of a footprint in the decaying leaves. Squatting, he studied the area more closely, now able to see the nearly invisible tripwire running beneath the thick underbrush.

Craig signaled the threat to his commanding officer. Brent acknowledged the danger and signaled for the rest of the squad to wait while Craig dealt with the problem. Slowly, methodically, the seven men continued toward their objective, alternating between bypassing and disarming the dozen explosive devices scattered along the way.

After thirty minutes of progress, they reached a small clearing and studied the rudimentary structure built from a combination of wood and mud situated in the center.

Tire tracks created deep ruts in the path between the structure and the dirt road leading away from it, but no vehicles were in sight.

Craig listened intently, alert for any sign of life. The absence of light from the windows and the lack of vehicles heightened his suspicions. Either their targets had already cleared out or this was a trap.

Brent's voice came over his communication headset. "Jay, do you see any heat signatures?"

"Negative."

"It looks like someone has been here recently, based on the footprints in the forest," Craig offered.

"Makes me wonder if someone tipped them off." Brent signaled Craig and Damian to check the area by the front of the structure, and he dispersed the rest of the team to secure the surrounding area.

As their teammates disappeared into the darkness, Craig and Damian traversed the twenty-five yards of open ground between the trees and the house. A tightness bloomed in Craig's chest, increasing with each step.

"Does it seem odd to you that we found so many booby traps in the woods, and yet there isn't any evidence of extra security here where they were staying?" Craig asked.

Damian inspected the front door. "No sign of explosives or alarms."

"Check the window." Craig motioned toward the one on the left, while he took the one on the right.

"Nothing."

"This doesn't make any sense."

"Let's check the perimeter before we try to enter," Damian suggested. He started around the side of the house, and Craig followed. Two more windows and a back door revealed nothing except the appearance of safe passage. Craig's reservations doubled.

Brent's voice came over the headset. "Status?"

"All entry points appear safe," Craig reported. "Looks a little too easy to me."

"Heading your way." A moment later, Brent appeared at the front corner where Craig and Damian continued to scrutinize the structure. "You didn't find any security measures?"

"Nothing," Craig confirmed.

"Something's not right."

"That's what he said." Damian pointed to Craig.

"The woods are filled with tripwires. I can't believe they wouldn't at least have alarms on the doors and windows. Unless . . ."

"Unless they want us to go inside," Craig finished for him.

Brent looked around the area. "I have an idea. Come on."

Ten minutes later, Craig stood at the edge of the clearing, flashlight in hand. He spoke to the man next to him. "Quinn, are you ready?"

Quinn's response was immediate. "Now."

Craig aimed his flashlight at the front door, his beam joined by Damian's. A moment later, Quinn took aim and shot a single bullet into the lock on the front door.

The whistle of the bullet was immediately lost beneath the booming sound of the ensuing explosion. Glass shattered, the ground rocked, and flames speared through what had once been doors and windows.

The Saint Squad instantly dove for cover. The ground shook with a second explosion, and Craig could hear fragments of the house impacting the nearby trees.

The smell of burning wood overwhelmed his senses, the smoke causing his eyes to sting. Several minutes passed before Brent signaled for them to split up and check the area once more.

The concern that some of Elazar's men were lying in wait proved to be unfounded. They all gathered at the edge of the smoldering fire, where the house had once stood.

Tristan was the first to speak, his lazy Texan drawl making the scene that much more surreal. "I think it's safe to say Elazar and his crew aren't here."

"You think?" Quinn asked.

Brent stared at the fire for a moment before his gaze returned to them. "The question is, where are they now?"

2

JANE SMILED FOR THE CAMERA, even though her insides were a jumble of nerves. She must be crazy to have agreed to this move. Leaving California, moving across the country, all while knowing her mother was still recovering from cancer treatments. What was she thinking?

The roar of a jet engine sounded, for a moment overshadowing the traffic outside the airport. Her mother waited for two other travelers to pass them on the sidewalk before she handed Sienna's cell phone back to her. "Tell me what you think."

Sienna stepped beside her to view the images. "These are great, Mrs. Napierski." Sienna shifted her attention to Jane. "I think we should use some of these when we do our big media blitz the beginning of October."

"You don't need pictures of me blasted all over the internet," Jane said with a shake of her head, her blonde hair catching in the faint breeze.

"Oh, come on, Jane. You're part of this adventure. A new chapter in my career, a new life for both of us." Sienna gave her arm a squeeze. "It'll be great."

"You're the boss."

"That sounds so weird." Sienna wrinkled her nose.

"I've been working for you for three years. I would think you'd be used to it by now."

Sienna seemed to consider that for a moment. "Nope. Still not used to it."

Jane couldn't help but laugh. Sienna Blake was one of the most well-known actresses in the US, yet the woman acted so blessedly normal that at times even Jane forgot they were employer/employee rather than best friends.

"Seriously," Sienna continued. "Can you upload those photos for me?"

"I'll upload them, and you can do what you want with them," Jane said. "You can bet that I won't be the one putting them online though."

"I know." Sienna lowered her voice and added, "But you'll help me do it."

Jane's mom moved forward and gave Jane a hug. "You two had better get going, or you're going to miss your flight."

Emotions clogged Jane's throat, and she tried to swallow them. "You take care of yourself."

"You know I will. Text me when you get to Virginia Beach."

"I will. Love you." Jane stepped from her mother's embrace and grabbed the handle of her suitcase. She started to turn toward the door, but her motion stopped abruptly when a dark-haired man bumped into her and caused her to stumble back several steps. Her suitcase fell onto its side, and her cell phone dropped to the ground.

Before Jane could blink twice, Sienna's bodyguard, George, was at her side with her phone in one hand and the handle of her suitcase gripped in the other. "Are you okay?"

"Yeah." She glanced around to see who had bumped into her, but the guilty party had already been swallowed up by the sea of bodies heading in and out of the airport.

"Are you sure you're okay?" Sienna asked, shifting so Jane was between her and George.

"Yeah." Jane glanced at her mom to ensure she had escaped harm. Giving her one more quick hug, she took a deep breath and headed for the airport doors and the new adventure that lay beyond them.

* * *

"What were you doing back there?" Abdul whispered in Arabic. "You're supposed to be blending in."

"That woman took a photo of us," Jamal Elazar said in a hushed tone.

"What?" Alarmed, he turned to see the two women who appeared to be in their early twenties.

"The blonde has a picture on her phone with us in the background. If anyone knows we're together, the entire US government will be looking for us."

The truth of Jamal's statement sent another spurt of trepidation through him. Logic surfaced, and Abdul forced calm into his voice. "Who would notice? Even if she puts it on social media, the likelihood of someone seeing it who would recognize us is slim at best."

"Don't you know who that is?"

Abdul glanced over his shoulder at the two women again. The brunette wore sunglasses and a ball cap, her ponytail feeding through the back of it. The blonde's hair fell several inches past her shoulders, a light dusting of freckles sprinkled across her nose. "I don't recognize either of them. Should I?"

"The brunette is Sienna Blake." At Abdul's confused expression, Jamal said, "The actress? Daughter of Sterling Blake, one of the most famous men in the world?"

"They don't appear to be looking for attention. Maybe the image won't be shared."

"I overheard them talking. Sienna mentioned using today's photos as part of a publicity campaign in October," Jamal said.

"When in October?"

"I don't know. She said the beginning."

"We have to stop her."

"By any means necessary."

Understanding reflected in Abdul's dark eyes. "Do you know where they're heading?"

"Virginia Beach."

"Find out what gate they're flying out of. Maybe we can snatch the phone before they board."

"What if we can't?"

"Then we'll be paying those women a visit during our time in DC." Abdul's expression darkened. "We did talk about testing out our new detonators."

"Yes, we did."

* * *

The limousine rolled to a stop, and Reed looked outside at his audience. Today he wasn't performing for his director. Instead, the paparazzi would be the recipient of his acting talents.

The driver glanced in his rearview mirror. "Are you ready, sir?"

"Let's wait another minute, Timmons."

"Yes, sir."

Reed drew out his cell phone and texted Sienna Blake, the costar in his new television series. *I'm here. Tell me when you're ready.*

The response came less than a minute later. *Coming out now.*

"Okay, Timmons. It's showtime." Though normally he was more than happy to open his own door, today Reed waited for the driver to circle around and take care of the task for him.

The scene now set, Reed stepped out of the limo. A few photographers glanced his way, but none of them lifted their cameras.

He wasn't surprised by the lack of attention. After all, his main role as an actor so far had been in a sci-fi television series in which the studio's makeup artist had made him unrecognizable. His short dark hair and blue eyes were the only features he had in common with his former character, and they were rarely enough for anyone to make the connection.

He had enjoyed flying below the radar as he'd adjusted to his new lifestyle as one of Hollywood's up-and-coming stars. His lead role in this new TV drama had the potential of bringing his fame to a new level.

Playing opposite his childhood friend had made the new job a true delight. Pretending to date Sienna was about to bring both of them and their show heavily into the spotlight.

Reed caught a glimpse of Sienna heading toward him, a single suitcase rolling behind her. He timed his forward progress so he reached the door the moment she stepped outside.

"Hey there." Reed leaned in and kissed her cheek. "How was your flight?"

The question wasn't even complete before the paparazzi sprang into motion. The half-dozen photographers jockeyed for position, and every camera aimed. As an actress, Sienna had made a name for herself, but in truth, as the daughter of one of the most well-known actors in Hollywood, Sienna had been born famous.

"Who's the new boyfriend?" one of the reporters asked.

"How long have you been together?"

"What happened to your military guy? When did you break up?"

Reed nearly laughed out loud. Sienna had been correct about the result of her arrival, right down to the questions asked. Adopting the role of protective boyfriend, he slipped his arm around her shoulders and guided her the first few steps toward the limo.

As expected, photographers moved into their path in their quest for more photos. The questions repeated.

Sienna looked at Reed apologetically. "Sorry, honey. I guess we're not a secret anymore."

"What's your name?" a balding man in his late thirties asked, snapping another photo.

"Reed Forrester."

"How did you two meet?"

This time Sienna answered. "Reed is my costar on our new television series *Beachfront*."

"When did you and your last boyfriend break up?" a dark-haired man called out. "Will you tell us his name now?"

"I will always be grateful for the time I spent with him, but as I'm sure you can imagine, a military career isn't very compatible with my schedule," Sienna said. "I do wish him the best for his future."

"If you'll excuse us, we have an early call time tomorrow." Reed guided Sienna through the crowd to where Timmons held the limo door open.

"Just one more photo," someone shouted.

Sienna pressed her hand into Reed's back, a silent signal for them to grant the request. They both turned and smiled for the cameras before climbing into the back of the limo.

"You have the address, right?" Reed asked as soon as Timmons slid behind the wheel.

"Yes, sir."

Ensuring some privacy, Reed hit the button to raise the window between them and the driver. He glanced out the car window. "Wow. You weren't kidding about getting the press out today. How did you get so many photographers here?"

"I had my assistant leak my travel plans." Sienna toed off her shoes. "Thanks again for being willing to help me out. Keeping my relationship with Craig out of the press is hard enough, but now that they think we're a couple, it will be so much easier."

"Pretending to date you is hardly a challenge. I have a feeling the publicity from today's little scene will generate a lot of interest in our show."

"Which will make our producers happy," Sienna said. "And Craig's commanding officer will be thrilled to have him out of the spotlight."

"I would think so. Navy SEALs don't seem the type to seek publicity."

"That's the truth."

"Are the two of you still planning on a Christmas wedding?"

"Yeah." Sienna reached over and put her hand on his. "But remember, that's top-secret info. Not even my parents know the details."

"Now I really feel honored that you told me about it."

"You should." Sienna withdrew her hand and raked her fingers through her long dark hair. "Of course, we have been friends since we were old enough to build castles on the beach."

"You mean since you were old enough to destroy my creations."

"I was only two. You aren't still holding a grudge, are you?"

"Only a little one." He stretched his legs out in front of him. "Are your parents going to be annoyed that my parents and I will be able to attend your temple ceremony and they can't?"

Sienna let out a sigh. "I wish they were active in the Church, but that's on them. I'm sure they'll be disappointed, but Craig and I will make sure they're included as much as possible."

"I have to say, it will be nice working with someone else who is Mormon for a change."

"Got tired of having all of those women hitting on you on your last project?"

"More like I was tired of trying to explain our values." Reed shrugged. "You know how it goes."

"That I do."

"I still can't believe how things fell into place for this show," Reed said. "Who would have ever thought we'd end up working together?"

When Sienna fell silent, an uncomfortable thought worked its way into his mind. The call from his agent six weeks ago about his audition for *Beachfront* had come out of the blue, but never before had he considered someone else might have been involved in bringing him to this point. "Wait a minute. Did you get me this job?"

"You got the job because you're a talented actor."

"Sienna?" Reed kept his eyes on her, noting the faint flush in her cheeks. "You did, didn't you?"

"No. Honestly, I didn't." She met his gaze, and he recognized her sincerity when she let out a little sigh. "I'm telling you the truth. I might have talked to the director about who would be good in this role, but your name was one of several I mentioned."

"I'm surprised they didn't cast Adam Pratt. He auditioned right before me."

"Adam did have a good audition, but so did you. And you were better prepared. That counts for a lot, especially in a television series."

"Well, I appreciate you mentioning my name. I was starting to think my agent wasn't ever going to find me a role outside of the sci-fi world."

"Now you just have to get used to being America's new heartthrob."

Reed rolled his eyes. "Yeah right."

"Oh, you know you're adorable." Sienna reached out and grabbed him by the chin. "Pretending to date me automatically makes you more popular."

"Uh-oh." He leaned back to free himself. "Your ego is expanding again."

She grinned at him. "Just stating the facts."

The car rolled to a stop, and Sienna reached for the door handle. Reed beat her to it. "I'll get that."

"Thanks." She shot him an amused look. "Cute and a gentleman. Definite heartthrob material."

Ignoring her teasing, he opened the door and waited for her to climb out before stepping out beside her on the sidewalk in front of her new home, a modest house that had been sectioned into three apartments. Timmons retrieved her suitcase from the trunk and set it beside her.

"I'm going to walk her inside, Timmons. I'll only be a few minutes."

"Of course, sir."

Reed took Sienna's suitcase for her. As soon as they were out of earshot of their driver, he asked, "Is your bodyguard here yet?"

"He should be here any minute." Sienna led the way to the stairs on the side of the house and then to the second-level unit. "Thanks for carrying that for me."

"No problem."

She unlocked the door and walked inside. She hadn't taken more than three steps when a man around his age moved into the entryway and scooped Sienna into his arms.

"You're home!" Sienna reached up and gave him a kiss in greeting, a look of absolute love and adoration on her face.

Though Reed had heard all about Craig from Sienna, this was the first time he had come face-to-face with the man. Craig turned, and his dark eyes landed on Reed. Though Craig was about an inch or two shorter than him, maybe six one, Reed sensed this man wasn't someone he would want to cross.

"You must be the new boyfriend," Craig said, humor in his voice. He kept his left arm hooked around Sienna's waist and offered his right.

"And you must be the real boyfriend." Reed shook the hand Craig offered.

"I really appreciate you helping us out," Craig said, repeating the sentiment Sienna had already expressed.

"It's not a problem." Reed moved to the door. "Sienna, I'll see you on set tomorrow."

"Thanks, Reed. And thanks for the ride."

Reed walked outside and headed for the limo. What would it be like, he wondered, to have a woman look at him the way Sienna looked at Craig?

3

SIENNA WATCHED REED LEAVE BEFORE she turned back to Craig and kissed him once more. "I can't believe you're here. How long are you in town?"

"Just tonight."

"Seriously?" Sienna's disappointment colored the single word. "Why did your squad come home for only a few hours?"

"Actually, I'm the only one who came home. I won the lottery and got to play errand boy."

Sienna forced herself to shake off her disappointment. Whether it was for one night or a full year, she was going to enjoy every moment she had with him.

"It was nice of the guys to let you win the lottery."

"How did you know they let me win?"

"Because they all remember how hard it is to be engaged while across the world from their fiancée." Sienna tilted her head to the left. "Am I wrong?"

"No, you're right." Craig's hand settled on her back, and he guided her toward the kitchen. "Are you hungry? I made some dinner."

"I'm famished. I don't like to eat on the plane."

"I know," he said. "How was your weekend in California?"

"Pretty good. Dad only tried to increase my security detail twice, but Grandma and Grandpa flew in from Phoenix and stopped him."

He stopped halfway down the hall. "Let me guess. Your grandpa helped keep your dad in line."

"Something like that. My assistant helped too. Jane is great at throwing logic at my dad and making him actually see it."

"Is Jane working for you again?" Craig asked.

"Yeah. She came back with me today. In fact, she should be getting here any minute. Do you want me to introduce you?"

"Maybe next time." He leaned down and kissed the soft spot where her neck curved into her shoulder. "I'm being selfish with these few hours we have together. You don't mind, do you?"

A delightful shudder rippled through her. "I don't mind."

"Besides, dinner's ready." He nudged her forward once more.

Sienna entered the kitchen and caught the scent of barbecue. "Is that . . . ?" She trailed off and peeked inside the oven. She turned, delight illuminating her features. "You made ribs?"

"I did." He picked up a hot pad from off the counter. "I was going to grill, but I didn't think it would look right for me to be hanging out on the deck after you staged being seen with another man."

"Is that going to be weird for you?" Sienna asked. "I know it didn't sit well with you when Adam Pratt and I went out on a fake date."

"That was different. We had barely started going out back then." He pulled the oven open and slid the ribs out and onto the stove. "Besides, it will be a lot easier for us to keep our wedding off the radar if no one knows we're together."

She lifted her left hand and stared at her bare finger. "I think the hardest thing is not wearing my ring."

"That's hard for me too, but we both know if you wear it in public, the press will follow you like hound dogs chasing a fox."

"True. It will be tough enough to make sure my parents are there without them leaking the details."

"You would think your dad would have figured out how to keep things private by now. He's been working in Hollywood for more than thirty years."

"You would think so," Sienna agreed. She glanced over at the kitchen table. Craig had already set it, as well as placing a carafe of ice water in the center of the table and a basket of what could only be her favorite crescent rolls beside it. "You're spoiling me."

"I wanted to make up for lost time." He began transferring the ribs onto a serving plate. "Can you grab the salad out of the fridge?"

"Sure." Sienna opened it and saw an apple pie sitting beside the green salad. "Apple pie?"

Craig put the ribs on the table and called over his shoulder. "I'm afraid that one is store bought, but I thought we could heat it up for dessert."

Sienna set the salad beside the ribs and slipped her hands around his neck. "Have I told you lately how much I love you?"

His grin flashed. "Once or twice."

She reached up and kissed him. "Just checking."

* * *

Jane stared out the car window at the lush foliage, instantly comparing it to the palm trees of Malibu. Virginia Beach and Malibu might both be located on the ocean, but at the moment, she felt like she was driving through a foreign country. The ocean was supposed to be to the west.

Even though she had accompanied Sienna on most of her trips since she'd started working for her, Jane had never worked on the East Coast before.

She thought of their travel from one side of the country to the other and wondered if she would ever get used to the first-class treatment. Instead of sitting in the crowded seating area by the gate at LAX, they had spent the hour waiting for their flight working in the Premier Lounge with a few other VIP passengers. When it had come time to board, one of the airline staff had informed them, and they had literally walked straight from the lounge onto the plane.

Of course, having George present to clear their path had ensured no one would bother them. She and George had accompanied Sienna only as far as the airport doors when they'd arrived in Norfolk. The photo op for Sienna and her new leading man had been staged, and Jane could only marvel at her employer's luck. Falling for the guy who would play opposite her for the foreseeable future would make life simpler. Sienna had dated a number of her leading men over the years, but Jane suspected this time things were different. Never before could she remember seeing Sienna so happy and content.

"You're awfully quiet," George said from the driver's seat. "Everything okay with your mom?"

"Yeah. The last scans looked good." Jane glanced at the man beside her. The forty-one-year-old ex-Marine had been working as Sienna's bodyguard for nearly a decade. George exited the highway, and a surge of excitement and anticipation flowed through her. A new beginning. She found herself looking forward to the possibilities.

Of course, after spending the past six months caring for her mother as she underwent treatments for breast cancer, anything outside the hospital and her mother's tiny one-bedroom apartment felt like freedom. The thought instantly sent a flood of guilt through her.

She had to get on with her life, Jane reminded herself. Her mother had said as much this morning before they'd left for the airport.

Sienna had been more than accommodating in letting her take a leave of absence during her mother's illness, holding her job as personal assistant until she could return to work. At the time they had made those arrangements, Sienna had been planning to return to California after finishing the movie she had filmed in Virginia. Instead, she had taken a job on a television series that had resulted in a permanent move.

"Are you nervous about the move?" George asked, interrupting her thoughts.

"A little," she admitted. "I've never lived outside of California for more than a few months before."

"It takes some getting used to, but I think you'll like it here." He pulled into the driveway of a modest-sized house. A wide porch wrapped around the left side of the structure, and she could see an exterior staircase that led to the second-floor balcony. "Here we are."

"Is this Sienna's place? I thought you were taking me to my apartment."

George motioned to the front door. "This is your apartment."

"I don't understand."

"The previous owners converted this place into three apartments. Sienna has the upstairs unit, and I have the one right below hers." He motioned to the staircase. "My front door is at the bottom of those stairs. Your place takes up the right side of the main level."

Jane stepped out of the car. A few seagulls flew overhead, and the scent of the ocean carried on the breeze. Then she heard it—the familiar pounding of water against sand. She moved to her right so she could see past the house. There it was. The Atlantic Ocean in their backyard.

"Sienna said she found me a place to stay, but I didn't expect anything like this."

"I have to say, there are times I really love our boss."

"We do have it pretty good," Jane said.

George dug a key out of his pocket. "Here's the key to your front door. Go check it out. I'll get the rest of your bags."

"Thanks." Jane took the key and grabbed the handle of her carry-on bag, hauling it and her computer bag up the front steps. She unlocked the door, stepped inside, and stared.

To her left, bookshelves lined one wall of the small study, a desk already in place to create her necessary workspace. To her right, light washed through tall windows onto the gleaming hardwood floor. Two wide leather chairs and a sofa were arranged around a square coffee table, each of the chairs large enough to hold two people. A flat-screen television hung above the marble fireplace.

Jane set her bags inside the door and wandered through the living area. On the far side of the room, she could see into a family-style kitchen. The breakfast area boasted a pine table and chairs beneath the windows that gave an amazing view of the beach. French doors provided access to the back deck, and Jane was delighted to see a grill and a patio table in place.

She continued into a short hallway on the far side of the kitchen and glanced into the full bathroom tiled in blue and cream. Moving forward, she discovered her bedroom with another set of french doors overlooking the water.

"Where do you want everything?" George called from the front door.

Jane used the main hallway to move from the kitchen to the entryway. "This place is amazing. Are you sure Sienna doesn't want the main level?"

"Positive. The upstairs unit is twice the size. This one has a bigger kitchen, but we both know Sienna rarely has time to cook."

"With that grill on the deck, we may have to rethink her eating habits."

George's grin flashed. "I'm already working on that."

"If we double-team her, she won't have a chance."

George nodded in agreement. "I'll put your bags in your room."

"Thanks." Jane retrieved her computer bag and set it in the office. Glancing out the front windows, a sense of wonder washed over her, and she found herself hoping Sienna's new job would keep them here for a very long time.

4

REED CLIMBED OUT OF HIS classic '71 Mustang and headed for the studio door. Although his new television series sometimes shot on location at the beach and at a local diner, they filmed most of their show inside this converted beach house.

His role as a self-made real estate mogul didn't stretch the imagination much. His father had started his real estate business before Reed was born, and Reed understood the business well. Their home in Malibu gave him plenty of exposure to those who had grown up with little concept of money or what it might be like to have a lack of it, but his parents refused to let him and his sister fall into that category. Regular chores, limited spending money, strict family meal times, and ridiculously early curfews had been his cross to bear during his childhood and teenage years.

Now, at the age of twenty-seven, he appreciated the gift of hard work and strong family values. He was also grateful he had stumbled into a friendship with the Blake sisters so early in life. His father had handled many of Sterling Blake's real estate dealings over the years, and Reed had ended up being pre-school buddies with Sienna's sister, Kendra, at the tender age of four. The family friendships had deepened from there.

Reed approached the oceanfront home that served as their primary set. From the outside, the house itself appeared modest compared to some he had seen in the area, but with its two stories and open living space, it served their purposes well. The kitchen and living room had been established as their primary sets, along with one of the upstairs bedrooms. Four of the five other bedrooms now served as dressing rooms. Makeup and wardrobe had taken over the master bedroom, with racks of clothes lining the interior walls.

He was nearly to the door when he saw Sienna's car pull up, George behind the wheel.

Sienna climbed out and started toward him. She must have noticed the photographers parked across the street because she kissed him on the cheek as soon as she reached him.

"Good morning."

"Good morning yourself." Reed lowered his voice. "How was the reunion last night?"

"Short-lived."

"You lost me."

"He was only home for the night. By the time he got back to his apartment, he probably only had about eight hours before he had to leave again," Sienna whispered.

"Any idea when he'll be back?" Reed asked.

"He doesn't know."

"Sorry. That has to be tough."

"It is what it is." She turned when a lovely blonde stepped beside her. "Reed, have you met Jane?"

"No, I don't think so."

"Jane Napierski, Reed Forrester," Sienna said by way of introduction.

"Good to meet you, Jane." Reed thought through their upcoming scenes for the day, unsure of the role Jane might fill in the guest cast members. "What part are you playing?"

"Actually, I'm Sienna's assistant."

"Oh, so you're here permanently, then."

Warmth and humor filled Jane's expression. "I'm not sure anyone can claim permanence when dealing with television, but I'm here as long as Sienna needs me."

"Jane is living in one of the downstairs apartments in my new place," Sienna offered.

"Nice." Reed felt a little twinge of envy. A beachfront house in a quiet neighborhood was a dream of his.

Two seagulls dive-bombed the area on the beach where they had staged a picnic yesterday. He would happily put up with such visitors if he could also wake to the sound of the surf outside his window and walk along the water's edge each morning, looking for seashells.

The salary from the show would more than pay for such accommodations . . . assuming they made it into a second season. After watching more than a few television and movie stars spend beyond their means, Reed wasn't about to make such a commitment until he was sure how their new show would be received.

He glanced over his shoulder at the photographers still snapping photos. At least Sienna's plans to get them in the headlines appeared to be working. Now if they could generate enough viewers in the early weeks, maybe he could upgrade from his current one-bedroom apartment into something more to his taste.

* * *

Reed Forrester. Jane had heard the name often enough over the years, but this was the first time she had ever seen him in person. She had to admit, his head shots didn't do him justice. Reed was one attractive man. Gorgeous blue eyes set in a strong face. The fact that he appeared to be as down-to-earth and friendly as Sienna was explained why her friend had chosen to date him despite the risks. Sienna was well aware of the challenges associated with an off-screen romance. Besides the stress of trying to maintain a relationship under the demands of their shoot schedule, a break-up could undermine everything they were trying to achieve professionally.

Jane followed Reed and Sienna to the studio, pleasantly surprised when Reed made a point of holding the door for both of them before bringing up the rear as they entered.

They were barely inside when a woman in her midtwenties approached with the day's scripts in hand. Her light-brown hair was cut short, and she moved with efficiency and purpose.

"Reed, Ken wants to see you before you go to makeup." She handed him a script and proceeded to give a second one to Sienna.

"Thanks, Toni." Reed turned to Sienna and Jane. "I'll see you later. It was nice to meet you, Jane."

"You too."

"You're Jane?" Toni asked and extended her hand. "Toni Erickson. I'm Reed's assistant."

Jane shook her hand. "Oh, yes. We've spoken on the phone. You worked with Sienna on her last film."

Sienna stepped forward. "Toni, I need to head to makeup. Would you mind showing Jane around?"

"I'm happy to."

"Thanks." Sienna put a hand on Jane's arm. "I'll see you later."

Jane nodded before speaking to Toni. "Thanks for holding down the fort for the past couple weeks. It couldn't have been easy handling both Sienna's and Reed's schedules."

"It wasn't a problem. They both took care of a lot of things themselves to help fill in the gaps."

"Well, I appreciate it regardless."

"How is your mom doing?" Toni asked. She must have seen the surprise on Jane's face because she added, "Sienna mentioned you stayed in California the past six months to help her through chemo treatments."

"She's doing much better, thanks."

"You must be so relieved."

"More than words can express," Jane said.

"Come on. Let's start over here, and I'll show you where you can set up."

Jane followed Toni through the main set, past two cameramen setting up, and into the main hallway. French doors sectioned off an office that was currently empty. Opposite it, in what was likely once a formal living room, six workstations had been created using long tables pushed against the exterior walls.

"You can set up over there." Toni motioned to an empty space.

"Thanks." Jane set her laptop bag on the office chair.

"If you want to come with me, I'll show you the rest of the set, and then you can get settled in."

"Sounds good. Thanks." Jane followed her back into the hallway, anxious to learn the lay of the land.

* * *

Abdul entered the sparsely furnished apartment, where Jamal was sitting at a folding table, a notebook in his hand, his pen moving over the paper rapidly. The sound of the door opening caused Jamal to stop and look up.

"Have you found her yet?" Abdul asked.

"In a manner of speaking." He tapped his pen against the notebook.

"Explain."

"I found Sienna Blake, but I haven't found the photo yet."

"For all we know, it could have already been uploaded."

"I've been monitoring her on social media, and there isn't anything there," he said. "It appears the two women were serious about waiting until October to use the photos."

"That buys us some time, but I don't want to wait to take care of this. We have to make sure the photos aren't shared with Sienna Blake's publicity people," he said.

"I have an address." He ripped off a piece of paper and held it up to reveal the notes scrawled across it. "If I eliminate Sienna Blake, there won't be any need for those photos to be in her publicity campaign."

He pondered the suggestion. "No, we try the subtle option first. An investigation into her death might bring the photos to light even faster."

"What is the subtle option?"

He waved at the two computers set up on the folding table in the kitchen. "We're going phishing."

* * *

Reed was halfway to his car when he remembered he was supposed to be dating Sienna. If they really were a couple, would he leave work without her?

He looked back at the door as it opened and saw Jane walk outside. Reed waited for her to close the distance between them. "Where's Sienna?"

"The producer wanted to talk to her."

"She's probably getting the same lecture I got this morning."

"About what?"

"The perils of dating your costar." He couldn't help but smile when he thought of his own encounter that morning with Ken, the show's producer. He had nearly confessed the truth, but the few lingering bystanders had been reason enough for him to keep his mouth shut.

Jane started toward the parking lot, and Reed fell into step beside her. "How was your first day?" Reed asked.

"Good. This set is amazing," she said. "I love that the beach scenes can be done right outside the back door."

"I gather that isn't normal." At her confused look, he added, "I've never worked on scene before. All of my previous projects were done at the studio."

"Really?"

"Yeah. Sci-fi tends to do a lot of work in front of the green screen."

Jane adjusted her computer bag so the strap was more firmly on her shoulder. "I imagine this is quite a change for you, then."

"It is, but it's been great so far. I love working with Sienna, and not having to spend hours in makeup before every shoot is a huge upside."

"I can only imagine." They reached the parking lot, and Jane asked, "How long have you known Sienna?"

"Since she stole my shovel and demolished my sand castle."

Jane's laughter rang out, a delightful sound that carried on the light breeze. "It's good to see you've decided to forgive her."

"I'm working on it. It was a pretty awesome castle."

Jane's smile stayed in place.

"There you are." Sienna approached, George walking behind her. She looked at Reed, humor dancing in her eyes. "Did you already get the lecture?"

"Oh yeah. I almost felt bad for putting Ken on the spot like that."

"Hey, if this is all he has to worry about as far as cast relations, this job is going to be the best," Sienna countered.

"True. Did you see what happened at the craft table today after lunch?"

"No. Why?"

"The kid guest starring in the next episode was complaining about not being able to play on the beach, so the caterers helped him build a castle out of leftover muffins."

"Craft services were okay with that?"

"Marshall may have been a little put out when he came looking for a blueberry muffin and found out they were all on the bottom," Reed said.

"That must have gone over well." Sienna looked at Jane. "Are you ready to go?"

"I am."

Reed leaned forward and kissed Sienna's cheek. "I'll see you later."

He pulled open both passenger doors and waited for Sienna and Jane to slide inside before closing them and offering a wave goodbye. Heading for his car, he glanced back as they pulled away and wished he weren't spending his evening alone.

JANE FOUGHT THE TUG OF emotion as she thought of the easy exchange between Reed and Sienna. She wasn't jealous, she assured herself. Rather, she wished she knew what it was like to have someone care for her that way. She had dated occasionally over the years, but never had she experienced the kind of connection that transcended casual dating to reach something more serious.

Though Sienna hadn't confided in her about her relationship with Reed, Jane had known her long enough to recognize this boyfriend wasn't like the ones who had come before. Perhaps it was the basis of friendship that made it different this time around, but whatever it was, Sienna's joy emanated from her in a way she couldn't quite describe.

"What are your plans for tonight?" Sienna asked, breaking into her thoughts.

"I don't know. I guess I'll spend some time unpacking."

Sienna shifted in her seat to look at her. "Seriously? I know you. You unpacked everything last night after we got in."

"Yeah, but I haven't made a run to the grocery store or figured out what I need in the kitchen," Jane said.

Sienna focused on George. "Sounds like we need to stop at the grocery store on our way home."

"We can pick up some hamburgers or steaks to throw on the grill," George suggested.

"You don't have to cook for me," Sienna said. "I think I still have some tamales in the freezer from Miguel's wife."

"Who's Miguel?" Jane asked.

"He's the real estate agent who helped me buy the beach house."

"Well, I think George is on to something. It wouldn't hurt for you to eat real food that isn't from a freezer or a restaurant."

Sienna fell silent for a moment, then said, "George does grill a pretty good steak."

"Yes, he does." Jane smothered a grin when she saw George wink at her in the rearview mirror. "Did you want to invite Reed over to join us?"

"Oh, that's a good idea," Sienna said. "It's probably been awhile since he's had a home-cooked meal."

"Is he the type who cooks by ordering online?" Jane asked.

"No, he actually loves to cook, but neither one of us has had a lot of time since we started filming."

"That's always her excuse," Jane said to George.

"I know," he agreed. "You'd think she would come up with something more original."

Sienna looked from Jane to George and back to Jane again. "Okay, I admit it. The kitchen and I aren't exactly on friendly terms. That's why I'm planning to marry someone who actually likes to cook."

"Good thing that worked out for you." George chuckled.

"A very good thing." Sienna took her phone out and sent a text. A moment later, she received a response. "Reed said he'd love to join us. I told him to come over at six thirty."

"In that case, I think we should divide and conquer." George pulled into a grocery store parking lot. "Sienna and I will get the steaks and fixings for salad, and you can get everything you need to make that cherry cobbler I like so much."

Jane laughed. "That I can do."

* * *

Craig looked over at the poor sap sitting across from him. The lieutenant was slumped forward with his head down, and what little part of his face was visible looked more green than white. The dark-skinned man beside Craig also appeared to have a bit of a greenish hue.

The carrier onboard delivery, or COD, as the cargo plane was known, jerked upward when it collided with another heavy gust of wind. Craig's stomach jerked with it, and he willed his body to settle.

The man beside him began another bout of dry heaves. He had emptied his stomach over an hour ago, but apparently, his body wasn't done protesting the rough ride.

Craig closed his eyes and forced himself to relax, his breathing slow and steady. He pretended he was on the water, waves rolling beneath his grandfather's speedboat, Sienna by his side. Even though they had been together for six months, at times he felt like he was living in a dream. The real dream would start as soon as he and his squad returned Stateside.

The plane jerked hard to the right and then to the left when the pilot compensated for the weather.

Craig's fingers tightened on the thick pouch he held on his lap, "Top Secret" stamped on the outside. The pilot had offered to secure it in the safe, but Craig's orders had been explicit. He was to maintain possession of the package at all times.

Slowly, the rough movement subsided, and Craig felt the plane descending. He opened his eyes; his sick and weary travel companions looked like they might never eat anything again.

The pilot signaled them to brace for landing. Craig crossed his arms over his chest and leaned back in his seat. A few moments later, his body jerked forward when the plane landed on deck and came to a sudden stop.

He took a moment to recover from the impact before he unclipped his harness and headed for the hatch. He nodded at the pilot. "Thanks for the ride."

"Anytime."

Craig climbed down the steps to the flight deck. When he passed through the doorway leading inside, he found Brent waiting for him. "You miss me?"

"We have new movement on the border of Abolstan and Syria." Brent held out a hand, and Craig passed him the envelope.

"I haven't looked inside yet. I never had time without people around."

"Let's get down to our boardroom and see what we've got," Brent said.

"Are the contents of that envelope really so important that you needed a courier?" Craig asked.

"Yeah, they are."

"Now I'm even more curious to see what's inside."

"That makes two of us."

* * *

Reed climbed out of his car, his eyes drawn to the surf beyond Sienna's house. He started toward the stairs leading to her apartment, but when he heard voices, he followed them to the back deck.

"Throwing a bagged salad into a bowl doesn't count," Jane said.

"Sure it does. I even bought dressing," Sienna countered.

"Did you think to buy any cucumbers or tomatoes?"

"No." Sienna jerked a thumb in George's direction, where he stood at the grill, as Reed came around the corner. "But George did."

"We really do have to work on your culinary skills," Jane said.

"There's one problem with that idea," Sienna said. "Complete lack of interest."

"Anything I can do to help?" Reed lifted the paper bag he held into their line of sight. "I picked up some rolls at the bakery, but I've been known to slice a cucumber on occasion."

"Hey there." Sienna motioned to the round table where four plates were already laid out. "We're eating out here. Pull up a chair and make yourself comfortable."

"Thanks." Reed set the rolls on the table, but he didn't sit. Instead, he moved to lean against the rail beside Sienna. A buzzer sounded.

"That's the cobbler. I'll be right back." Jane started toward the back door of the main-level apartment. She glanced back as she reached for the knob. "George, where's the stuff for the salad?"

"It's in my refrigerator. I'll get it for you."

"I can get it if you want," Reed offered.

"Thanks." Spatula in hand, George waved in the direction of the stairs leading to the second level. "It's the door at the bottom of the stairs. The stuff is in the crisper drawer on the left."

"Be right back." Reed entered George's apartment, surprised by the generous size of the living room. Sunlight streamed through the windows and splashed light onto the table in the dining area. He walked into the L-shaped kitchen and glanced into the hallway beyond that presumably led to the bedroom and bathroom.

Reed made his way to the refrigerator and retrieved the bags of vegetables. When he returned outside, George and Sienna were deep in discussion about the merits of blue cheese on steak. Leaving them to their debate, Reed knocked twice on Jane's back door and pushed it open, the scent of cherry cobbler heavy in the air.

"That smells amazing."

"Hopefully it will taste that way." Jane tugged an oven mitt off her hand and set it aside. "Come on in."

"I come bearing gifts."

"Great." She retrieved a cutting board from a cabinet and set it on the counter.

Reed opened the bag and started laying out the ingredients: bagged salad, a tomato, a cucumber, an avocado, and a bell pepper. "Do you have an extra cutting board?"

"You really don't have to help."

"I don't mind. I like to cook."

"That's good. Sienna needs all the friends she can get who know their way around the kitchen." Jane washed her hands before turning to face him.

"Sounds like you know her well."

"When you work together and go to church together, it's hard not to get close."

"Wait." His eyebrows shot up. "You're LDS?"

Jane looked up, surprised. "Yeah."

"Me too."

"I never realized that," Jane said.

"I haven't reached the stage in my career where everyone is trying to dissect my life."

"That's about to change."

"So Sienna keeps telling me." Reed accepted the cutting board she handed him and selected a knife from the wooden block on the counter. "How long have you been working for her?"

"Three years. I started at the end of my senior year in college."

"How did you manage taking classes and working at the same time?"

"I started out doing an internship for the studio, and we became friends. Sienna realized she needed an assistant to keep up with everything, and she offered me a job. It was only a few weeks until graduation, so her dad's assistant helped out until I could work full-time."

"You were a theater major, then."

"Computer science, actually." Jane fished around the cabinets until she found a bowl large enough to hold a salad. After dumping the bagged lettuce into it, she retrieved a second cutting board and sliced the avocado.

"How did you get an internship at a movie studio with a computer-science degree?"

"The studio was upgrading their internet security, and I got one of the intern positions. It's like they say: timing is everything."

"Isn't that the truth." Reed finished slicing the bell pepper and moved on to a tomato. "Do you enjoy your job, or are you hoping to find something else in your field?"

"I love my job." She shrugged. "The truth is, I'm good at computer science, but I didn't really like it that much."

"And you majored in it because . . ."

"By the time I realized I didn't want to work in a computer field, I was too close to graduation to quit. It seemed more logical to graduate and go back for a master's degree if I decided to change."

"Sounds like it turned out for the best all around."

"It did."

The door opened, and Sienna walked in. "The steaks are ready."

"Perfect timing. We're about done here." Jane combined the rest of the ingredients and picked up the bowl.

Sienna waved them outside. "Come on. Let's eat."

6

"Anything?" Brent asked the moment he walked into the boardroom they had been assigned to on the USS *Ronald Reagan*.

Craig looked up from where he sat between Seth and Quinn at a row of computer stations. "Intel is looking into the different modes of transportation and trying to narrow down where these guys went after abandoning their hideout. Nothing so far."

"Where's Amy?" Brent asked, referring to his wife, who also served as the squad's intelligence officer.

Seth swiveled away from his computer, where he was currently searching through intel reports on Abolstan and Syria. "She's in CIC checking for updates."

"I thought she went to the officers' mess to see what they're serving for dinner," Quinn said.

"Quinn, you're enlisted," Brent reminded him.

"Yeah, but I have friends who are officers."

Seth studied him for a brief moment. "So, they're having steak tonight?"

Tristan walked in behind Brent, a grin on his face. "Quinn, you were right. You can smell the steak from two compartments over."

"Is Amy getting some for us?"

A line appeared on Tristan's normally smooth brow. "I thought you asked her."

"It's your turn. I convinced her last time."

"Boys, can we talk about this later?" Though Brent's comment was phrased as a question, the underlying command hummed beneath it.

"Did you find out what's in that pouch I brought back?" Craig asked.

"Oh yeah. You guys have got to see this." Brent held up a thick envelope and carried it to the worktable in back of the room. He glanced around and took stock of who was missing. "Are Jay and Damian still working out?"

Seth nodded. "I told them to be back at 1600."

"We'll catch them up when they get here." Brent slid the contents free of the envelope and spread the papers on the table. "Satellites caught movement at an airstrip near Elazar's hideout an hour after we watched it explode."

Craig looked at the images taken from far above. Multiple vehicles were parked by a small jet, two people visible by one of the trucks. The runway was nothing more than a narrow strip of pavement at the edge of a wooded area. "Any idea where these guys are now?"

"Or what they're up to?" Seth asked.

"Two days after these pictures were taken, a challenge inspection of a chemical-weapons-related facility in Syria showed a discrepancy in their records."

"What kind of records are we talking about?"

"Chemical toxins. Weapons grade." Brent paused. "This plane was spotted in Damascus day before yesterday."

"Where is it now?"

"It was traced into Abolstan, but from there, we think these guys crossed the border into Turkey."

"Are you telling us they let me go all the way to Virginia and back to carry the news that we lost them?" Craig asked.

"No." Brent shuffled through the papers until he found the two he wanted. The first revealed an airline reservation for a charter plane from Ankara, Turkey, to Vancouver, Canada. The second page appeared to be a surveillance photo from an airport.

Brent's jaw tightened briefly before he continued. "The names on the reservations are aliases, but we caught a break. Interpol forwarded these photos through the CIA."

"Wait. Isn't that . . . ?" Quinn began.

"That's right. It's Jamal Elazar." Brent held out the picture and slowly swept it in front of each of them. "Get a good look. The last time he was spotted was when Abdul Maleb was still alive and they were caught together on surveillance video outside of Cairo. At the time, Jamal had a thick beard and was twenty pounds heavier."

Alarm sounded in Seth's normally calm voice. "And he's in Canada?"

"Yeah. Intel believes this group is behind the theft of the toxins."

"If they're in North America . . ." Craig began.

"They're already making a move," Quinn finished for him.

"Yeah," Seth agreed as the hatch opened behind him and Amy entered. "But how are they transporting the bomb? Chemical weapons would likely be picked up in an airport security scan no matter how they tried to package it."

"Not bomb," Amy interrupted. "Bombs."

"Excuse me?" Brent stared at his wife.

"Intel estimates that with the amount of toxin stolen, we could have up to three bombs."

Seth studied the photos. "My guess is two."

"How do you figure?"

Seth tapped a finger on the photo of the runway in Syria. "Look at these vehicles. See how the front fender is smashed in on this one?"

"Yeah. What about it?" Brent asked.

Craig saw the answer when his eyes drifted to the satellite photos from the runway in Abolstan. "This is the same truck."

"Two trucks in Abolstan. Two trucks in Syria two days later," Seth tapped on the damaged fender in the Abolstan photo. "These are the same vehicles."

"They booby-trapped their hideout so we wouldn't find any evidence of what they were building," Craig said.

"That's my guess."

"Having two trucks doesn't necessarily mean that's how many bombs they created," Amy said. "The size of these devices doesn't have to be terribly large."

"How big do you think they would be?"

"Best guess, the size of a large duffel bag. Maybe twice that."

"If they used a charter plane to fly the weapons into Vancouver, they might be able to smuggle them across the Canadian border into the US," Tristan said.

Brent put his hand on Amy's shoulder. "I want you to check with the captain to see if we can get our orders changed."

"I already did."

"How soon can we get a transport?"

"First thing tomorrow."

Jay came through the hatch with Damian right behind him. "You all look serious. What's going on?"

"Pack your bags," Brent said. "We're going home."

* * *

Jane leaned back in her chair as she watched the men on either side of her polish off their cobbler. She had taken only a small serving for herself, her body not used to eating at this time of day.

"This was amazing." Reed set his fork down and blew out an appreciative breath. "Jane, you may have missed your calling."

"I don't know about that," Jane began.

"Wasn't I brilliant in hiring an assistant who can cook?" Sienna asked, her eyes bright with humor.

Reed chuckled. "I'm sure that was the number-one thing you were looking for."

"Okay, so it is possible I recognized Jane's organizational skills too." Sienna pushed back from the table. "We should get a picture of us together."

"I'll take it." George stood.

"Jane, do you have your cell? Mine's been acting up."

"Sure." Jane handed her phone to George. "Come on. Let's get all three of you." George motioned for all of them to gather at the railing. Jane expected Sienna to take position in the middle, but Reed stepped between them and slid one arm around Sienna and the other around her.

"Okay, smile everyone." George took several photos before handing the phone back to Jane. "Here you go."

"Let me see." Reed stepped beside her and looked at the screen. "Can you text that to me?"

"Sure." Jane opened her camera app and started scrolling through the images. "Which one do you like the best?"

He leaned closer, the scent of his aftershave tickling her senses. He pointed to the first one. "That one looks good."

Jane clicked on it.

"Wait. Scroll over." Reed pointed to the image immediately before it. "When was that taken?"

"When we were at the airport."

Sienna edged forward. "Is that the one I want to use for my promos?"

"Yeah."

"I like it," Reed said. "Jane, can you send me that one too?"

"Sure." Jane selected it and opened her contacts only to realize she didn't have Reed's number.

Reed must have read her mind because he held his hand out. "Here. I'll put my number in for you."

Jane handed him her phone.

Sienna leaned against the rail. "We should use tonight's pictures for the promo too."

"I'm sure anything with the two of you together will trend," Jane said.

"You're probably right," Sienna agreed.

Reed handed Jane's phone back to her. "It's hard to believe how much attention we got from me picking you up at the airport."

"We're just getting started," Sienna told him. "By the time we start releasing these promo photos, *Beachfront* is going to be on everyone's radar."

"I hope you're right," Reed said.

"She's right." George waved at the house. "She wouldn't have bought this place if she wasn't sure she would be here for a while."

"I may have to follow your example." Reed paused. "Next season."

Jane sensed Reed's hesitation and wondered at the cause. Was he hesitant to buy his own place because he was worried the show wouldn't succeed? Or was he hoping his relationship with Sienna would influence his decision? Either way, she hoped Sienna would keep this house. Jane was quite certain she could happily live with this view for the rest of her life.

7

SIENNA COLLAPSED ONTO HER COUCH and let out a sigh of exhaustion. The last scene of the day was supposed to have taken only fifteen minutes to shoot but had instead stretched into nearly two hours. She was glad she had thought to send Jane home early. Sienna had used the excuse that she was going out with Reed to give Jane some much-needed time to herself. Though they had picked up a few things at the grocery store the night before, she knew her assistant well. Jane wasn't going to operate at peak efficiency until she had her house in order. Literally.

Once Jane's car arrived on Friday, their schedules wouldn't be so tied together, and Jane would have more flexibility to run her personal errands. Only two more days. Sienna settled against the plush cushions and pulled her cell phone from her purse. She clicked the button on the screen to open her email, annoyed that it had decided to operate at a snail's pace. Three times she had tried to check for messages, and each time, the screen flashed for a moment before going back to the home screen.

When the same thing happened again, she moved across the room and powered on her laptop. All she wanted was to see if Craig had messaged her and to find out when she would see him again.

While her computer powered on, she went into the kitchen and retrieved a glass of orange juice. When she returned, the screen didn't show anything except the powering on button.

"Seriously?" Annoyed all over again and impatient, she pocketed her phone and headed outside. If she couldn't get her electronics to work, she would recruit help from someone who could.

Barefoot, she padded around the front of the house and rang Jane's doorbell. When Jane didn't answer right away, Sienna wondered if she had taken a walk. She rounded the corner to the back deck and looked out at the beach. Sure enough, Jane was visible near the water's edge.

Sienna descended the wooden stairs leading to the sand and made her way to Jane's side. "Hey, Jane."

"Hi. I thought you had plans for tonight."

"I did, but they got interrupted when my phone and laptop decided to stop working. Any chance I can borrow your laptop to check my email?"

"No problem." Jane fell into step with Sienna as they started toward the house. "What's wrong with yours? Do you want me to take a look at it?"

"Would you mind?"

"I'd be happy to. If you want, I'll see if I can fix it while you're using mine."

"That would be great. Thanks." When they reached the back deck, Sienna headed for the stairs.

"I'll leave the door open for you."

"Okay. I'll be right back." When Sienna walked into Jane's apartment a few minutes later, Jane's laptop was already powered on and waiting at the kitchen table.

Jane held out her hand. "I'll trade you."

"Good luck. I've never had it bog down this bad." Sienna handed hers over.

"Let's take a look."

Both women sat at the table, and Sienna opened her email. Her smile was immediate when she saw the message from Craig. It widened when she read his words. He was coming home.

* * *

Jane's first security scan revealed a virus unlike any she had ever seen. The moment she deleted it, files appeared to replicate in another part of Sienna's hard drive. While Sienna read through her emails and did whatever else it was she needed to do on the internet, Jane searched for the parasitic files slowing down Sienna's laptop. Unfortunately, every time Jane eliminated one problem, she found a thread that led to another.

"How's it going over there?" Sienna asked.

"I don't know where you picked this up, but you've got a nasty virus."

"Can you fix it?"

"I'm trying. Is it okay if I hang on to your computer tonight?"

"No problem, but don't stay up too late working on it. We have a seven o'clock call time in the morning."

"What makes you think I'll stay up too late?"

"I know you. Besides, it's almost ten now. I say we both get some sleep, and you can bring that with you to work. You should have some downtime since the director and producer aren't used to relying on you yet."

"That's a good idea." Jane looked up when Sienna stood. "I'll see you tomorrow."

"Seriously. Get some sleep."

"I will." Jane watched Sienna leave before adding, "Tomorrow."

Minutes stretched into hours as Jane continued her efforts. At one thirty in the morning, she found a brief flash of success when the computer began operating at normal speeds. Three minutes later, the illusion of accomplishment was shattered when she rebooted the computer only to find the problem still present.

"Okay, you win," Jane muttered to the now-black screen. "I'll deal with you later."

She started to power it off when a string of code flashed in front of her. Her heartbeat quickened. This wasn't a random virus Sienna had picked up. The program infecting her computer had been planted on the hard drive deliberately. Jane didn't know who was behind it, but of one thing she was certain—someone was spying on Sienna.

* * *

Reed rolled his shoulders against the tightness that had settled there; he'd spent too many hours on the couch last night going over his lines.

He approached the studio, surprised to see a police cruiser parked beside it. A wave of alarm washed over him, and he searched for anything else out of place. The man guarding the parking lot entrance had a companion today, the two men flanking the gate that kept the locals from entering.

Three paparazzi were parked across the street but appeared unaffected by whatever had caused the change.

Uneasy, Reed rolled down his window as he pulled up to the gate. "Good morning, Troy." Reed motioned to the police car. "Is everything okay?"

"As far as I know." He hit the button to let Reed through. "Have a good day, sir."

"You too." His hands clenched the wheel as his mind whirled. Could the police car be here as a prop? He couldn't think of any scenes it would fit in. And why had the number of security guards increased? With another quick look around, Reed parked his car and headed inside.

A handful of people were setting up in the living room, including his assistant, Toni. He caught a glimpse of Jane near the hallway by the producer's office.

"Hey, Jane. Do you know what's going on with the police car outside?" he asked.

"I'm afraid that's my fault," she said, her voice low.

"How is it your fault?"

She waved him farther into the hall. Through the glass doors, Reed could see Ken, their producer, speaking with a uniformed policeman, as well as George and Sienna.

Jane dropped her voice to a whisper. "Sienna was having trouble with her computer last night. When I was trying to fix it, I found a snooper program. Someone was deliberately spying on her electronic activity."

"That happens all the time."

"I know, but her phone was messed up too," Jane said. "After what happened on her last movie, Ken wanted to make sure the police were kept in the loop."

"I guess that makes sense." Reed knew Sienna had dealt with sabotage issues on her last film, but he couldn't begin to comprehend what it would be like to have to deal with such safety concerns. He motioned down the hall. "And the cops are here to talk about security?"

"Yeah. George insisted."

"Do you have any idea what their plan is?" Reed asked.

Before Jane could answer, the office door swung open, and George poked his head out. "Jane, can you come in here for a minute?" George asked. "Reed, you too."

Curious as to why he was being summoned, he followed Jane into the office and closed the door behind him. Reed motioned for Jane to take the empty seat beside Sienna, choosing to stand beside George at the back of the room.

"Reed, did Jane bring you up to speed about the need for extra security?" Ken asked as he lowered himself into the chair behind his desk.

"She gave me the highlights."

"Good." He waved a hand toward the police officer standing in the corner opposite him. "Officer Hensley has been assigned to the studio for our normal workweek. He'll coordinate with our security team to make sure we don't have any unwanted visitors on set."

"I'm surprised the police force is willing to dedicate someone to a single issue like this," Reed commented.

"*Beachfront* has the potential of bringing a lot of revenue into Virginia Beach. The police chief wants to protect that," Ken explained.

Officer Hensley spoke now. "Once the culprits behind the most recent threats against Miss Blake are apprehended, my department will be able to scale back our presence."

"What about Sienna's laptop and phone?" Jane asked. "Do you have a computer forensics expert to trace the snooper programs?"

"We will send the laptop and phone to the FBI lab, but Miss Blake said she would also like to use another resource that may be more efficient."

"What resource is he talking about?" Jane asked Sienna. "This is a bit out of my league."

"Don't worry," Sienna assured her. "I wasn't talking about you this time."

"Then who?"

Ken shifted his attention to Reed. "I understand Sienna's boyfriend has some Navy SEAL friends who can help out."

It took a moment for Reed to realize that Ken had clearly misunderstood Sienna and assumed he was the boyfriend she was referring to. "Sienna's absolutely right. I'm sure our Navy SEAL friends would be happy to look into this for us, but how will that work if you are sending the laptop and phone to the FBI?"

"I can create a copy of the hard drive for them," Jane suggested. "Basically, I would use a clean laptop and create a mirror."

"That would work," Officer Hensley agreed.

"Good. I'll let you two make the arrangements," Ken said.

"I'll also put a call in to the FBI to see if they have any similar cases," Hensley added.

Ken placed both hands on his desk and pushed himself up. "In the meantime, Jane, please pick up a new laptop to use for this mirror of yours and arrange to get Sienna a replacement cell phone. You can give the new number to whoever needs it."

"Yes, of course."

"I believe that's all we need to discuss for now. Reed and Sienna, you're overdue in makeup."

Sienna stood. "Heading there now."

Reed opened the door and waited for the women to exit before following behind them.

"I'd better go order that new phone for you," Jane said.

"Thanks for everything, Jane," Sienna said.

"I'll see you later."

"Bye, Jane." Reed followed Sienna up the stairs leading to the makeup room. When she reached the landing halfway up, he caught a glimpse of her face.

"Hey, are you okay?" He reached out and took her by the arm to stop her. "I know you're used to extra security, but . . ."

She let out a sigh, and he could see the mask of confidence drop away. "I still can't believe this is happening again. When Jane told me why my computer had stopped working, I was sure there must be some other explanation. Then George looked at it and agreed with her. Someone is spying on me. Or stalking me."

He gave her arm a gentle squeeze. "You're afraid you have a stalker like your sister did."

"I was so excited last night when I found out Craig is coming home. Then, within hours, I discover my life isn't my own again."

"Come here." Reed pulled her into his arms. "Focus on the good news, and let everyone else deal with the bad."

"I'm trying."

Reed heard footsteps and, moments later, saw Jane at the bottom of the stairs.

"I'm sorry to interrupt," she said, backing away.

"It's okay." Sienna stepped out of the embrace and faced her assistant fully. "Did you need something?"

"Yes. I wanted to find out if you want a California prefix for your new phone number or if you would rather have one from Virginia."

"Let's go with a Virginia number this time. Maybe that will help me blend in."

"Hate to break it to you, kid," Reed said, "but you aren't ever going to blend in."

Her eyes narrowed. "I think you just insulted my acting talents."

"Insult you? Never." He took a step forward. "I value my life."

"Crush a man's sand castle when you're a baby, and he's scared of you forever." Sienna started forward. "Come on. Let's get to work."

8

ABDUL ENTERED THE SECOND-LEVEL APARTMENT that had become his base of operation since arriving in DC. The scent of cumin, caraway, and turmeric lingered in the air, evidence of the meal he had shared with Jamal and Munjid at midday. Munjid, his younger brother, had come ahead to Washington to secure their accommodations. Now they would work together to exact a simultaneous attack on two US targets.

He could hear movement in the kitchen, but he headed instead for the open living area to his right. As expected, Jamal sat at a portable table, his attention on his computer.

"What's the latest on the actress?" Abdul asked.

"The address we had for her was incorrect, and I haven't been able to trace the GPS signal on Sienna's cell phone." Jamal gestured toward the screen but didn't look up. "I've been monitoring her computer and phone for the past two days, but it appears she has stopped using both since last night."

"Could she know we're watching her?" Abdul demanded.

"She's an actress. How could she know such a thing?" Jamal dismissed the idea with a wave of his hand. "She must be too busy working to be using them."

"Did you find the photos?"

"No." Jamal's confidence faded away only to be replaced with frustration. "I've looked through everything. The other girl must not have sent them to her yet."

"For all we know, they could have already been uploaded."

"I don't think so. I heard them talking, and Sienna was the one who wanted to put them online. I also couldn't find anything when I searched the internet."

"Now what?"

"I don't think we have a choice. We need to find these women. They're the only ones who can prove you're still alive."

"And how do you propose we find them?" Abdul asked. "Virginia Beach isn't a small town, and you said you haven't been able to trace Sienna's GPS signal."

"No, but I should be able to hack that part of her phone or access the IP address of her laptop when I'm in the immediate area."

"Take Munjid with you."

"We'll leave tomorrow."

* * *

Jane couldn't get the image of Sienna and Reed out of her head. She didn't know why the memory of them embracing on the stairs kept playing over and over in her mind. After all, it wasn't like Jane hadn't been around when Sienna had dated Joseph Hurst in London while they had been filming a movie there or when Sienna had gone out with the producer's son during another project in California. Still, that was no reason for her to obsess over Sienna's new boyfriend.

Moving to her kitchen window, she watched the last rays of light dancing over the incoming waves. Despite her exhaustion from a ten-hour day at the studio, she headed outside, a pair of shoes in her hand rather than on her feet. She made her way across the deck and down onto the sand.

Her stomach clenched as the day's events replayed in her mind once again. She wanted to know about these friends of Reed's who they were planning to ask to look into the tracking software.

She drew closer to the surf, the bite in the air contrasting the heat of the daylight hours. Her toes dug into the sand, the minutes stretching out as she watched the crash of waves.

"What a great spot."

Jane whirled around at the sound of Reed's voice, her right hand lifting to her chest as though she were trying to keep her heart in place.

Reed closed the distance between them. "Sorry. Didn't mean to startle you."

"It's okay."

"You look cold." He shrugged out of his jacket. "Here." He draped it over her shoulders.

Jane shivered, but it had nothing to do with the cold. Annoyed at her reaction to him, she struggled to find her voice. "Thanks."

"Is everything okay? You looked like you were in another world."

"Yeah. It's just going to take some time to get used to living here." She pointed at the lingering rays of sunlight bouncing off the water. "I'm used to the sun setting in the ocean. This feels backward."

"It is, but then, I suppose folks from the east would think the same thing about California."

"I suppose." She looked out at the water. "You're from California too, aren't you?"

"I am. Born and raised. I grew up down the road from the Blake family."

A gust of wind sent a shiver through her, and she slipped her arms into the sleeves of the jacket Reed had lent her. "Are your parents in the business?"

"No. Dad made his fortune in real estate. What about your family? What do they do?"

"My mom is in banking, and my younger brother is in his senior year at Cal State Northridge."

"And your dad?"

"He was living in New Orleans last I heard."

"You're not close?"

The thought of her father, or rather her lack of a traditional one, put her feet in motion. She took several steps down the beach before she looked to her left, where Reed now walked beside her.

"I'm sorry," he said. "I didn't mean to pry."

"It's okay. I just don't think about him much." The breeze teased her hair, and she tucked a wayward strand behind her ear. "Dad took off right after my brother was born."

"How old were you?"

"Five."

"Old enough to remember, too young to understand."

"I never thought of it that way. One day he was there. The next he was gone. Other than an occasional birthday or Christmas card, I haven't heard from him in more than ten years." She stopped walking and looked at him. Really looked. He was the perfect height for an actor, two or three inches past six feet. Not too tall to make casting difficult, but tall enough so his leading ladies could wear heels. His features were classic in every way. Straight, narrow nose, strong cheekbones, gorgeous eyes.

A flush worked up her neck and into her cheeks when she realized those baby blues were staring back at her.

"It's interesting how things that happen at such a young age can affect us for so many years," Reed said.

"What do you mean?"

"Not knowing what it's like to have your father's support must affect you somehow, just as having one has influenced my decisions over the years."

"Does your dad give you lots of advice?"

"He's more of a sounding board." Reed shifted his gaze to the ocean. "And the truth is that if he hadn't chosen to move to Malibu when I was a kid, I wouldn't be here now."

"What do you mean?"

"Sienna had a part in me getting this role. If I hadn't known her, I'm not sure I would have been invited to audition, much less been offered the job."

Sienna. The name crashed over Jane like a bucket of ice water. What was she doing out here walking on the beach with her best friend's boyfriend?

"I should get back." Jane turned toward the beach house. "Where is Sienna anyway?"

"I'm not sure. I came over to see if you had dinner plans and saw you walking on the beach. I never made it to Sienna's door."

"You wanted to know if I had dinner plans?" Jane asked, confused.

"You, Sienna, George," Reed clarified. "I had fun last night, and I was hoping for a repeat performance. That, and I thought everyone could use a distraction after dealing with the police today."

Immediately, Jane's chest tightened, and her steps faltered.

"I'm sorry. I shouldn't have reminded you." Reed put his hand on her arm. Then, in a gesture she had seen and envied that morning, he gathered her into his arms. "No one should have to live with fear like this."

Jane's arms came up around his waist automatically. "I'm not the one who should be scared."

"Maybe not, but I know you're worried about Sienna." His hand rubbed up and down her back.

She breathed in the lingering scent of his aftershave, her stomach jumping into her throat as he drew her even closer.

"Everything's going to be okay." The words tickled her ear and sent a new wave of unexpected sensations rolling through her.

"Well, hello." Sienna's voice sounded behind her. "Reed, I didn't know you were here."

Sienna was standing on the deck above them, a flash of surprise visible in her expression. Jane pulled back, and Reed's arms dropped to his sides.

"Hey, Sienna. I came over to see if you guys had eaten dinner yet," Reed said as though he went around hugging women who weren't his girlfriend all the time. Maybe he did. "I thought we might order something in."

Feeling ridiculously awkward, Jane took off Reed's jacket. "Thanks for letting me borrow this." She started up the steps. "I'd better get some work done. I have a few things to do before tomorrow."

"Are you sure?" Reed asked. "I'd love it if you could join us."

Jane looked from Reed to Sienna and back again. "I'm sure."

With one last glance at the couple, she headed inside, twin emotions working through her that she was only now beginning to recognize: guilt and jealousy.

9

REED WATCHED JANE RUSH INTO her apartment. He looked at Sienna with a sense of bewilderment. "Was it something I said?"

"Beats me." Sienna walked down the steps to meet him on the sand. "Did I interrupt something?"

"No, not really."

Sienna tucked her hand into the crook of his arm. "You two looked pretty cozy."

"She was feeling unsettled about what's going on with you." Reed reached out and patted her hand. "Speaking of which, any word on when Craig's getting back?"

Absolute joy filled her voice. "Tomorrow."

"Having him around should make you feel a bit safer."

"Some, but the truth is his schedule is so unpredictable I never know when I'll get to see him."

"Then I guess it's a good thing you have friends to hang out with who won't mind when you stand them up."

"For sure."

"Now, about dinner." Reed escorted her up the steps and onto the porch.

"I still need to prep for tomorrow," Sienna said with a wrinkle of her nose.

"I happen to know someone who would love to run lines with you."

"In that case, Chinese food?"

"Sounds perfect." Reed motioned to the front of the house. "Let me grab my script out of my car. We can work while we wait for dinner to get here."

"Okay. I'm going to see if George wants anything."

"I'll meet you upstairs." Reed headed to his car, replaying in his head the scene when he had hugged Jane. The gesture had been so natural he hadn't thought anything of it until she had pulled away so suddenly, her cheeks flushed.

He unlocked his car and retrieved his script from the front seat, where he'd left it. When he turned back toward the house, he noticed the lights glowing from Jane's apartment.

He nearly detoured to her front door to ask once more if she would join him for dinner, but he forced himself to continue to the stairs. Maybe if the invitation came from Sienna, Jane would be more likely to change her mind.

* * *

The moment Reed left her apartment, Sienna powered on the new laptop Jane had picked up for her that afternoon. Though Sienna was anxious to see if Craig was online, she followed the security protocols Jane had given her to make sure no one would be able to monitor her activity.

Relief flooded through her when she logged onto Skype and saw the little green dot next to Craig's name. She clicked the button to video chat, and he answered three seconds later.

"Hey, gorgeous. How are you?"

The simple question was all it took for tears to form.

"Hey, what's going on?" Craig asked. "Is everyone okay?"

Sienna took a deep breath and swallowed back the rising fear and unsettled emotions. "Everyone's fine," she said.

"Then what's with the tears?"

"Remember how I was having problems with my computer and I had to borrow Jane's to talk to you yesterday?"

"Yeah. What about it?"

"Jane was trying to fix it for me, and she found some sort of snooper program."

Instantly, Craig straightened. "A snooper program? As in, someone has been spying on you?"

"Yeah. And that's not all. My phone was messed up too."

"Do the police think someone is targeting you specifically?"

"That's their guess," Sienna told him. "I hope I didn't overstep on this one, but I said I wanted you and your friends to take a look at my stuff as well as sending it to the FBI lab. The lab was expected to take a few weeks to look at it."

"That's fine. We're due back home tomorrow afternoon."

"Will Brent be okay with it?"

"I'll check, but I'm sure it'll be fine."

Sienna picked up her new cell phone and unlocked the screen. "Let me give you my new number."

"I'll get it from you when I get home," Craig said. The look on his face reminded her that they weren't using the most secure form of communication.

"Okay. Text George when you get here. I'd love to meet you when you arrive."

"Will do, but for now, I want to hear how the rest of your day went."

"Are you trying to distract me?"

"Yep," Craig admitted.

A giggle escaped her, contrasting the tears that had been threatening a moment before. "You know, you're good at that."

"I'm even better in person," Craig promised.

"I miss you."

"I miss you too. What do you say we have a nice laid-back dinner at your place tomorrow to celebrate my homecoming?"

"Will you have your gun with you?" Sienna asked.

"Always."

"Then it sounds perfect."

* * *

Reed couldn't explain why, but sometime between running lines with Sienna and throwing out the empty takeout containers from dinner, his mood had soured. George had come to Sienna's long enough to share their meal before leaving them alone to prepare for tomorrow. Jane had apparently chosen to eat and work alone.

He unlocked his door and flipped on the light five minutes before ten. One look at the elegant black chairs angled toward the flat-screen television made him wish he had found something unfurnished. Even an empty apartment would have more personality than the one he was currently occupying. His mood took another downward turn.

He picked up the remote and turned on the TV to keep him company. When the infomercial voice filled the room and insisted he needed to join their weight-loss program, he clicked the power button again. Maybe he would stick with silence.

A sigh escaped him, and he tried to shake off his bad mood. At least his evening with Sienna had been productive. Now that he was alone, though, he could admit he had been disappointed that George had been the only one to join them for their meal. He couldn't, for the life of him, figure out why Jane had retreated so suddenly when they had returned from the beach. He had thought they were getting along well, but with the way she had run off, he wondered if she had simply been tolerating his presence.

His cell phone rang, and he pulled it free of his pocket to see his mother calling. "Hey, Mom. Is everything okay?"

"Yeah, I just haven't talked to you lately."

"I'm afraid I can't talk long. I have an early call tomorrow." Reed wandered into his kitchen and retrieved a cup from the cabinet by the refrigerator.

"Oh, sorry. I keep forgetting about the three-hour time difference."

"How's everything in California?"

"We're all fine. Your sister changed her major again."

"What is it this time?" Reed asked. Isabel was only a sophomore in college, and she had already run the gamut from anthropology to education.

"Accounting."

"Maybe she should stick with this one," Reed said. He poured himself some water and wandered back into the living room. "We could use a good accountant in the family."

"You sound like your father. Speaking of which, your dad wanted to know when you'll be in town next."

"Probably not until Thanksgiving. Other than a couple of weekends, I don't have any other breaks scheduled."

"We may have to make a trip your way, then."

"You're always welcome." Reed took a drink of water and looked around his living room. He had no doubt that the moment his father saw the cookie-cutter floor plan, he would have the local real-estate listings in front of him within five minutes. Choosing to let the topic of a visit drop, he said, "Sorry, Mom, but I need to get going."

"Okay, honey. I'll talk to you soon."

After they said their goodbyes, Reed headed into his bedroom. The deep-blue-and-cream bedspread pulled the colors out of the seascape that hung on the far wall. Silk flowers in a crystal vase topped the round table beside a cream settee, another touch that screamed "an interior decorator has been here."

It wasn't that he had something against professional decorators, per se, but he preferred living in a space that had at least a few personal touches.

He dropped his car keys and cell on the table, wondering if a few family photos would make this place feel more like home. He picked up his phone again and looked through the most recent images.

He stopped when he reached the picture of him with Sienna and Jane, the Atlantic Ocean in the background. Warmed by the memory of their evening together, he selected the photo, along with the one of Jane and Sienna at the airport in California. Continuing his search, he added one of him and his family at a Japanese restaurant the night before he moved to Virginia.

After he sent the images to the local Walmart to be printed, he browsed the website to look at frames. Not sure what he wanted, he decided to wait to buy some until he picked up the photos. By this time tomorrow, his apartment was going to start feeling more like home.

10

FOR THE FIRST TIME SINCE arriving in Virginia, Jane didn't look forward to going to the set. She felt foolish for the way she had rushed into her apartment last night, but the truth was she needed some time to sort out her feelings. A lengthy phone call last night with her mom hadn't helped distract her as she had hoped it might. Instead, when her mom had asked about the people she worked with, Jane had struggled not to think about Reed.

He wasn't like Sienna's other leading men. Over the past few days, Jane had found him to be friendly, down-to-earth, and a gentleman in every way. He was precisely the type of guy she would love to date. That realization had been reason enough for her to hide out in her apartment last night. She couldn't think about Reed that way. Reed was with Sienna, and Jane wasn't about to cause any problems between them. If only she didn't have to see him all the time.

She walked out her front door, surprised that her car was parked outside. The 1989 gold BMW had been her first car, one she had bought used during her first year of college. Though her income could support buying something more modern, she hadn't been able to bring herself to retire a vehicle that still ran perfectly fine. At least, it ran fine now that she had dumped three hundred dollars into the latest repairs.

"Hey, Jane." George approached from the sidewalk and held out her spare set of keys. "I was about to bring these to you."

"Thanks." She took the keys from him. "When did my car get here?"

"A couple hours ago."

"At four in the morning?"

"Yeah. The driver called last night to find out when he could deliver it. When I told him what time we have to be at the studio today, he agreed to bring it by early."

"You should have told me. I would have gotten up to take delivery."

"You're still adjusting to this time zone. That wouldn't have helped you any." George took a step toward his apartment. "I assume you'll want to drive yourself today."

"Yeah, but do you mind if I follow you over? I haven't gotten my bearings yet."

"No problem. We'll leave in ten minutes."

"Sounds good. Thanks." Keys in hand, Jane headed down the front steps and unlocked the door. She had filled her car with her belongings and decided to make good use of the next few minutes. She managed to unload the contents of the back seat and most of her trunk before George and Sienna came outside.

Lifting the last two boxes, she quickly carried them inside and added them to the mound now cluttering her entryway.

After grabbing her laptop bag, she locked her apartment and jogged across the lawn. George pulled out of the driveway and waited for her to start her car.

She clicked her seat belt in place and put the car in gear. Maybe now that she had her freedom back, she would be able to find a way to avoid Sienna's captivating costar.

* * *

Reed took his mark opposite Sienna on the living room set. His lines fresh in his mind from last night's session, they had to run through the scene only twice before the director was satisfied.

"Take ten while we set up for the next one," Marshall said, dismissing them.

Sienna immediately headed to where Jane was standing by one of the cameras. "Do you have my phone?"

"Yeah." Jane handed it to her as Reed stepped beside them.

Sienna tapped the screen, and instantly her face lit up. "I'm going to read my messages."

As Sienna headed for her dressing room, Toni approached. "Do you need anything before I go get the updated script?"

"No, I'm good. Thanks, Toni."

"Okay. I'll be back in a few minutes."

Reed watched Toni head for the stairs before he turned to Jane. "We missed you last night. Did you get your work done?"

"Some of it, at least." She tucked a lock of her blonde hair behind her ear. "I'd better go check on wardrobe for the next scene."

"I'll walk up with you." He started toward the stairs. "What are you doing tonight after work?"

"Me?" She glanced around at the crew members working nearby.

He caught the look of alarm on her face and realized belatedly that he shouldn't be asking her out in front of other people when everyone thought he and Sienna were a couple. "You and Sienna."

"Oh." She relaxed visibly. "I don't think Sienna has any plans."

"I thought maybe we could grill some hamburgers or something."

"I see you've joined the 'make sure Sienna eats real food' bandwagon."

"I have a feeling you don't have time to cook a lot either with this job," Reed said.

"It's not so bad. I threw together a shrimp pasta salad last night. I can usually eat that for a few days, even after I share some with Sienna and George."

"Sounds like something that would go great with burgers."

Her lips lifted into a half smile. "It does."

He stopped in the hall outside of wardrobe. "Tell Sienna and George I'll pick up everything for burgers on my way to your place."

"I can pick the stuff up," Jane said.

"I think it's my turn," Reed insisted. "You guys fed me last time."

"I don't mind. Really," Jane countered. "I have to run some errands for Sienna this afternoon anyway."

Reed looked at her skeptically. "Are you sure?"

"I'm sure." Jane pulled her phone from her pocket and clicked until she got to her list before showing it to Reed. "See?"

He scanned it; Walmart was one of her planned stops. "What does Sienna have you picking up at Walmart?"

"A few things for the house."

"If you're going there anyway, could I get you to do me a favor?"

"Sure. What do you need?" Jane scooted to the side of the hall when one of the lighting techs came out of the bedroom used for the upstairs set.

Reed gave the newcomer a nod of greeting before turning his attention back to Jane. "I had some photos printed that should be ready. I also need frames."

Jane began typing another note on her phone. "How many and what sizes?"

"Three 5x7s. I don't really care about the style. Something simple."

"I can do that."

"Here." Reed reached into his pocket and retrieved his wallet. He slid a credit card out and offered it to her. "You can pay for my stuff with this."

"I can take care of it, and you can pay me back. It won't cost that much."

"It's easier if you use this. I almost never carry cash, unless I'm traveling."

"Okay." Jane took the credit card and slid it into the back of her phone case. "I'll give this back to you when you come over tonight."

"Sounds good." Reed waited for Jane to walk through the door before following her inside. "Hey, Delilah. How's it going?"

"Good," the woman with red streaks in her hair answered. "Did I hear someone say they were going to Walmart?"

"I am this afternoon. Why?"

"Could I ask a huge favor?"

"Give me a list," Jane said in response.

"Sorry," Reed said. "I think I opened up a can of worms."

Jane offered a good-natured shrug. "It's no big deal. The work of an assistant is never done, and it's never dull."

Reed watched her retrieve Sienna's clothing for the next scene and head for the door. He wasn't sure why her reference to herself as an assistant irritated him. As she disappeared into the hallway, it struck him. He had asked for a favor from a friend, but she saw herself as an employee. He was going to have to do something to change that. Sienna's stand-in boyfriend or not, he enjoyed being around Jane, and he wanted to find out if she felt the same way.

11

JANE PARKED IN FRONT OF her apartment and found Reed standing on her porch. Her stomach lurched at the sight of him. His normal business suit from wardrobe had been replaced by khakis and a T-shirt that was several shades darker than his eyes.

She blew out a frustrated breath. She had no business noticing his eye color or his broad shoulders or anything else about him. And why was he on her front porch in the first place? If he were with Sienna like he was supposed to be, maybe she would stop thinking like this.

Before she managed to gather her things out of the front seat, he jogged across the narrow patch of lawn and pulled open her car door.

"What can I help with?"

She tried to imagine Sienna standing beside him. "Actually, if you can get the stuff out of the back, that would be great." She climbed out, her laptop bag in one hand and three plastic grocery bags in the other.

Reed opened the back door, and Jane bumped her door closed with her hip. "Does all of this come in?" he asked.

"Everything back there does. The stuff I got for wardrobe is in the trunk, but it can stay there until I go to the set tomorrow."

"Okay." Reed collected the rest of the groceries and followed her inside. He waved at the stack of boxes by the door. "Looks like you still have some unpacking to do."

"That's the stuff I had shipped in my car. I'll start on those tonight." Jane led the way into the kitchen and set everything on the table. Reed dropped his load beside hers.

"Do you want me to help you put everything away before I start making the hamburgers?"

Jane hadn't expected Reed to use her kitchen to prepare the food. Thinking it best to keep a professional distance between them, she retrieved the hamburger meat and handed it to him.

"I can take care of all this. Do you want to take the stuff for tonight up to Sienna's apartment?"

He looked up at her, confused. "Didn't she tell you Craig was getting home today?"

"Craig?" she asked. The name sounded vaguely familiar, but she didn't know why.

"Yeah." He stared at her for a moment and must have sensed her confusion. "You know. Her Navy SEAL."

"Oh, right." Embarrassed that she didn't remember the name of the man who had saved Sienna's life several months earlier, she turned away and retrieved a mixing bowl and a plate.

"Do you have any onion or seasoned salt?"

"The spices are in the cabinet above the stove, but I'm afraid I don't have a whole lot up there yet."

"It's okay. I can make do." He began digging through the spices while Jane put away the rest of the groceries.

She opened the bag filled with frames. "I almost forgot. I have the stuff I picked up for you."

"How did the photos turn out?"

"I didn't look." Jane opened her backpack and slid the protective envelope out from where she had stored it next to her laptop to keep the photos from bending.

Reed abandoned the food and came over to take the envelope from her.

"I picked up six frames. I figure I'll take whichever ones you don't want." Jane looked around the professionally decorated apartment. "I thought a few pictures might make this place feel more like home."

"That's why I printed these." He pulled them free and spread them out on the table. "What do you think?"

She looked down, surprised that she was in two of them. With Sienna, of course, but that didn't completely erase the oddity of Reed having a photo of her that he intended to display in his apartment.

Not sure what to say, she focused on the picture of the three of them from a few nights ago. "That one turned out better than I thought. I love the view of the water in the background."

"Me too."

Her gaze wandered to the third image. "Is this your family?"

"Yeah. That's my mom, dad, and little sister. This week she's decided to be an accountant."

Confused, Jane looked up at him. "How old is she?"

"Twenty. She's been through a few college majors already."

"She still has time to decide."

"Sometimes I think she keeps changing her mind to tease my mom. Mom's quite the planner. It about drove her nuts when I decided to pursue acting after college."

"I didn't realize you went to college. Weren't you with your last series for a few years?"

"Almost three. I started a few months after I graduated." He selected one of the frames and proceeded to put a photo in it. "Before that, I'd only done a few bit parts in movies and guest starred on a TV show."

"It's still pretty amazing that you've done so much already, especially with squeezing college in there."

"I guess."

"Did you serve a mission too?" Jane asked.

"Yeah. Minneapolis."

"Sounds cold."

"Oh yeah." He framed the next two pictures. When he completed his task, he laid them out on her table. "What do you think?"

Reality stared back at her. There she stood in framed color, a commoner beside royalty. Hollywood royalty, but a king and queen nonetheless. "They look good."

"I think so too." His eyes still on the photos, he moved closer, and his arm brushed against hers. A jolt shot through her, and for a moment, she didn't move, couldn't move.

She looked up at him and found herself captured in his gaze. The interest she saw reflected there both surprised and stunned her. Time stopped, and everything fell away but him.

He moved in front of her, their bodies still close. "I started to ask this earlier, but too many people were around. Would you go out with me sometime? Are you busy Saturday?"

Her stomach jumped, and for a brief moment, the word *yes* hung on the tip of her tongue. Then she remembered.

"How could you ask me such a thing?" Jane took a deliberate step back. "Sienna is my best friend. I would never do something like that to her."

"Something like what?"

"Just because you're on television doesn't mean you can have a girlfriend and then pick up whoever you want on the side." Anger and indignation rose inside her. "I thought you were better than that."

He stared at her, appearing truly shocked. Did he have so few scruples that he thought this kind of behavior was normal?

When he didn't respond, she retreated another step. "I need to get some air."

Jane dashed out the door, leaving Reed to stare after her.

* * *

Reed watched Jane exit out the back door onto the deck, her words still rolling through his brain. Girlfriend? Where did she get the idea . . . ?

The flash of understanding hit him like a brick that had been hovering over him for days. Did Jane really think he and Sienna were a couple? How could she not know about Craig? "Jane, wait!"

He rushed onto the deck to discover Jane had come to a screeching halt. He followed her gaze to where Sienna stood, her arms wrapped around Craig's neck, her lips pressed to his.

Jane looked at Reed, wide-eyed, a combination of shock, disbelief, and sympathy illuminating her features.

Craig must have sensed their presence because he pulled away from Sienna and shifted his attention to them. As he had done the first time they'd met, Craig slid his left arm around Sienna's waist and offered his right hand.

"Hey, Reed. How's it going?"

"Doing well, thanks." Reed stepped forward and shook his hand. "Glad to see you made it back okay."

"Thanks." Craig's gaze moved to Jane. "I don't think we've met. You must be Jane."

Numbly, Jane nodded.

"I'm sorry." Sienna smiled brightly at Jane. "Jane, this is Craig." She lowered her voice to a whisper. "Of course, we don't talk about him in public."

Confusion became Jane's dominant expression.

"Are you two joining us for dinner?" Reed asked when she didn't respond. "We were about to grill some hamburgers."

"Sounds great," Craig said. "I have to run a quick errand first, but we should be back in an hour or so."

"We'll see you then," Reed said.

Jane continued to stare after them, turning so she could watch Craig open the door of his truck for Sienna to climb in.

"I guess Sienna forgot to fill you in about Craig."

Jane's eyebrows drew together, and a wrinkle of concern marred her forehead. "I don't understand. Your girlfriend was just kissing that guy, and you're okay with it? What kind of relationship is this?"

"A friendship."

"Friendships are based on trust."

"Yes, and I trust that Sienna and her fiancé will be very happy together."

"Fiancé?"

"Fiancé," Reed repeated. "They started dating last winter around the same time her sister got married."

"I'm obviously missing something. She had me set up the press at the airport to catch the two of you together."

"That was an act." Reed leaned back against the deck railing. "Craig is a Navy SEAL. It wouldn't be good for his career to be paired with Sienna, at least not at the moment. I guess there's some mission he's been working on that makes it necessary for him to stay out of the spotlight."

Understanding dawned in her eyes. "So you made it look like you and Sienna were a couple so no one would think to look for her mystery man."

"Right. Everyone knew they were together after he saved her life, but with the upcoming release of *Beachfront*, they wanted to make sure he stayed in the shadows."

Her cheeks colored. "I had no idea."

"Sorry. I figured Sienna told you." He waved in the direction of the spot Sienna and Craig had occupied moments before. "Judging from Sienna's reaction when she introduced you to Craig, she thought you knew what was going on too."

Jane dragged her fingers through her hair. "I feel like an idiot."

Finding her embarrassment endearing, he pushed away from the rail and took a step closer. "I have to ask you something."

"What?"

"Were you avoiding me on set because you thought I was Sienna's boyfriend or because you didn't want to be around me?"

Her gaze met his. "I'm not the kind of girl to go after someone else's boyfriend."

"And I don't cheat." He put both hands on her arms. "Now that everything's out in the open, would you go out with me sometime? It would have to be low-key so it doesn't look like I'm dating someone behind Sienna's back, but I'm sure we can figure something out."

"I'd like that." She offered him a smile. "We should probably start on dinner."

"We have a little time before they get back. How about a walk on the beach?"

"I love the ocean at sunset." She looked out at the glistening waves.

"Me too." His hands slid down her arms to clasp her hands. "There's just one thing I need to do first."

"What's that?"

He leaned forward, stopping when his lips were a breath away from hers. He waited until the surprise melted into awareness and anticipation.

The moment he kissed her, a jolt shot through him, coursing through his veins. An unexpected longing grew from somewhere deep inside him and slowly worked its way into every part of his being. The scent of the ocean and the garden roses wound around them, mixing with the moment they created together.

He pulled back, his surprise reflected in the sea of green staring back at him. He took two breaths to steady himself, but he didn't trust his ability to speak. Instead, he brushed his lips against hers once more.

Time stalled, the world melting away until all his senses were filled with her. The breeze teased her hair, and he reached out to comb his fingers through it. He drew her closer, and something snapped into place like a missing puzzle piece finding a home.

When he pulled back a second time, everything tilted for a moment before righting itself into a brighter, more vivid image of what had existed moments before. Staring at her flushed cheeks and bright eyes, he took several breaths before he managed to find his voice. "I've been thinking of doing that since I met you."

Her lips curved. "I've been trying not to think of doing that since I met you."

He chuckled. Taking her hand, he started toward the steps. "Come on. Let's take a walk on the beach, and you can tell me what else you've been trying not to think about us."

When she didn't respond other than to fall into step beside him, he stopped to look at her once more. She had a serious look on her face. "I want there to be an us. Are you okay with that?" he asked.

"I want this too, but it's not going to be easy."

He gave her hand a squeeze. "Nothing worth having ever is."

12

WAS THIS REALLY HAPPENING? JANE strolled beside Reed along the deserted beach, amazement and disbelief filling her. Dozens of concerns about her growing infatuation for Reed had worked through her head, but she had never imagined this outcome.

A thread of annoyance threatened when she thought of how Sienna had neglected to confide in her, but she pushed that emotion back. From Sienna's earlier reaction, she suspected Reed's assumption was correct. Obviously Sienna thought Jane had already known about her true relationship with Craig.

"You realize we're going to have to be pretty inventive when we go out on dates," Reed said, breaking into her thoughts. "At least Sienna was kind enough to buy a place on a private beach."

The mere mention of future dates left her giddy inside, like a teenager about to experience her first kiss. But reality quieted some of the butterflies dancing in her stomach. "I'm more concerned with how things will be at work. I don't have acting talent like you and Sienna."

"It'll be easier than you think," Reed said as though he had already worked through the logistics in his mind. "Everyone believes Sienna and I are a couple, and they all know you keep her calendar. It makes sense that we would talk all the time."

"I guess that's true . . ."

"Don't worry." He stopped near the water's edge. "I should probably tell you that you're the only person I want to date."

The right side of her mouth quirked up. "I imagine it would be really complicated trying to date others while you're paired with Sienna."

"Even if Sienna and I weren't in the middle of this publicity stunt, I wouldn't want to go out with anyone else."

Surprised by the intensity in his eyes, Jane reached up and kissed his cheek. "I feel the same way."

* * *

"I can't believe this is happening to you again." Craig parked his truck beside the building where his squad kept their offices when they were in town.

"I can't either," Sienna said.

Craig heard her fear and reached out to take her hand. "Don't worry. We'll get it sorted out."

"I know you have a lot going on. If you don't have time to look at my computer, I can see if Charlie might be able to speed things along," she said, referring to her brother-in-law at the FBI.

"No. I'm glad you asked us to get involved. I'll feel more comfortable knowing what's going on. And I don't want you to fall too low on the police department's priority list." He turned off the engine and collected the case that contained Sienna's phone and laptop from the back seat. He circled around the truck and opened the door for her.

"You aren't going to get into trouble for helping me, are you?" Sienna asked.

"No. I already talked to Brent." Craig took her hand and started up the sidewalk. "He told me to secure everything in our office so we can look at it tomorrow in our spare time."

"I know you and your squad. You don't have spare time."

He opened the door for her. "Okay, so maybe Seth and I are planning to go in early tomorrow."

Sienna's left eyebrow winged up. "Who did you bribe to give up their lunch break?"

"Tristan and Damian."

They passed through the main entrance and started down a hallway on the left. "Tell them thank you for me."

"I already did. If it takes more than a couple hours to sort through everything, you may have to order some pizza for them."

"Let me guess. Quinn and Jay are the next two you're going to hit up for help."

"Yep. A couple of large pepperonis and they'll do about anything for you."

"I remember that about them."

Craig stopped at the door to the space he shared with several other members of his squad and used the cypher lock to gain access. Once inside, he headed for the black vaulted filing cabinet in the corner. He spun the dial and worked through the combination before opening the bottom drawer. He placed the case inside and secured it once more. "Okay, we're all set."

"I really owe you for this."

"I know." Craig crossed to where she waited by the door. Slipping his arms around her waist, he lowered his mouth to hers for a kiss. "I'm going to enjoy collecting."

"I'm sure you are." She pulled back when footsteps sounded in the hall behind her. "Come on. Let's go get dinner."

Craig's hands remained at her waist, holding her in place. When her eyes lifted to meet his, he gave her another brief kiss. "I really missed you."

"I missed you too."

* * *

Jane looked up from the tomato she was slicing when the door opened and Sienna walked in.

"Did you forget to tell me something?" Jane asked. Through the window, she could see Craig now standing by the grill, chatting with Reed and George.

"I don't think so. Why?"

"The publicity stunt . . ." Jane prompted her.

A wrinkle formed on Sienna's brow. "What are you talking about?"

"I'm talking about how I thought you were really going out with Reed." Jane set the knife aside, her earlier embarrassment now transforming into frustration. "All this time, I thought you were so happy because of him, but you were really engaged to someone else."

"I am so sorry." Sienna's cheeks flushed. "Jane, I could have sworn I told you about Craig."

The remorse on Sienna's face chased away the worst of Jane's annoyance. "Things were pretty crazy the last few months with my mom's treatments." She let out a sigh and tried to give Sienna the benefit of the doubt. "Maybe you mentioned it and I forgot."

"We both know better. You remember everything."

Jane motioned to where the men stood beside the grill. "Poor Reed. I really thought he was asking me out while he was still dating you."

"I bet you let him have it."

"You could say that."

Sienna's gaze followed Jane's before she looked back at her, seemingly catching the crux of the problem. "Wait. You and Reed?"

Jane smiled. "Yeah."

"Now I'm really sorry," Sienna said. "I had no idea you were thinking of him that way."

"I was trying not to because I thought he was your boyfriend." Needing something to do with her hands, Jane slid the sliced tomatoes onto a serving plate.

"Yeah, I guess that would have made for an awkward conversation. Can you forgive me?"

Jane let her gaze meet Sienna's. "I'm working on it."

"You know what this means, don't you?" Sienna asked.

"What?"

"I can go out with Craig in public again."

"I'm not following," Jane said. "What does my dating Reed have to do with you and Craig?"

"Publicly, I'm dating Reed. We can double date."

"I saw you and Craig together. I don't think anyone would see the two of you in the same room and not be able to notice the sparks flying."

Sienna cocked her head to one side. "You're exaggerating."

"No, I'm not." Jane shook her head. "Besides, won't the press recognize Craig from when he saved your life?"

"I doubt it. They don't have any clear shots of his face. Besides, when Reed and I are in the same room, that's where the cameras will be aimed. People see what they expect to see."

Jane pondered the truth of her statement. "I guess you're right. I was convinced you and Reed were a couple, and I normally spot the stand-in boyfriends."

The back door opened, and Reed walked inside. "Do you have a clean plate to put the burgers on?"

"Yeah." Jane picked one up off the counter. "Here you go."

"Everything should be ready in five minutes," Reed said.

"Thanks."

"Hey, Reed," Sienna said. "I was just telling Jane we should double date sometime."

"That's a great idea," Reed agreed. "I've been wanting to drive to Williamsburg and check out Busch Gardens."

"You and your amusement parks."

"What can I say?" Reed asked. "I like roller coasters."

"You two may be the perfect pair." Sienna jerked her thumb at Jane. "We've spent our share of time at Disneyland."

"You're never too old for Disneyland," Jane insisted.

Reed nodded. "I agree completely."

13

Jane opened her eyes, her mood as bright as the sunlight streaming through her window. She swung her legs over the side of the bed, and immediately a grin stole over her face as the memories of last night rushed through her.

Eager to get her day started, she showered and dressed.

She was halfway to the kitchen when her alarm went off. She couldn't remember the last time she had woken before her alarm, especially not by a full thirty minutes. Since arriving in Virginia, she hadn't managed to roll out of bed without hitting the snooze alarm at least twice until today.

Her heart fluttered with anticipation. The idea that she couldn't show her true feelings for Reed gave her some trepidation, but she decided to believe Reed and Sienna's assumption that people would see what they expected to see. For now, she was going to enjoy knowing that an interesting, fun, exciting man wanted to spend time with her.

Jane popped a piece of bread into the toaster and poured herself a glass of juice. The sound of the surf pounding against the sand gave her a sense of home. Deciding to enjoy her extra few minutes this morning, she buttered her toast and carried it and her juice out onto the deck.

Though she expected the temperature would reach the nineties today, with the breeze blowing in off the water, she debated if she should go back inside to grab a sweatshirt to ward off the chill.

"Jane Napierski?"

Jane whirled to face the source of the deep male voice, her juice sloshing over the side of her cup.

"Sorry. Didn't mean to startle you." The man appeared to be in his mid-thirties, his expression serious.

Instinctively, Jane reached for her back pocket, where she normally kept her cell phone only to realize she had left it inside. Her breath shuddered out, and fear snaked through her.

He reached into his suit jacket and produced a leather case the size of a wallet. He flipped it open to reveal his identification and badge. "Darren Rinzler. FBI. I'm working on the Blake case."

The sharpest edge of her fear receded, but enough remained to leave her skeptical. She looked out at the water, and her logic surfaced. In California, she could judge the time based on the sun's position over the ocean. Even though the sun was coming up on the wrong side of it, she didn't have to look at the clock to know it was still shy of seven thirty.

She suddenly wished she had taken a closer look at his badge. "It's a bit early to be calling on people, isn't it?"

"Normally, yes, but I got the message from Sienna Blake earlier that you would be available to come into our office today."

Tension settled in her neck and spread outward. "She didn't tell me anything about that."

"The message I got came through her brother-in-law," Agent Rinzler said. "Apparently Sienna thought you could shed some light on the electronic trackers you found on her computer." He must have sensed Jane's apprehension because he took a step back and waved toward her door. "I'm happy to wait here if you would like to call her."

"Thanks." Jane gave him a wide berth and made her way back into her apartment. She flipped the lock to give her some sense of security before retrieving her phone from her kitchen counter.

She hit Sienna's name on her favorites list.

"Hey, Jane. I was about to call you," Sienna said by way of greeting. "My brother-in-law is sending an FBI agent to pick you up this morning. They thought you might be able to help narrow down the source of the virus on my computer."

"He's here now." Jane let out a sigh. "Sienna, we really need to work on your communication skills."

"What?"

"It's a little unsettling to have some guy show up at"—she glanced at the clock—"seven thirty-two in the morning and not know he was coming."

"Sorry about that."

"I guess you're okay with me coming to work late today."

"Of course. I can manage."

"In that case, I'll see you later." Jane dumped the rest of her juice down the sink and set her glass on the counter. After she pocketed her cell phone and collected her purse, she walked out onto the deck.

She found the FBI agent waiting for her there. "Sorry about that. After everything going on lately, we're all a little cautious," she said.

"Understandable." Agent Rinzler started around the side of the house toward the street where he had parked. "It's about a half-hour drive from here. I can give you a ride and bring you back, or you're welcome to follow me over."

"I'll follow you."

He pulled a business card from his wallet and handed it to her. "The address of my office is on there in case we get separated. My number is on there as well."

"Okay. I'll see you there." Relieved to be able to rely on her own transportation, she walked to her car. She slid behind the wheel, her emotions finally settling enough for disappointment to replace her fear. She would much rather go to work where she would see Reed than deal with computer issues. But if this sacrifice of her time could help the police get closer to finding Sienna's stalker, it would be worth it.

* * *

Reed listened halfheartedly to Toni as she ran through the day's schedule, his eyes shifting toward the door each time it opened. He had to remember not to smile when he thought of how things had turned out with Jane last night. After all, to everyone he worked with, today was simply another day, not the first day of a new relationship with an intriguing, delightful woman.

The door opened again, and he looked up in anticipation. When Sienna walked inside without Jane, a bubble of disappointment surfaced.

"Reed?" Toni's voice broke into his thoughts. "Did you hear me?"

"Oh, sorry." Reed forced himself to look back at his assistant. "What time did you say I'm on set this morning?"

"Eight thirty." Toni looked at him suspiciously. "You seem distracted. Is everything okay?"

"Yeah." Reed glanced down at his watch. "I'd better get changed. I'll see you later."

He pulled his phone from his pocket, hoping to see a message from Jane. A seed of worry took root. Last night when he had left Jane's house, everything had been great. All of the misunderstandings were behind them, and they had talked about seeing each other this morning. So where was she? One of the new security guards passed him and heightened his concern.

Not one to stew over the unknown, he sent her a text. *Everything okay?*

His hope for an immediate response wasn't realized. He went into his dressing room and changed his clothes for his first scene. When his phone chimed, he snatched it up; Jane's message shone on his screen. *Everything's fine. Had to make a detour on the way to work.*

When are you getting here?

Not sure. Probably be there around lunchtime. I'll text you when I'm on my way.

Thanks. See you soon.

K.

Disappointed that he had to wait to see her, he pocketed his phone and headed for the set. At least this morning, he would be shooting an intense scene where he was supposed to feel a lot of frustration. He wouldn't have any trouble getting into character.

* * *

Jane passed through the door Agent Rinzler held open and looked around the reception area. She had expected to see something like the police stations she had seen on television. Instead, a receptionist sat at a curved desk more reminiscent of a corporate office than a law enforcement agency.

"Debra, can you please sign Miss Napierski in?"

"ID please." The woman in her fifties extended her hand.

Jane handed over her driver's license, signed the visitor log, and a moment later clipped on her visitor badge. She slid her license back into her wallet and fell into step beside Agent Rinzler.

They reached a conference room separated from the large bay of cubicles by a wall of glass. Inside, six chairs encircled an oval table, and a flat-screen hung on the wall.

Agent Rinzler pulled open the glass door and waited for her to enter before pulling it closed behind him.

As soon as they were alone again, Jane said, "What do you think I can help with?"

He sat across from her and waved at someone through the glass. "We would like you to walk us through everything you did on Sienna Blake's computer."

A woman opened the door and walked inside carrying a laptop.

"This is Naomi Albert. She's one of our forensic computer specialists."

Naomi slid into the seat beside Jane. She opened the screen and pushed the computer in front of Jane. "Since you were the person searching for the problem, I need you to walk me through everything you did."

"You realize I spent hours working on this, right?"

"I do." She gave Jane an apologetic look. "What I'm trying to do is decipher what code on here is from your diagnostics and what is from the invasive software."

"Okay." Jane leaned forward in her seat and tried to remember the details of how Sienna's current nightmare had started.

Agent Rinzler plugged a cable into the USB drive and turned on the flat-screen so the agents could see everything Jane did without needing to look over her shoulder.

"I have a keystroke logger installed on this laptop, so we won't have to worry about documenting everything ourselves," Naomi said.

"Do you think once you see what I did that you'll be able to trace the person who did this?"

"Our computer techs will keep working on it, and I know the navy has a few of their people looking into it too," Agent Rinzler told her.

"I hope someone has better luck than I did," Jane said.

"We'll all keep trying," Naomi promised. "Something is bound to break sooner or later."

"I hope it's sooner."

"Me too."

14

WITH HIS TEAMMATES' HELP, CRAIG followed the electronic trail from the snooper program on Sienna's laptop to Niger, through Budapest, London, Sao Paolo, Tokyo, Paris, Tunis, Sydney, and back through London and Tokyo again.

"Any luck so far?" Brent asked from his office doorway.

"Whoever did this was good. The signal is bouncing all over the world. Africa, Europe, Asia, South America. Even Australia," Craig said. "At this point, I feel like I'm running in circles."

"Maybe you are."

"What do you mean?"

"Have you hit any cities twice yet?" Brent asked.

"London and Tokyo."

"Both easy places to route signals through." Brent leaned on the edge of the empty desk opposite Craig. "Anything in the US?"

"No." Craig's brow furrowed. "In fact, there's nothing anywhere in North America."

"That's odd," Brent said. "I would think if Sienna picked up a stalker, it would be someone here in the States."

"She has a movie being released in the UK in a few months, but from what I understand, the promotion hasn't started yet."

"What about her last couple movies? I know one just released here in the States last month, but wasn't there one that hit Amazon Prime recently too?"

"She did mention something about that."

"Since her movies are available digitally, her stalker could be anywhere."

Craig raked his fingers through his hair. "Yeah, but I'm not going to rest easy until I'm sure he isn't anywhere near Virginia."

"Keep at it. If you don't find anything by this weekend, I suggest you take a break. From what Charlie said, the FBI hasn't had any luck either. Maybe a few days off will help us find the insight we're lacking."

"You're right. I just don't want to assume everything is okay and find out the hard way we were wrong."

"Can't say I blame you."

Craig clued into Brent's earlier comment. "Wait, is there something going on this weekend?"

"My brother-in-law has a box reserved for us at the Nationals game on Saturday."

"I assume you're talking about Amy's brother who plays for the Marlins?"

"That's the one. Matt thought it would be a nice coming-home present for us and our wives," Brent told him. "Of course, Sienna's invited too."

"I'm sure she'd love that, but we're supposed to be staying out of the spotlight right now."

"Which is why Matt got us box seats. Since it will only be us and his parents, we don't have to worry about people listening in on our conversations."

"Any chance you can snag two extra tickets for me?"

"Probably. Why?"

"Because Sienna is supposed to be dating her costar. I thought it would be nice to have him and his date join us to keep the gossip down."

"Good idea. I'll give Matt a call to see if he can get us the extra tickets." Brent hesitated a moment. "We will need to clear the costar and whoever he brings as a date though. The last thing we need is someone showing up who will take pictures of us and throw them up on social media."

"Reed is a childhood friend of Sienna's, so I doubt we have to worry there. I'll make sure to mention it though."

"And his date?"

"Sienna's assistant." Craig smiled. "From what I understand, Jane deals a lot with the press. Sienna trusts her."

"That's the important thing." Brent started for the door. "We've got time on the shooting range in fifteen minutes. Better secure what you're working on. We'll get a couple of the guys to help you out this afternoon."

"Do I need to come up with some kind of bribe?"

Brent's grin flashed. "Nah. It's either help you or pack parachutes for tomorrow's jump."

"I hate to say it, but I'm pretty sure they'd rather pack chutes than sit behind a desk."

"I guess you haven't met Master Chief Ninzo."

"Can't say that I have."

"Trust me," Brent insisted. "If it's a choice of working for him or helping you, they'll be here."

* * *

Jane took a right turn, certain she hadn't been to this particular area of town before. When she left the FBI office, she had turned on her GPS to guide her home. Of course, the GPS was actually programmed to the pizza place six blocks away from her house, but it was close enough to get her into familiar territory without risking having her home address in her phone in case it was lost or stolen.

The navigation voice told her to take a left turn, and Jane checked the directional display on her GPS unit. Why was it sending her south? She should be heading north. Two blocks later, she was directed to take yet another turn that would send her in the opposite direction to where her instincts told her to go.

She supposed there could be traffic on the freeway that would cause the GPS to reroute her, but after spending hours digging through computer code, she was ready to get back into familiar territory. The complexity of the tracking program on Sienna's computer worried her more than she wanted to admit.

Annoyed with herself for not paying better attention when she'd followed Agent Rinzler to his office, she read the street signs as she passed. Butts Station Road. Certainly she would have remembered that one. The lowering sun to her right sent a ripple of trepidation through her.

If someone tried to find Sienna through her laptop and phone, was it possible they could have hacked her phone too? The thought was so out in left field that she felt silly even entertaining it.

The navigation system told her to take the next right, and her sense of unease increased. "Better safe than sorry," she muttered. She reached out and powered off her GPS as well as her cell phone. And turned left.

Using the sun to confirm her direction, she took a turn at the next main street and headed north in the hopes of finding the interstate. She glimpsed a silver Camry as it changed lanes and followed behind her. Was it her imagination or had she seen that car before?

She shook her head. Paranoia. Her time working with the FBI today had given her a healthy dose of it. She was seeing things. Silver Camrys were one of the most common cars in the country. She passed through an intersection and noticed the sign indicating she should turn right to get to the interstate.

Blowing out a breath, she signaled and moved to the left lane, proceeding to make a U-turn at the next light. She glanced in her rearview mirror, her heartbeat quickening. Two cars behind her was a silver Camry.

* * *

Reed paced back and forth across George's living room.

"Reed, if you don't sit down, I'm going to tie you up," George said from where he stood at the kitchen counter rubbing spices onto the ribs he was marinating for tomorrow's dinner.

"Are you sure she's on her way home?"

"She said she would be home in time for dinner."

"When she texted me this morning, she told me she would see me by lunchtime."

"I doubt she knew how much detail the FBI wanted when she sent you that text," George said.

The oddity that Jane would communicate through George struck him. "How come she texted you about when she was coming home instead of me or Sienna?"

"I texted her to find out when she would be home."

Reed paced to the window and looked out again. Nothing. He walked back to the kitchen. Again.

"Reed, how about you shuck this corn for me?" George picked up a large grocery bag with a half-dozen ears of corn still in it.

Grateful for something to do, he pulled the first ear out and opened the lid of the garbage can so he could discard the husks as he worked. Every time an engine sounded outside, he looked through the window in the hope of seeing Jane's car.

He couldn't explain why he was so worried about her, but something had been grating on him since he left the studio and found out Sienna hadn't heard from her either. He shook his head and tried to grasp at common sense. He had really only started dating Jane yesterday. For all he knew, she might be the type to stop at a dozen places on her way home. Maybe she went shopping or had decided to eat out instead of coming straight home.

But he didn't think so.

Reed finished with the corn and looked at his watch again. Jane should have arrived at least thirty minutes ago. He pulled his phone from his pocket. "I'm going to call her."

"Go ahead. It will make both of us feel better."

Reed dialed her number, the fingers on his free hand tapping against his leg while he waited for the call to connect. Finally, it connected only to go to voice mail.

"It went straight to voice mail."

"Try again."

Reed called a second time. Again, Jane's recorded voice came on, telling him to leave a message. Immediately, he dialed a third time to receive the same result.

Reed shook his head. "Nothing."

George looked at his watch. "Okay, now you've got me worried."

Footsteps sounded on the deck, followed by a knock at the door. George wiped his hands on a kitchen towel and answered it, stepping aside to let Sienna in.

"Have you guys heard from Jane lately?" Sienna asked. "I thought she would be back by now."

George tossed the towel aside. "I'm going to call the FBI office and see if she might still be there." A minute later, George lowered his phone. "The office is already closed for the day."

Sienna pulled her phone from her pocket. "I'll see if Charlie can give us the number of the agent who came to get her today."

Worry churned in Reed's stomach. "I'm going to feel pretty ridiculous if she drives up and we find out she stopped for sushi or something."

"Jane doesn't eat sushi," Sienna said before speaking into the phone. "Hey, Charlie. Sorry to bother you, but we can't get ahold of Jane, and we're getting pretty worried here. Do you have anyone we can call to find out if she's still at the FBI office? The main number is going straight to voice mail."

Sienna fell silent for a moment and then said, "Thanks. I appreciate it."

"Well?" Reed asked the moment she hung up.

"Charlie's going to make some calls. He said he'd get back to me."

"I hope he doesn't take long. I'm not very good at this waiting game," Reed said.

George looked from Reed to Sienna. "He's not exaggerating."

15

Sienna paced to the window to stand beside Reed. Her brother-in-law had yet to call her back, and the past twenty minutes had felt more like twenty hours.

"Maybe her car broke down," Sienna said, searching for any logical explanation as to why Jane hadn't arrived home yet. "I know she had some work done on it right before she had it shipped."

Reed lowered his phone after yet another attempt to call her. "Her phone is still going straight to voice mail."

That, Sienna couldn't explain. Not only was Jane diligent about keeping her phone charged, but she also carried a portable battery pack and an extra power cord in the event that she did lose power during the day.

For the past few days, they had all been so focused on Sienna's safety. Could Jane's safety have been in jeopardy as well? And why would anyone mess with both of them?

Sienna's phone rang, and she snatched it up before reading the caller ID. "Hello?"

"Sienna, I talked to the agent who worked with Jane today," Charlie said. "He told me she left his office at three thirty."

"That was three hours ago."

"I know. I checked your local traffic and didn't see anything that should have caused her to be so late."

"Could she have been in an accident?" Sienna asked.

"My counterpart in Virginia checked with the local authorities. Nothing popped up with her description."

"I know her car is too old to have GPS on it, but what about tracing the GPS on her phone?"

"Technically, I'm not supposed to do that until she's been missing for twenty-four hours."

"Charlie . . ."

"But I did anyway." He interrupted before she could finish voicing her protest.

"And?"

"Her phone isn't registering. Best guess is that it's turned off." Charlie paused before asking, "Would Jane think to turn her cell off if she thought she was being followed?"

"I don't know." Sienna considered the possibility. "She might, especially since we just went through the trouble of replacing my phone and making sure my GPS signal isn't traceable."

"I'm going to call the agent I'm working with out there to see if he'll put a BOLO out on her and her car."

"Charlie, you don't think someone is after her because of me, do you?"

"I don't know," he said. "I'll call you as soon as I have anything."

The line went dead, and Sienna stared at her phone for several seconds before daring to look up at Reed's worried expression.

His voice was thick when he managed to speak. "He thinks something happened to her."

"He doesn't know, but he's asking the local authorities to help." Sienna lowered herself onto the chair by George's front window. "I think he's worried that whoever was messing with me might also be preventing Jane from coming home."

Reed's jaw tensed, and he stared out the window again, no doubt to give himself a minute to control his emotions. He shook his head. "This can't be happening."

Sienna put her hand on his shoulder. "I can't tell you how many times I've said that same thing over the past year." She fell silent until she was sure she could speak without choking on her words. "I got through it before, and we'll get through this now."

"She's got to be okay."

"She certainly has a lot of prayers being offered on her behalf right now."

The rumble of an engine sounded outside, and Sienna could feel Reed's muscles stiffen. "It's her!"

* * *

Reed bolted for the door and sprinted to the driveway, reaching Jane's car before she could open her own door. He tried to open it, but it was locked. As soon as he heard it click, he tried again, this time succeeding.

"Are you okay? Where have you been?" Reed asked. "We've been worried sick."

Jane's hand trembled when she reached for her purse, and Reed noticed the lack of color in her cheeks. The moment she stood, he pulled her into his arms.

Sienna put her hand on his back. "Let's get inside."

Realizing Sienna was trying to protect them from the possible prying eyes of the paparazzi or anyone else who happened to recognize them, he slipped one arm around Jane and the other around Sienna.

George passed them. "I'll make sure her car is locked up."

"Thanks, George." Reed instinctively headed for Jane's front door. As soon as they were inside, he asked again, "Jane, what happened?"

She reached out and put her hand against the wall as though to steady herself. "I'm not sure."

"It took you over three hours to get home," Sienna said. "Did you get lost?"

"Kind of." Jane ran her fingers through her hair, pulling it back from her face for a moment before letting it fall back into place. "I tried using my GPS to get home, but it felt like it was sending me in the wrong direction. Then I started worrying that someone might be trying to find you through me, so I turned off my phone and tried to backtrack."

"That doesn't explain why it took so long," Reed said. "Or why you're so pale."

"I was heading back to the freeway when I noticed a familiar car. I was afraid I was being followed, so I passed the entrance and detoured to see if the car stayed behind me."

"Did it?"

Her breath shuddered out. "Yeah."

"What happened?" Sienna asked anxiously.

"I drove around for a while, hoping to lose him. I even ran a red light, but he didn't back off. Finally, I found a fire station and pulled in there. A couple of firemen were out front. When I told them I thought I was being followed, they all looked at the car and it took off."

"Did you get the license plate or anything?"

"I wrote it down." She pulled a scrap of paper from her purse with a series of letters and numbers scrawled on it. "The fire chief said he would pass the information on to the police. Then he followed me to the closest gas station so I could gas up, and he gave me directions to get back here."

"That must have been terrifying for you," Sienna said. "Jane, I am so sorry. This probably has something to do with whoever tampered with my computer and phone."

"Whoever it is, maybe now we'll be able to find him," Reed said.

"I hope so." Sienna held up her phone and stepped toward the kitchen. "I'm going to call Charlie to let him know Jane made it back here."

Reed pulled Jane into his arms again. "I was so worried about you."

"I'm sorry I didn't call. I should have asked the fire chief to let you all know where I was, but I was so anxious to get home, I didn't think about it until I was already on the road again."

"It doesn't matter now. You're home, and you're safe."

"How long do you think we can stay that way?" Jane leaned back so she could see his face, and Reed saw tears shimmering in her eyes. "If someone really did hack into my GPS, who knows what they're capable of."

"Now you're really scaring me," Reed said. "Did you manage to get a good look at the person following you?"

"No. He always left a car or two between us."

"Sounds like a pro."

"I can't think of what that kind of pro would want with me unless it was to get to Sienna."

Sienna returned from the kitchen, and her voice wavered when she asked, "What would a pro want with me?"

"I have no idea." Reed saw the way the color had drained from her face. "I think you should call Craig though."

"I already texted him." She drew a shaky breath. "If whoever was following Jane was really looking for me . . ."

"That means they know more about you than we thought," Reed finished for her.

"I'm not liking the sound of this," Sienna said.

"Neither am I."

16

CRAIG WOKE IN THE MIDDLE of the night, a new sense of clarity struggling to break through his semiconscious brain. He and his squad had spent hours trying to trace the snooper program on Sienna's laptop and the virus that had infected her phone. Even Seth hadn't been able to break out of the loop of public servers and hidden domains.

All of them had noticed the same thing: no sign of any signal going through the United States. The hope that the perpetrator was some foreign fan with more tech savvy and curiosity than malice had bloomed over the past week when no additional signs of a threat had surfaced.

Yet, for the past two days, something had been nagging at him like a memory on the tip of his brain that refused to be recalled.

Fear resurfaced, an overwhelming feeling that whoever had tunneled their way into Sienna's electronics was really in the US. After all, if he or anyone on his team pulled a stunt like this, they would avoid sending any signal through where they were really located.

His brain now whirring, he swung his legs over the side of his bed, grabbed his cell phone from his bedside table, and hit a number from his favorites.

Fifteen seconds later, a groggy Damian answered. "*Qué?*"

Craig responded in Spanish, knowing all too well that his teammate's brain took a minute to shift into English. "*Necesito ayuda.*" Simply translated: I need help.

"*Qué necesitas?*"

"Are you awake?" Craig asked.

"*Sí.*"

Craig nearly smiled. He couldn't count how many times their conversations bridged languages. "I've been thinking about how none of the signals on the snooper program have been going through North America."

"Or Central America," Damian added, now awake enough to speak in English.

"I think whoever is spying on her is here in the US"

Damian must have followed his logic because he didn't hesitate before he asked, "What can I do to help?"

"I want to do a threat analysis on her place and where she works. I thought we could have our morning run through her neighborhood before we check out her house and the beach."

"I bet Brent would let some of the other guys help too."

"I'll ask him in the morning," Craig said, feeling a little more at ease. At least in the morning he would feel like he was doing something to help ensure Sienna's safety.

"What time is this run of ours starting?"

"0500," Craig said, not bothering to look at the clock. "That will give us time to look over Sienna's house before we report to base."

"I'll see you then."

"Thanks, Damian."

"*De nada.*"

* * *

Jane tried to ignore the tightness in her chest as she walked out of her apartment Thursday morning. Every time she thought things were falling into a routine, something changed.

She had been excited about exploring the changes in her relationship with Reed, but she could do without the fear that came from her experience yesterday. She peered out her window at a police car parked across the street and mustered her courage before walking outside.

George stood watch at the corner of the deck, where he could see her front door as well as the stairs leading to Sienna's apartment. He glanced in her direction. "Are you ready?"

"I think so." Jane gripped her purse.

"Sienna will be right down," George said. "I want you to ride with us."

"I was going to ask if I could anyway," Jane admitted. "After yesterday, I'm not anxious to do any driving."

"That's understandable." The door opened overhead, and Sienna descended the stairs.

Instantly, George whisked everyone to the car, his eyes scanning the area. As soon as they were inside, he made a call.

"Ready?" George asked whoever answered on the other end. He seemed to have received the expected answer because he hung up and started the car.

They pulled out onto the street, and the police car took up position behind them. "Are we really getting a police escort to work?" Jane asked.

"For the next couple days anyway." Sienna twisted around in her seat to look at her. "My brother-in-law called in a favor."

Feeling a little more secure, Jane let herself relax in her seat. "Tell him thank you for me."

"I will." Sienna studied her. "Are you sure you're okay to work today?"

"Yeah," Jane said, trying to convince herself as much as Sienna. "Besides, I really don't want to be alone."

"No chance of that," George muttered.

Jane noticed a look pass between George and Sienna. "Am I missing something?"

"You got Sienna worried enough yesterday that she's calling in some extra help," George said.

"What kind of help?"

"Craig and a couple of his friends are going to stop by today," Sienna said. "Craig wanted to check out the beach access and make sure the set is secure."

"Won't that be awkward having Craig around when you're supposed to be dating Reed?" Jane asked.

"It'll be fine," Sienna said. "Besides, I thought I could have you be our liaison between Craig and the producers today. You know what's really going on, and it will also let the two of you be seen together before we go to the game on Saturday."

"Are you sure you still want to go to the game?" Jane asked. "That's a lot of people."

"And no one expects us to be there," Sienna reminded her. "Besides, I think it will do all of us some good to get out of town for a few hours."

George glanced at her in the rearview mirror. "I agree with Sienna. Having you two with the Saint Squad for the day will give me and the security company I hired time to do a detailed assessment of what enhancements we need to make to the house."

"The Saint Squad?" Jane asked.

"Craig's squad," Sienna elaborated. "We'll have fun. You'll see."

* * *

Jamal entered the apartment and gave a frustrated shake of his head.

"You didn't get it?" Abdul asked. He waited for his brother to follow Jamal inside before asking, "What happened? You spent days hacking into this woman's phone. Her GPS should have led her right to where we wanted her."

"She must have shut it off," Jamal said. "It appeared to be working perfectly, and then suddenly, she took a wrong turn and kept changing her direction."

"I think she noticed one of us," Munjid added. When he didn't clarify who had been spotted, Abdul guessed his brother's inexperience had been the cause of the problem.

"Have you found where they're staying?" Abdul asked.

"Not through their electronic signals . . ." Munjid began.

Abdul caught the gleam in his brother's eye. "But you found another way."

"We think so," Munjid said.

"The police department dispatched a squad car for protection detail a few hours after we lost her," Jamal added.

"You think they were sent to her house."

"That's precisely what we think." Jamal tapped his phone against his palm. "We won't be able to get to her with the extra security, not without risking being seen."

"Then perhaps we need to get caught."

Munjid looked from Abdul to Jamal and back again. "I don't understand."

"Jamal said someone has been trying to trace our signals. If they catch who they're looking for, those efforts will stop," Abdul said. "It's like in a game of chess. Some pawns can be sacrificed; others need to guard the prize."

Though his brother's confusion remained, understanding dawned on Jamal's face. "I'll take care of it."

* * *

Craig glanced at the spot across the street where two paparazzi leaned against a car, their cameras hanging around their necks. Turning his back on that annoyance, he continued along the edge of the studio property with Jane at his side. "I don't see any sign of intruders."

"How can you tell?" Jane asked.

"See the wave patterns along the fence line?" Craig squatted down beside the fencing that separated the private beach belonging to the television studio from the stretch of sand that serviced the residents beyond. He checked it for tampering before straightening. "Those rocks over there create a rip current through this area. Someone trying to access the set from the ocean would struggle to get to shore."

"You could do it though, couldn't you?" Jane asked.

"I could do it, but if I were going to break in here, I would come from the rocks over there and try to get through the fence before I would choose a water entry." Craig saw Damian approaching from the far side of the beach. When he reached them, Craig asked, "Anything?"

"No." He spoke rapidly in Spanish and gave a subtle nod toward the waves crashing on the rocks.

Craig said something to him before Damian started back toward the parking area.

"What did he say?"

"Oh, sorry. He tends to slip into Spanish when he isn't thinking about it." Craig started toward the house, where shooting was currently taking place. "He suggested a surveillance camera be installed on that side of the beach. He agrees that it's the most likely place for an intruder to try to get in."

Jane fell into step beside him. She didn't know this man well, but she found herself trusting him. "Do you think whoever was following me yesterday was really the same person who was spying on Sienna?"

"It's hard to say. The FBI is checking out your cell phone to see if they can find any evidence of tampering, but so far, no one has said anything."

"I'm starting to wonder if I was just being paranoid," Jane said.

"Always follow your instincts," Craig said. "I tell Sienna that all the time. It's better to be paranoid than to find out you ignored a prompting that could save you from a world of hurt."

"I guess if you put it that way, I don't feel so silly."

They reached the parking lot where Damian and one of his other teammates waited for him.

"Jay, did you see any problems?" Craig asked.

"A couple of suggestions for enhanced security but nothing indicating a prior breach."

"That's good news," Jane said. "Do you want to meet with the producer?"

"We need to get back. We have a dive this afternoon," Craig said. "I'll type up our notes and bring them over tonight."

"If it's easier, you can email them to me," Jane suggested.

"I'm avoiding electronic communication with both you and Sienna at the moment."

Jane recognized the wisdom in that decision. "Smart. I'll see you tonight."

Craig lowered his voice and leaned closer. "Tell Sienna I'll be over around six."

"I will."

"Good meeting you, Jane." Jay lifted his hand in a wave and headed toward the car they had all arrived in.

"You too." Jane turned and headed for the door. Despite the reassurances by the three Navy SEALs, she was eager to get inside to safety.

17

CRAIG HEADED FOR HIS OFFICE ten minutes later than he had planned. His early-morning run along the beach near Sienna's house had morphed into an early-morning briefing with the police officers stationed across the street.

Their report of no unusual activity should have given him some sense of comfort, but he felt like a pawn in a chess game, and he still had no idea who the players were.

"Craig," Brent called out as he passed his office.

Craig paused in Brent's doorway. "Hey, sorry I'm late. It took longer than I thought when I checked in with Sienna's security detail this morning."

"That's not what I wanted to talk to you about." Brent waved him inside and motioned to his computer screen. "I got a call from Charlie a few minutes ago."

"About?"

"They have a lead." Brent waited for Craig to circle his desk so he could see his computer monitor. "They searched through the logs we sent them and managed to narrow down the origin."

"Where is he?"

"They found hits in Atlanta and Chesapeake."

"Chesapeake, Virginia? That's less than twenty miles away."

"I know."

"Do they know who our guy is?"

"They're still working on that."

Frustration rose up inside Craig. "So we still don't have any idea why he is after Sienna and Jane."

"Charlie thinks he was using Jane to try to find Sienna," Brent said. "Best guess is that he's some sort of stalker. The FBI is sending Sienna's laptop and phone to one of their best computer forensics specialists. It sounds like the guy has been on leave for the past few weeks after the birth of his first child. They're hoping he can identify who's on the other side of the keyboard."

"I can't wait for that to happen," Craig said.

"I'm sure Sienna and Jane feel the same way."

"And Reed."

"Reed?" Brent asked.

"Sienna's costar. He's the one coming with us to the game on Saturday."

"I look forward to meeting him."

"He seems like a good guy." Craig headed for the door. "You'll let me know if you hear anything else?"

"You know I will."

"Thanks, Brent."

"Anytime."

* * *

Nerves fluttered in her stomach when Jane heard the knock on the door. Even though it had been three days since her relationship with Reed had changed, this would be their first real date. Added to that, she was about to go to a public event where the man she was interested in had to pretend to be interested in someone else. Talk about a tangled web.

She opened the door to find Reed standing across the threshold, a faded blue T-shirt hanging comfortably over his torso and cargo shorts completing the outfit. He had his keys in one hand and a ball cap in the other.

Reed's lips curved into a smile. "Hey, beautiful. Are you ready to go?"

Her cheeks reddened at the unexpected compliment. "I think so." She slipped on the sandals she had left by the door and picked up her purse.

The moment she stepped outside, Reed put his hat on, and she laughed. "Why are you wearing a Dodgers cap to a Nationals' game?"

"I like the Dodgers."

"Yes, but the Dodgers aren't playing in the game we're going to."

"Doesn't matter."

Footsteps sounded on the stairs leading from Sienna's apartment. The moment Sienna and Craig rounded the corner, Sienna gave Reed a disapproving look. "Really, Reed? Don't you think you can leave that hat home for one game?"

Reed shook his head in mock disappointment. "How you managed to grow up in LA and end up a Diamondbacks fan is beyond me."

"Maybe it's a good thing the Diamondbacks aren't playing either," Jane said.

"Probably," Craig agreed.

"Reed, seriously. We're supposed to be blending in," Sienna said. "That hat is going to make you stand out."

"Don't worry." Reed grinned. "If anyone notices us, I'll make sure I give you a big sloppy kiss on your cheek."

Sienna wrinkled her nose. "Ew."

"Hey, that would have you trending on social media by the end of the day," Jane said.

"Thanks, but no thanks," Sienna said. "I don't mind trending but not like that."

Jane stepped between them and put one hand on Reed's back and the other on Sienna's. "Come on, you two." She guided them toward the car. "Time to go."

Reed flashed a smile at her. "This is going to be fun."

* * *

Reed changed lanes on the interstate, his cap now lying on the console between him and Sienna. He glanced briefly at his childhood friend. "Okay, I have to say this is pretty sad that you can't even sit next to the guy you're planning to marry."

Sienna motioned toward Craig, who sat in the back seat beside Jane. "Yeah, but you never know when the paparazzi are going to show up."

"We're driving on I-95 at seventy miles per hour. I doubt anyone is going to get a photo of us here."

"Not here necessarily, but we have to park sometime."

"Minor details," Reed said.

Craig leaned forward. "In my line of work, we stick with the Boy Scout motto: Be prepared."

"At least we're able to travel together in the same car," Jane put in.

"True." Reed glanced at her in the rearview mirror.

"And if someone does catch us and we happened to hit a couple of news cycles, there will be that much more interest when they start airing our promos," Sienna said.

"Sounds like I need to leak some photos of you two today," Jane said.

"As long as they don't include any sloppy kisses," Sienna said.

"You are no fun," Reed countered.

Ignoring the banter between them, Craig spoke to Jane. "Maybe you should leak the photos after we're on our way home. We'll have a lot more fun if we don't have to worry about everyone cluing into Sienna's presence at the game."

"Good point. I'll post them on our way back."

"In the meantime," Sienna began, shifting in her seat to look back at Craig and Jane, "which one of you is going to help me hide Reed's ball cap from him?"

"I don't go to any ball game without this hat."

"But we aren't going to see the Dodgers. We're watching the Nats and the Marlins."

"So?" Reed's shoulders lifted. "That doesn't mean I can't make sure everyone knows where my allegiance lies."

"I think if we double-team him, we can take him," Jane told Sienna.

"Or we could have Craig take care of it for us," Sienna suggested. "I figure a Navy SEAL should be able to handle such an easy challenge."

"Hey, leave me out of this," Craig said. "I'm not about to mess with anyone when it comes to a favorite team."

"Sounds like we're on our own," Sienna said.

Jane leaned forward. "I'm sure we can come up with something."

Sienna appeared to be deep in thought, and Jane noticed the way her friend's eyes brightened with amusement. "Actually, I think I do have an idea."

"I don't suppose you're going to share it with me in front of Reed."

"We'll talk later."

"Reed, I'm afraid you may have taken on more than you can handle," Craig said.

"I don't know about that."

* * *

Jane couldn't stop the grin when Reed followed her inside the suite at the baseball stadium and automatically removed his hat. Granted, they had received a few odd looks as they'd made their way from the gate to where they were watching the game.

When Sienna caught her eye and winked, Jane had to bite the inside of her cheek to keep from laughing. Clearly, Sienna had known their seats were indoors, even though when she had issued the invitation, she had simply said she had extra tickets to the game for them. Reed had probably thought as she had, that they would be outside with the rest of the fans. Instead, they were situated on the third level with a window overlooking the infield. The suite itself had a long table where their group would be able to eat while enjoying the game.

"You made it," the tall, dark-haired man nearest them said.

"Hey, Brent. This is Reed Forrester and Jane Napierski," Craig said. "Jane, Reed, this is Brent Miller, my commanding officer."

"Ah, the boss." Reed shook the hand Brent offered.

"Something like that."

"Brent's brother-in-law is Matt Whitmore," Craig added.

"On the Marlins?" Reed asked.

"That's him." Brent waved at the tall, slender woman across the room. "That's my wife, Amy, over there with her parents."

"Isn't that . . ." Jane began.

Before she could finish her question, the distinguished man in the corner crossed to them. He greeted Craig and Sienna before turning to Jane and Reed. "You must be the other boyfriend and girlfriend."

Jane's smile was immediate. "I guess you could say that."

"Senator Whitmore, it's good to see you again." Craig shook the older man's hand.

"You too, Craig. We were hoping you and Sienna would be able to make it."

A striking couple entered: a tall, blond man who was a younger version of the senator and a woman who was the blonde version of Sienna.

Jane put her hand on Sienna's arm. "You didn't tell me your sister was coming."

Sienna turned toward the door. "Kendra!"

"You're here!" Kendra rushed across the room and hugged Sienna.

"Hey, trouble," Reed said to Kendra, hugging her in turn. He looked up at her husband. "Charlie. It's good to see you again."

"You too, Reed." Charlie's gaze landed on Jane. "I don't think we've met. I'm Charlie Whitmore."

"Jane Napierski."

"Good to meet you."

Jane looked from Charlie to the senator to Brent, her gaze finally landing on Sienna. "I'm confused. You're all related?"

"In a roundabout sort of way," Senator Whitmore said. "Brent married our daughter, Amy. Our youngest son, Charlie, married Sienna's sister, Kendra."

"And we're all here to watch your other son play baseball."

"That's right." The senator motioned across the room to where a handful of people in their twenties and thirties chatted. "If you're not already confused, wait until you meet the rest of the gang."

Craig took over the introductions, rattling off names, beginning with Tristan, the easy-going Texan. Then Quinn, the dark-haired, quick-witted man who had his arm around his wife, Taylor. Seth, the exceptionally tall, dark-skinned man and his pregnant wife, Vanessa.

More people were ushered in, led by Jay and Damian.

Jane had expected to feel like an outsider, but she found everyone to be welcoming, even going out of their way to include her and Reed in conversations.

When Jane sat down at one of the tables, Jay's wife, Carina, took the seat beside her. "Jane, you've known Sienna for a long time, right?"

"About three years. Why?"

"I'm trying to design her wedding dress—"

"Wait. You're Carina Wellman? The fashion designer?" Jane asked.

Color washed into Carina's cheeks. "It sounds so weird to hear my name said like that, but yeah, that's me."

"We've talked on the phone," Jane said. "You designed Sienna's gown for the last Emmys."

"Oh, yes. I hadn't put that together," Carina said. "You're her assistant who was in California."

"That's right." Jane took a sip of her soda. "What can I help you with?"

"I was hoping you might have some insights I can use to make her dress more personal." Carina waved across the room to where Sienna was chatting with Craig. "You know how hard it is to get Sienna to sit still long enough to brainstorm."

"Yes, I do."

From his seat on the other side of Jane, Reed leaned forward. "Maybe you could figure out a way to weave in the Dodgers' logo."

Carina's elegant eyebrows drew together.

"Ignore him," Jane insisted with a shake of her head. "He and Sienna have been feuding about their baseball allegiances since we left Virginia Beach."

"Just trying to help," Reed said.

Jane caught sight of the nachos Brent was carrying to the seat a few spots down from her. "Reed, do you think you could get me some of those nachos? They look so good."

He eyed her suspiciously. "Do you really want some, or are you trying to get rid of me?"

"I would never try to get rid of you," Jane said.

Reed rose from his seat. "Carina, do you want anything?"

"I would love a water bottle."

"I'll be right back."

The moment Reed headed for the suite attendant, Carina turned to her. "Now, about the dress—"

Before Carina could finish her sentence, Mrs. Whitmore approached. "Oh, are we talking about Sienna's wedding?"

"We are."

"I love the temple at Christmastime."

"The temple?" Jane looked from Carina to Mrs. Whitmore. "Are you LDS?"

"I am."

Carina waved to encompass the room. "The whole squad is, except for Damian."

"Seriously?" Jane asked. "How did that happen?"

"When the squad was formed, someone up the chain of command decided to put the Mormon boys together," Carina explained. She smiled when she added, "My husband actually learned about the Church when he joined the squad."

"He converted?"

"He did."

"So you're LDS too?" Mrs. Whitmore said.

"Yes. I grew up in the gospel," Jane told her.

"I'm surrounded," the man behind her said, his Hispanic accent evident.

"You know, Damian, surrender is an option," Carina said.

"That's what you always say." He motioned to the window. "Time to stand. The game is about to start."

The first notes of the national anthem rang out, and Jane stood. Out of the corner of her eye, she noticed the way the SEALs stood at attention, their absolute respect for their country nearly palpable. A shiver ran through her, and a new depth of patriotism bloomed. She lived in the land of the free, and she was looking at the men who embodied the expression "the home of the brave."

18

REED REPLACED THE NOZZLE AND screwed the gas cap back on his car. He looked up at the convenience store beside the gas pumps, where Jane, Sienna, and Craig were standing at the counter paying for their purchases. When they returned to the car, Craig approached him by the driver's side door.

"You ready?" Reed asked.

"Yeah, but it dawned on me that it's way too dark for anyone to see into your car now," Craig said.

Reed caught the gist of his comment. "Maybe we should give Jane a turn navigating for me."

"My thoughts exactly." Craig opened the back door and motioned Sienna inside.

A minute later, they were on the road again, now seated beside their respective dates. Reed slid his hand over and laid it on Jane's.

Jane turned her hand palm up and linked her fingers with his. "That was a lot of fun." She glanced back at Craig. "I really like your teammates."

"They're good guys," Craig said.

"That was nice of Jay to invite us to their barbecue next weekend," Jane said.

"Are you sure it's okay for us to crash the party?" Reed asked. "It seems like a pretty big group for a backyard barbecue."

"Not at Jay and Carina's house. It's enormous, and they're on a private beach."

"How does a navy lieutenant afford a place on the beach?"

"Apparently, Carina came into some money a couple years ago," Craig told them. "It happened before I joined the team, so I don't know all the details, but Jay's parents live on the second floor of their place, and Jay and Carina live on the third."

"What's on the first?" Reed asked.

"A couple of guest rooms, the rec room, and an indoor lap pool."

"Sounds amazing," Jane said.

"It is." Sienna leaned forward in her seat. "Reed, even your dad would approve."

Jane glanced at Sienna before looking at Reed, confused. "Your dad?"

"He's a real estate agent," Reed said.

"He's not just any real estate agent," Sienna added. "Barry is one of the top agents in Malibu. He's the guy everyone trusts."

"Having your dad for a client didn't hurt his reputation," Reed said dryly.

"Maybe you should let him have you for a client," Sienna suggested.

"I don't know . . ." Reed said. This conversation wasn't a new one, but it was more than finances that made him hesitate. He didn't want to make such a major purchase until he was prepared to build a real home. He wasn't sure he was ready for that kind of permanence at this point in his life.

Jane rubbed her thumb over the back of his hand, and he took a quick look in her direction. Then again . . .

Sienna pressed on. "You should at least meet with an accountant, or you're going to get killed with taxes. Just creating a business to funnel your income through isn't going to be enough."

"So you keep telling me."

"You may be older," Sienna teased, "but I'm wiser."

Reed simply shook his head. "I have no response to that."

"Reed, you're a very smart man," Craig said with complete sincerity.

"Hey!" Sienna protested. Reed didn't see the elbow Sienna jabbed into Craig's side, but he heard the quick expulsion of breath. "You're supposed to be on my side."

"I am," Craig insisted. "I was simply admiring Reed for his wisdom in knowing when to retreat."

* * *

Jane walked into church behind Sienna, with Craig and Reed trailing behind them. The rowdy group of baseball fans she had spent last night bantering with now sat in the back three pews, the men in their white shirts and ties, the women in dresses, all exhibiting calm demeanors.

Jane nearly smiled at the memory of Amy and Vanessa's rather loud debate about whether the manager of the Marlins should have used a pinch hitter in the eighth inning.

Seth stifled a yawn, the only outward indication that none of them had gotten much sleep last night.

Sienna stopped and waited for Craig to take the seat in the back pew by his teammate, Damian. Jane bit back a smile. For a guy who was so adamant about not being LDS, he looked pretty comfortable sitting in the chapel.

Realizing that Sienna was orchestrating their seating arrangements so they could sit beside their respective boyfriends, Jane waited for the rest of her friends to take their seats so that Sienna was sitting between the two men. She had to remind herself not to reach for Reed's hand when she sat beside him. Despite the blood-pumping kiss he had given her last night when he'd dropped her off, publicly he was still Sienna's boyfriend.

In front of Jane, Carina yawned and looked back at her. "Is it just me, or did morning come faster today?"

"It's not just you," Jane said.

Reed stretched his legs out in front of him and leaned back in his seat. "If I start snoring—"

"Don't even think about going to sleep," Sienna warned. She leaned forward so she could see Jane clearly. "We can take turns elbowing him to keep him awake."

"You guys are no fun," Reed complained.

"We're in church. We're here to be spiritually fed, not to have fun." Sienna managed to keep a straight face, but humor danced in her eyes as she delivered her line.

"I think we should do both," Reed countered.

The bishop stood to begin the meeting, and a hush fell over the congregation. Jane settled back in her seat, appreciating the sensation of being surrounded by friends who shared her beliefs.

* * *

Craig let himself enjoy the weekend with Sienna, but when he hadn't heard from the FBI by Monday afternoon, he picked up the phone and called his future brother-in-law. Charlie answered on the second ring.

"Hey, Craig."

"Charlie, sorry to bother you, but is there any news about Sienna's stalker?" Craig asked as he headed from the helipad toward his car.

"Nothing yet," Charlie said. "I got a call from the agents we had monitoring Sienna's house and work. They didn't see anything out of the ordinary."

"Any luck on tracing the signal of whoever was monitoring her phone and computer?"

"We ran into the same problems you did. The signal circles through so many cities it's impossible to figure out where it originated."

"So we're back to where we started."

"I'm afraid so." Charlie was clearly frustrated. "I do have a piece of good news though."

"What's that?"

"Our guys also tried to track Sienna's signals through her phone and laptop and weren't able to find her through the GPS signals on either."

"That makes sense. I put a scrambler on both after the last problem she had. You can only access her GPS if you have the right code."

"Your efforts paid off. Even though whoever bugged her electronics could see what she was doing on the internet, they couldn't access her location."

"At least that's something."

"The local police have agreed to maintain a higher presence in the area of her studio. Other than that, there's not much else we can do at this point."

Craig's stomach clutched at the thought of Sienna once again finding herself in danger. "I appreciate you looking into things for us."

"Least I can do," Charlie said. "Most likely, this was some tech-savvy fan who wanted to get closer to Sienna. Now that he's been cut off and we haven't seen any further attempts at access, hopefully he'll give up."

"We always hope."

"I know," Charlie said. "Hope for the best. Prepare for the worst."

"It's how we've been trained."

"I'm praying neither of us needs our training this time around."

"That makes two of us."

19

JANE STIFLED A YAWN AS she made her way to the production office. The six o'clock call time shouldn't have bothered her, but even after two weeks in Virginia, her body hadn't quite adjusted to the eastern time zone.

Toni looked up from the copy machine when she walked in. "Good morning."

"Morning," Jane said. "Are those today's scripts?"

"The first two anyway. I heard the director talking to the writers this morning. Sounds like some scene changes are in the works."

"I hate it when they change things last minute."

"I know what you mean." Toni crossed to her and handed her Sienna's scripts. She looked around before lowering her voice. "Do you know what's going on with Reed and Sienna?"

"What do you mean?"

"I've hardly seen them together for the past few days."

"They're together all the time," Jane said, hoping she sounded casual.

"Not lately."

"They were at the Nationals game on Saturday."

"I saw some of the Twitter feed on that, but you know how this business is. You can never tell what's real and what's staged." She glanced at the empty hallway. "I was pretty bummed when I found out they were dating. Reed is such a great guy."

A little surge of jealousy surfaced, but Jane quickly pushed it aside. Reed had been working with Toni for weeks before Jane had arrived. She had to believe that if he had had any interest in Toni, he would have already acted on it. "Reed is a great guy," Jane managed to say. "It's great that he and Sienna have such a good relationship."

"In this business, you never know how long these things will last," Toni said. "I thought for sure Sienna was going to end up with the guy who saved her life a few months ago. That sure ended fast."

Jane chose her words carefully. "Some things are meant to be, and some things aren't."

"True."

"I'd better get to wardrobe," Jane said.

"Okay. If you see Reed, let him know I have his scripts."

"I will." Jane left the room. The moment she turned the corner, she ran into Reed.

The right corner of his lips lifted, and she could tell he was fighting the smile trying to form. "Hey."

"Hey." Her heartbeat quickened, and she tried to sound casual. "Toni was looking for you. She has your dailies."

Apparently cluing in to his assistant's close proximity, he lowered his voice. "Dinner tonight at your place?"

Jane nodded. She added in a whisper, "You need to say that to Sienna in front of some people today."

His eyebrows furrowed. "Any particular reason?"

"I'll explain later."

* * *

Craig was on the third mile of his run when his phone rang. He pulled it from his pocket and noted the caller ID. When he saw Charlie's name illuminating the screen, he slowed to a walk. "Hey, Charlie. What's up?"

"We have a lead," Charlie said. "Our computer forensics team analyzed the search logs your squad sent them and managed to pin down the origin. Our guy's name is Xavier Guadalupe. We've confirmed that he lives in Atlanta, but he's been staying in Chesapeake for the past few weeks. That's consistent with what we saw in the logs."

"Do they have him in custody?"

"Not yet. They think he drove back to Georgia after he checked out of his rental yesterday," Charlie said.

"So Sienna is safe for now."

"Yeah. We have agents in Atlanta heading to his apartment. With any luck, they'll have this guy in custody by the end of the day."

"Keep me posted."

"I will."

As soon as Craig hung up, he broke into a run and headed back toward his barracks. He was half a mile out when his phone rang again.

This time Brent's name popped up on his screen. "Hey, Brent," Craig greeted him breathlessly. Again, he slowed to a walk.

"We're up," Brent responded, his words clipped.

"When and where?"

"Helicopter pad. One hour."

"Do we know how long?" Craig asked.

"Negative."

"See you then." Craig took a minute to send a vague text to Sienna, letting her know just enough of what was going on, and then picked up his pace. He didn't have time to talk to her in person and didn't want any information in his text to get picked up by anyone else. Three minutes later, he reached his room and headed for the shower. Who knew when he would get that luxury again.

When he arrived at the helicopter pad with fifteen minutes to spare, he approached Brent. "Any more details on our mission?"

"Intel got a tip on our missing toxins."

"Where?"

"We're headed back to Abolstan."

"Great," Craig muttered.

Brent waved toward the chopper. "Load up. We lift off as soon as everyone's here."

"Roger that."

Craig stored his duffel and offered a silent prayer, both that his squad could neutralize this latest threat and that Charlie was right that by the end of the day, Sienna's newest stalker would be silenced for good. He was ready for both of them to find some peace.

* * *

Jane entered Sienna's dressing room carrying her wardrobe for the day. "The director said he wasn't sure if we would get to the kitchen scene this afternoon, but I grabbed the outfit just in case."

"Thanks." Sienna's cell phone chimed.

Jane watched her friend's expression go from elated to disappointed in the space of a heartbeat. "Everything okay?"

Sienna motioned for Jane to close the door. As she did so, Sienna held up her phone. "Craig texted to tell me he's shipping out."

"He's only been in town for a week."

"I know."

"How long will he be gone?"

"Not sure."

"I'm sorry, Sienna. I guess this means the barbecue at Jay's house will be postponed."

"Not necessarily. The wives tend to get together anyway. Riley always says that if we wait for the guys to be in town to enjoy life, we'll miss half of it."

"That's probably true." Jane thought about the difference between the intended barbecue and what it would be like with everyone's significant others out of town. Everyone's except hers. "Maybe we should bring George with us. He and Reed can grill if the squad isn't back by then."

"I already invited George. He enjoys being around Craig's squad."

"We also need to stage some more pictures of you and Reed together having fun."

"Why? The ones of us at the ballgame are still circulating," Sienna said.

"Yeah, but a few people here at work are wondering about you two. If you want to keep up the charade, some new photos would go a long way in killing the rumors."

"Who have you been talking to?"

"Toni. She's got quite the crush on Reed."

Sienna must have sensed Jane's insecurity. "Don't worry, Jane. Reed only has eyes for you."

"I don't know about that," Jane countered. "But it is my job to make sure it looks like you're the object of his affection."

"Right." Sienna let out a sigh. "We'll take more pictures."

"And you should leave from work together for the next few days."

"Yeah. I guess with all of the computer security stuff, we stopped worrying about keeping up pretenses."

A knock sounded on the door.

Jane pulled it open; one of the production assistants was standing on the other side. "Yes?"

"They're ready for Sienna on set."

"I'll be right there," Sienna called out.

Jane closed the door and handed Sienna the purse she would carry in the next scene. "Thanks."

When they reached the set, Reed looked at her, his expression brightening when his eyes locked on Jane's. Sienna gave her arm a little squeeze before she crossed to him. She whispered something in his ear, kissed his cheek, and, a moment later, walked onto the set.

Toni appeared beside Jane in an instant. "I guess they are still together," she said disappointedly.

"As much as they've ever been."

"Bummer."

* * *

Throughout the day, Reed made a point of seeking Sienna out. They chatted about their fake dinner plans in front of the cameramen. He draped his arm around her shoulders when they were reviewing some last-minute script changes. They ate lunch together. And every time he saw Jane, his curiosity heightened. What had caused her to be so concerned about appearances at work?

They had been dating for two weeks, and up until today, no one seemed to have been the wiser.

Toni approached as he headed for the door leading to the beach. Clear skies had altered their director's plan for today, causing all of them to prepare for work in the heat and humidity of August in Virginia. "They're ready for you."

"Thanks." Reed started for the door. "How hot is it out there?"

"You probably don't want me to answer that question."

"Right." He stepped outside, enveloped by the overly warm day. Makeup was going to have their work cut out for them to keep everyone looking fresh for the upcoming scenes. At his entrance, the director waved him over and announced the scene.

"Places."

Reed took his mark, instantly distracted when he faced the beach and saw Jane standing at the water's edge. He wasn't sure what she was doing down there other than perhaps taking a late lunch break. He had been disappointed when she hadn't eaten with him and Sienna.

"Reed," Marshall called out.

Reed instantly straightened, forcing his mind to recall his lines and the emotions he was supposed to portray. Sienna entered, and they set about shooting their first scene. When they finally took a break, he lowered himself into the canvas chair that boasted his name across the back and looked out at the water again. And Jane.

As though she hadn't moved a muscle during the past hour, she still stood a few feet from where the surf sprayed over the sand.

Sienna sat beside him and leaned over to whisper in his ear. "I'm going to Carina's house tonight with some of the other wives."

"Maybe I'll hang out at my place, then," Reed whispered back.

"Let me know if you want company." Sienna looked out at the water briefly. "Probably best not to text right now since certain people have access to your phone when you're on set."

"Seven o'clock," Reed said, his voice low. "Can you pass on my address?"

"I can do that."

20

CRAIG STUDIED THE INTEL REPORT, praying it was right. Elazar's group had been found. Or so they hoped.

Unlike the rugged camp they had infiltrated over a month before, intel believed the eight men known to associate with Jamal Elazar were living in a house in the center of Khalar.

"Getting in there unseen isn't going to be easy," Jay said from his right.

"We have two days to figure out how to do exactly that," Brent said. "A helicopter is scheduled to take us in, and another round of satellite photos will be available tonight at 2100."

"I'm thinking broad daylight," Tristan suggested. "We get dropped off outside the city before dawn and go native."

"It's worked before," Quinn said.

"Last time, Damian nearly got himself shot when he pretended to be drunk," Tristan said.

"I did not," Damian said. "I had everything under control the whole time."

"Jay, identify possible landing sites," Brent ordered. "Quinn, secure our weapons. Seth, I want you to take care of our wardrobe, and I'll work with Tristan to plot our path into the city once we land."

"What about me?" Damian asked.

"Work with Craig on how to infiltrate the structure," Brent said. "I want to meet with everyone in four hours to go over our initial mission plan."

The squad dispersed to carry out their various assignments, the gravity of the missing toxins heavy on their minds.

* * *

Jane nearly didn't answer the phone when she saw her mom was calling, but the realization that she hadn't talked to her in nearly a week sent a ripple of guilt through her. "Hi, Mom."

"Hi, honey. How are you?"

"Doing okay. Just busy getting adjusted to the new job."

"It's been almost three weeks. If you aren't already on top of everything, your schedule must be crazy."

"A little bit. How are things with you?"

Jane listened to her mother recount the latest about her neighbors and coworkers.

"You haven't said much about the people you're working with," her mom finally said. "Are they nice? Any new friends worth mentioning?"

Jane swallowed the whole truth and offered only a small piece of what was going on. She didn't want to open the conversation of how she was dating the man who was constantly appearing in the press linked to Sienna. "Everyone's really nice. Still getting to know them."

"Well, I know you probably have a dozen things to do for Sienna, so I'll let you go."

"Okay. Thanks for calling, Mom. I love you."

"Love you too."

Jane hung up and headed for her car. She followed the GPS on her phone to the address Sienna had given her. A few minutes later, she parked in the lot outside Reed's apartment.

The building he lived in rose three stories, balconies visible in neat rows facing the ocean. Other than a few towels hanging over the wrought-iron railings and a few pieces of furniture, one balcony looked identical to the next.

She took a moment to identify which door belonged to Reed and promptly headed the other direction to make sure she wouldn't be noticed. Pretending to be lost, she circled the back of the complex before approaching his door and knocking. Taking five minutes to traverse what should have been only thirty feet made her feel ridiculous. Did going to her back door have the same effect on Reed?

The door swung open. "Come on in."

Reed stepped back to let her enter, astutely keeping the door between them in case the paparazzi had managed to learn where he lived. Jane knew the press thus far had left Reed alone, for the most part, but now wasn't the time to take chances.

As soon as the door closed behind her, he leaned forward for a kiss. "I have to admit, you have me curious. What was going on at work today?"

"Someone asked me what was going on with you and Sienna. They thought you two broke up."

"And you were making sure the rumors got squashed."

"Something like that." She let her gaze sweep over his living room. Trendy furniture that looked like it should be on a showroom floor, artistic touches on the walls. She noticed the framed photo of her and Sienna on a bookshelf, along with the picture of his family.

"Come on in and sit down," Reed said, leading her further inside. "I thought we could order in and watch a movie."

"That sounds good." She sat on the couch, the stiff leather cold against her skin when she leaned back.

"Did you pick out this furniture?" Jane asked.

"No." Reed sat beside her. "Sorry. I know the couch isn't that comfortable."

"Then why did you buy it?"

"I didn't. The apartment came furnished."

"Maybe you should find something you can furnish yourself," Jane suggested.

Reed stretched out his arm, his fingers grazing her shoulder. "I have that same thought every time I walk in the door."

"Reed, if you don't like living here, then why don't you move?"

"I don't know. Too much effort, I guess."

"Anything worth having is worth the effort."

He shifted and leaned toward her, his mouth covering hers. Sensations shot through her, and his fingers worked their way from her shoulder to her neck as though to hold her in place. When he pulled back, his face was close to hers. "You're absolutely right. Anything worth having is worth the effort."

* * *

They were ready. The Saint Squad's insertion three miles outside of Khalar had occurred without incident, as had their 0400 jog into the city.

Now, with white keffiyehs covering their hair, sandals on their feet, and weapons concealed in their traditional Arabic robes, the seven men strolled the streets, each of them coming from different directions. Walking in silence, Craig and Brent approached the back of their target location.

"In position," Quinn announced through the communications headsets they all wore.

"Me too," Jay said quietly.

Craig couldn't see either of the men in their hiding places, but he knew from their mission plan that Quinn was on sniper duty on the rooftop across the street, and Jay had the vantage point from a building on the next block over.

"Let's go," Brent said. "Straight in, straight out. Nice and simple. No weapons unless absolutely necessary."

"It doesn't seem right that we're going in with tranquilizer guns after they tried to blow us up last month," Damian said.

"The more we neutralize without alerting their neighbors, the better," Brent reminded them.

"Sometimes I hate it when that practical side of you comes out," Tristan said.

Brent ignored him. "Do we have heat signatures?"

"Affirmative," Jay reported. "Five heat spots. One is isolated upstairs. Two by the back door and two more by the front."

"Secure the ground level first," Brent ordered. "Are the entry points clear?"

"No sign of booby traps on the front door," Seth reported.

"We're clear," Craig added from his position beside Brent.

"On three," Brent said.

Craig edged closer to the back door and adjusted his grip on his weapon, his finger now on the trigger of his tranquilizer gun. The countdown echoed through his head, followed by a burst of movement.

Craig kicked open the door, and Brent led the way inside, his gun raised. Craig followed, his eyes immediately drawn to the two men inside scrambling for the automatic weapons lying on the table between them.

Brent's rapid words spoken in Arabic didn't have the desired effect. Instead of stopping their intended action of securing their weapons, the men grabbed and aimed.

Brent and Craig fired one shot each. Both targets slumped to the floor in front of them. The SEALs rushed forward and used zip ties to secure the men's hands in case they didn't sleep as long as intended.

"Clear," Craig said into his headset as soon as he finished.

"Clear," Damian repeated, indicating the scene in the front of the house mirrored the one in the back.

"Four down," Brent said quietly. "Jay, movement upstairs?"

"Negative," Jay responded.

Using hand signals now, Brent motioned for Craig to take the lead.

His weapon at the ready, he made his way up the wooden stairs to his left. Through his headset, he could hear Jay directing them onward.

"Target in the southwest corner, fifteen feet to your left."

Craig hesitated four steps from the top, waiting for Brent to signal him to go ahead. He swung his gun in the direction Jay had indicated, and he was facing a door. Together with Brent, they moved to either side. Craig reached for the knob, but it was locked. He pulled a tool from his vest. With their presence already announced from the previous noise downstairs, he didn't want to wait to see if whoever was on the other side wanted to try some blind target practice. Craig quickly picked the lock and wrapped his fingers around the knob.

Brent nodded, and Craig opened the door.

The man inside lifted his hands in surrender, absolute terror evident on his bruised face. "Don't shoot! Don't shoot!" he cried in English flavored with a British accent.

"Search him," Brent told Craig.

With Brent covering him, Craig moved forward, checking to make sure the man hadn't booby-trapped himself before conducting a more thorough search for weapons. The man winced when he patted down his legs, and Craig noticed the way a torn piece of his shirt had been wrapped around his calf. "He's clean."

"Who are you?" Brent asked.

"Terry Walters." His eyes darted from Brent to Craig and back again. "You're Americans?"

"That's right," Brent said.

"I'm attached to the British embassy in Ankara. I was on an inspection in Damascus when I was kidnapped."

"Why did they kidnap you?"

"They needed to know how to transport the chemical toxins safely by air." The man's eyes watered. "I'm sorry. They threatened to send a bomb into London harbor if I didn't help them."

Brent's jaw tightened. "Can you walk?"

Terry held his hands out. "I think so."

"Bring him with us, but first check him for trackers," Brent told Craig.

Craig retrieved a scanner from one of his vest pockets, sweeping it over the man. "He's clean."

"Then let's go." Brent reached out to help Terry up, Craig supporting him on the other side.

The other man's legs immediately gave way beneath him. "Sorry," he mumbled.

"We've got you," Brent said.

After the first few steps, Terry seemed to find his balance, and they made their way downstairs.

As soon as they did, Seth met them by the front door. "We photographed and tagged everyone, but none of them is Jamal Elazar."

"He left for America weeks ago," Terry announced.

"What?"

"He's the one who transported the bombs."

"To America?" Brent asked.

"Yes, to America."

21

JANE CARRIED THEIR POPCORN BOWL to the sink and turned on the sprayer. Even though she and Reed had spent time together nearly every day since she'd arrived in Virginia, she still couldn't quite wrap her mind around her current reality. So many times she had been referred to as "plain Jane" growing up and in college, and now she was dating a handsome, interesting man who made her feel like she was the most special person in his world.

"Don't worry about that," Reed said. "I can clean up."

"I don't mind." She finished rinsing the bowl and set it aside. "Thanks for tonight. I had fun."

"Me too." He wrapped his arms around her and lowered his lips to hers.

Jane fell into the kiss, her skin tingling beneath his touch. Her heart bounced high in her throat, and her stomach started its now familiar fluttering.

He drew her closer, causing a new wave of goose bumps to surface. She breathed in his aftershave and the lingering scent of popcorn. The wall clock chimed over and over, announcing midnight's arrival.

Jane pulled back. "I should go."

"When I buy a house, I'm going to make sure I don't get a grandfather clock."

The oddity of his comment made her smile. "Why?"

He gave her a quick, teasing kiss. "Because I don't want the reminder of how late it is."

"Whether you hear the chimes or not, midnight arrives every night."

"Yeah, but I'd rather not think about it." He released her and scooped his keys off the counter. "Come on. I'll follow you home."

"You don't have to do that," Jane said. "I only live a couple miles from here."

"Jane, it's after midnight in the summer in a tourist town," Reed said. "I won't sleep easy unless I'm sure you made it home okay."

"That's very sweet."

"Not sweet. Practical."

The sentiment touched her more than words could express. Her heart stumbled in her chest. Not sure she could find words, she reached up on her toes and kissed him once more. Her voice was husky when she managed to say, "Whatever you call it, thank you."

* * *

"What's the latest?" Craig asked the moment Brent walked into their board-room on the USS *Ronald Reagan*.

All conversation among the rest of his squad ceased, everyone anxious for news.

"Terry's story checked out," Brent said. "The British confirmed that he disappeared during an inspection mission. They were working with Interpol to locate him."

"Which means we really could have chemical weapons in the United States," Tristan said gravely.

"It also means we know who we're looking for. Terry confirmed that Jamal Elazar left for the United States several weeks ago," Brent told them.

"I can't begin to imagine what kind of chaos a chemical weapon would cause if it went off in the States," Quinn said.

"Intelligence is working on it. With the electronic markers we put on the men in Khalar, we hope they'll lead us to Jamal."

"And if they don't?" Craig asked.

"We pray that someone identifies his location before it's too late." Brent walked farther into the room and dropped a stack of photos on their work-table. "Intelligence already identified three of the four men we encountered. The good news is that they will likely see this as a rescue mission . . ."

"Which means they may not realize we put a marker spray on all of them."

"That's what we're hoping." Brent spread the photos out. "For now, familiarize yourselves with these photos. It's possible we may get pulled in on the intelligence side of things, especially with what's at stake."

"How long until we head Stateside?" Jay asked.

"I'm working on that," Brent said. "As soon as I have an answer, you'll all be the first to know."

* * *

Three wrong turns had put him more than forty minutes behind. Abdul swallowed his frustration. He couldn't risk using a GPS signal and letting someone track him from the dock to his new base of operations. Even though Jamal was an expert at hiding his electronic activity, Abdul wouldn't take the chance that someone might be able to trace the origin of the tracking software on Sienna Blake's computer back to him. Unfortunately, the paper maps he was using instead of a GPS hadn't told him about the roadwork along the route he had chosen.

When Abdul finally approached the new apartment he had rented, he pulled into the parking lot at the restaurant next door.

"Why are you parking over here?" Munjid asked.

"If anyone finds us, they'll block off the entrance to the building complex. We can't take a chance of getting trapped."

"I'm starting to wonder if you're cautious or paranoid."

"Probably both."

Munjid twisted and looked at the two oversized duffel bags in the back of the van. "How long are we holding on to the explosives? It makes me nervous having them both together."

"Now you're sounding paranoid." He chose a spot that abutted the grassy barrier between the two parking lots.

"For good reason. Those bombs make me nervous."

"Regardless, they're your responsibility now," Abdul told him. "Jamal needs to keep his focus on making sure those photos don't compromise our plans."

"How long until Jamal relocates with us?"

"He will meet us here in a few days, after he is sure we aren't being followed," Abdul said.

"I think you are paranoid."

Abdul turned off the engine. "Trust me on this. I know what I'm doing."

"I trust you," Munjid said. "A few more weeks and America's capital will never be the same."

* * *

Sienna carried a veggie platter from Carina's kitchen and set it on a patio table with the other appetizers. Jane followed her with the deviled eggs.

"Thanks." Carina continued putting water bottles and soda into a cooler.

"You're welcome," Sienna said. She looked out at the stretch of private beach two stories below, appreciating the solitude Carina and Jay's house provided. "Is there anything else you need help with?"

"Actually, yeah." Carina motioned inside. "I need the key to the storage closet to get some more chairs out. Can you grab it for me? It should be on my key ring in my purse."

"No problem." Sienna headed back inside and found Carina's purse on the kitchen counter. She opened it in search of the keys, surprise surfacing when she saw a chrome-plated pistol tucked inside. The idea that one of her girlfriends would feel the need to carry a weapon hit her, and she had to remind herself that Vanessa also carried a handgun all the time.

Sienna hoped Craig never expected her to walk around armed. She really didn't like guns. After digging Carina's keys out, she walked outside. "Here you go."

"Thanks." Carina unlocked the door to the storage closet, and the two of them set out more chairs around one of the patio tables.

Amy emerged from the house, carrying a case of soda. "Okay, I think this is the last of it."

"Great. Can you put those in the other cooler?" Carina asked.

"Sure."

Sienna waited until Amy finished her task before she asked, "Have you heard anything?" If anyone knew where the guys were, it would be Amy. As the squad's intelligence officer, she often arranged their transportation.

"Brent said he would check in with me today, but I haven't heard from him yet," Amy said. "With any luck, he'll call in the next hour or two."

"I was really hoping they would be home for tonight." Carina motioned to Reed and George standing by the grill. "At least I didn't have to cook."

"George and Reed both love to grill." Sienna smiled. "Jane and I have a bet over who wins the battle of the spatula tonight."

"I think Reed is going to edge George out," Jane said.

"I don't know. George is bigger." Sienna instinctively raised her voice to be heard over the sound of an approaching helicopter. She didn't think to look up until Jane pointed skyward.

"What in the world?" Jane stared at the helicopter that had taken position over the beach.

"It can't be," Carina said.

"Yes, it can." Amy laughed. "Now I know why Brent was late calling me."

"Wait." Jane looked from Amy to Carina to Sienna with an expression of wonder. "Is that the Saint Squad?"

Sienna couldn't keep the grin from spreading across her face. "It is."

They watched two black ropes fall from the open doorway. Two men rappelled down. The moment they hit the sand, they unhooked and stepped clear. Then two more took their place. As soon as all seven men reached the ground, one of them waved his hand and the helicopter rose.

Sienna rushed toward the stairs leading from the deck to the beach, several other sets of footsteps pounding behind her. She had barely reached the sand before Craig was in front of her, his arms encircling her.

"Hey, there," he said.

Sienna couldn't help but laugh. "You certainly know how to make an entrance."

"I told you I would be here if I could." Craig waved in the direction of the retreating helicopter. "Brent convinced our pilot to drop us off at home instead of making us go to the base first."

"Sounds like a good command decision," Sienna said.

"I thought so."

Behind them, the other members greeted their wives, and two by two, they started up the stairs to the deck, with Quinn and Taylor leading the way.

"It's my turn to grill," Quinn insisted as he reached the top.

"No, you grilled last time," Tristan countered.

"They'll never change," Taylor said.

Amy chuckled. "Just watch."

As the two men debated over who should get to grill, Seth passed them both, said something to George and Reed, and accepted the spatula George handed him. By the time Quinn and Tristan noticed the hand-off, Seth was already flipping burgers.

Jane approached Sienna and Craig, motioning to the grill. "Looks like we both lost the bet."

Sienna laced her fingers with Craig's. "That's okay. I feel like I won anyway."

22

ABDUL NOTICED THE SILENCE. RATHER, he had enjoyed the peace until he realized it was out of place. He looked over at Jamal tapping away at his computer. If it hadn't been for the trouble with the actress, he would have insisted the laptop be left behind or destroyed. Electronics made him nervous. Unfortunately, to battle effectively, sometimes they were a necessary evil.

"What's wrong?"

"I finally isolated the cell phone number of the woman who was with Sienna Blake at the airport in Los Angeles."

"And?"

"I'm trying to create a mirror of her phone so I can see what she has."

"How much longer will it take you?"

"I'm almost done." He hit a few more keys and did something to change the image on the screen. "I'm ready."

Abdul watched Jamal download hundreds of photos. After a moment, he opened some and began scanning through them. Minutes passed, images of the beach and a house dominating the most recent pictures. Impatience simmered inside him and threatened to boil over until finally Jamal clicked a button and the scene from the Los Angeles airport appeared before them.

Both men leaned closer. Part of Jamal's head appeared in the corner of the frame, but not enough of him was visible for him to be identifiable.

"We've been chasing after these women, and this is all they had?" Abdul asked, a hard edge in his voice.

"There was no way of knowing what was in their photo," Jamal said. He clicked another button, but this time Jamal had moved into the frame.

Both men fell silent. Jamal looked up at him, clearly concerned the authorities would notice him if this photo went out. "Maybe they'll use the other one," Jamal finally said.

"It's risky," Abdul said.

Jamal clicked to the next image, and both men gasped. Not only was Jamal's face clear, but whoever had taken the photo had also managed to get Abdul facing the camera head on.

"We no longer have a choice," Abdul said. "How can we get her phone? Will the photos help us locate her?"

"Yes, but it will take time to find her house," Jamal said. He seemed to ponder for a moment. "I have another idea that may work better."

"What's that?"

"Now that I have her phone information, I can plant a virus in her operating system. If it works as intended, it will wipe out all her information."

"Do it."

"I'll take care of it today," Jamal said. "What about Sienna Blake?"

"Find her house. It's time to take care of this problem once and for all."

* * *

"Seriously?" Jane stared at her phone with a combination of frustration and trepidation. She knew of several people who had upgraded their phones in the last few months who had suffered from a total loss of data, but after what Sienna had gone through with her phone and laptop, Jane wasn't sure what to think when her screen went black. In a complete role reversal, she headed for Sienna's apartment. She knocked, waited, and knocked again. When Sienna finally answered, her hair was wet.

"Sorry. Didn't mean to catch you in the shower," Jane said apologetically.

"That's okay. What's up?"

Jane took a deep breath and let her fears spill out. "I'm afraid my phone may have been hacked like yours was."

"Seriously?"

Jane nodded. "I think so."

"Come on in." Sienna stepped aside, waiting until Jane was inside before speaking again. "I'll call Craig and see if he can take a look at it."

"Thanks. I appreciate it." Jane lifted her hands. "I don't know how I'm going to make it through the day without my cell though. I keep your calendar on it."

"We'll make it work," Sienna promised.

Jane stared at her friend. "Sienna, is this ever going to stop?"

"Yes," she said with certainty. "But I don't think some extra prayers would hurt."

"I've already got that covered."

"That makes two of us."

* * *

Craig looked up when Damian walked into their office. Damian took one look at the cell phone on his desk and said, "Not again."

"Again."

"Same thing?" Damian asked.

"I don't think so." Craig lifted the phone to reveal a completely black screen. "I don't know why Jane was targeted, but the security measures on her phone were pretty extensive. I think whoever was trying to hack in probably got frustrated and decided to wipe everything out instead using some kind of virus."

"This doesn't make any sense."

"I know."

"Sounds like you need to call the FBI again," Damian said.

"I already left a message for Charlie Whitmore."

"At the rate we're going, Charlie may need to transfer back to Virginia. I think he's spending more time on cases out here than anywhere else."

"He has a vested interest. The last thing he wants is for his sister-in-law to be anyone's target."

"True," Damian agreed. He motioned toward the door. "Everyone is waiting in Brent's office for morning prayer."

"I think I should be the one to offer it," Craig said. "I have a lot to pray for today."

* * *

Craig wasn't sure if he should be annoyed or grateful that Charlie hadn't told him Xavier Guadalupe had yet to be apprehended by the authorities. It wasn't until Craig had called Charlie about Jane's cell phone that he had learned the truth.

Admittedly, Craig didn't know how he would have managed to keep his focus during their last mission had he known Sienna's stalker was still on the loose. His stomach knotted up every time he thought about how he had left the country while Sienna had still been in danger.

Charlie had been kind enough to give him daily updates, but so far, the past three days had simply been the same conversation repeated over and over. No news. The FBI was continuing their search.

Craig glanced at the clock on his dashboard as he headed to Sienna's apartment. It was nearly six o'clock, and he had yet to get his daily phone call from Charlie. Impatient, Craig dialed Charlie himself.

The phone rang only once. "Craig, I'm sorry I didn't get a chance to call you earlier, but I got stuck in meetings all day."

"Do you have news?" Craig asked.

"I do." Charlie paused, and Craig could hear fingers tapping on a keyboard. "Our agents picked up Sienna's stalker early this morning."

"Do we know why this guy was tracking Sienna?"

"He's denying any involvement in the hacks. He insists he was in Virginia Beach to write a book," Charlie said.

"Write a book?"

"Yeah. Apparently he was coauthoring a technical manual on computer security."

A trickle of discomfort ran down the center of Craig's back. "Was there anything on his search history about Sienna?"

"He visited her page on IMDB, and he watched one of her movies on Netflix two weeks ago, but that's all we found."

"Doesn't that seem odd?" Craig asked. "If he's really fixated on her, I would think he would have been checking up on her all the time."

"Our tech guys think he has another computer stashed somewhere," Charlie said. "They're checking pawn shops in Atlanta and Virginia Beach to see if he might have wiped it and sold it off."

"For a case that's solved, it sure has a lot of questions that haven't been answered."

"I know, but these things take time."

"I'm not the most patient man when it comes to my fiancée's safety." Craig pulled up in front of Sienna's house.

"I know how you feel," Charlie said. "I'll make another call to the agent conducting the interrogation. From what I understand, Guadalupe has already been charged. At this point, it's simply a matter of seeing if he'll crack and confess to his actions and motives."

"And if he doesn't?"

"We'll put the evidence before a jury. I doubt we'll have trouble getting a conviction."

Craig tried to push aside the seed of worry that wouldn't quite die. "Thanks for the update."

"You're welcome. Give Sienna my best."

"I will. Thanks, Charlie."

"Anytime."

23

"It's over?" Sienna asked, skepticism and hope battling within her.

"The agents picked up Xavier Guadalupe an hour ago." Craig took a glass from the cabinet beside Sienna's refrigerator and filled it with water. "His computer had the tracking program on it that was used on your laptop as well as the code that made it impossible for my squad to back trace his signal."

"If it was impossible for the Saint Squad, how did the FBI find him?"

"Apparently they had someone who was better at breaking code than we are." Craig took a drink of water and set his glass aside. "This Xavier guy is good, better than anyone we've come up against before."

"He must be good if neither you nor Jane could find him."

"The cops are going to stick around through tomorrow so George has time to work with the security consultants on making sure your alarm system hasn't been compromised," Craig said. "I would also suggest you have Jane get a new phone, and we'll put an extra layer of encryption on it."

"I will." Sienna crossed to him and wrapped her arms around him. "Thank you for everything."

"I didn't do much," Craig said. "The computer forensic guy who traced Xavier is the hero this time."

"It doesn't matter who gets the hero title," Sienna countered. "As long as the job gets done."

"True, but this was pretty anticlimactic."

"What do you mean?"

"No one came at us with guns or kidnapped anyone. We didn't have to defuse any bombs or rescue anyone from a moving vehicle." Craig's shoulders lifted. "Pretty boring."

"Honey, sometimes boring can be good." She reached up and kissed him, enjoying the familiar warmth that seeped through her. A smile crossed her face when she pulled back and added, "And if this is what you call boring, maybe we should try it more often."

His grin flashed. "Whatever you say."

* * *

Jane peeked out her kitchen window when a knock sounded at her back door. Her heart lifted when she saw Reed standing on the deck, a brown paper bag nestled in the crook of his arm. She pulled the door open. "Hey there. Come on in."

"I brought Chinese food. I thought we could use a night off from cooking." Reed set the bag on the table. "How are you holding up?"

"Better now that Sienna called," Jane said. "Did you hear the news?"

Reed shook his head.

"I just got off the phone with her. The FBI caught the guy who was stalking her."

"That's great news." Reed's phone chimed, and he pulled it out. After he read his text message, he pocketed it again. "That was Sienna telling me the same thing."

Jane held out a hand and watched it tremble. "I don't think it's sunk in yet."

"You had quite a scare the other day." Reed's eyebrows drew together. "If the guy is in custody, why is there still a cop car parked outside?"

"Sienna said they were going to stick around through tomorrow, until after the upgraded security system is installed."

"Smart," Reed said. "You can never be too careful."

"So I'm finding out." Jane crossed the kitchen and pulled out two plates. "Did you want a fork or chopsticks?"

"Chopsticks for me."

She dug two pairs from the back of her silverware drawer and carried everything to the table as Reed filled their water glasses. "Did you want to eat inside or out on the deck?"

"Let's eat in here," Reed said. "It's still hot outside."

As soon as they were seated, Reed folded his arms. "Do you mind if I offer the blessing?"

"That would be great. Thank you."

Warmth washed over her as he spoke words of gratitude, not only for the food before them but for her continued safety too. When he closed the prayer, she reached out and put her hand on his. "Thank you."

He leaned forward for a sweet and simple kiss. "You're welcome."

His phone sounded again, and Jane expected him to check his latest message. When he didn't, she said, "If you need to check that, I don't mind."

"Finding time together is hard enough with this whole publicity stunt going on. Whoever wants to talk to me can wait." Reed gave her hand a squeeze. "I'm here to be with you."

"You know, I kind of feel sorry for all your fans."

"Why is that?"

"I don't know if they'll ever appreciate what a great guy you are." She picked up a container of rice and passed it to him. "Every time we're together, I find I like you even more than I did before."

"Believe me, the feeling is mutual."

* * *

Jane felt like celebrating. This morning she had walked outside and gotten into her car without worrying that someone was going to show up uninvited. Okay, so she may have looked around a couple times as she'd crossed the lawn, but the worst edge of fear had dissipated. She hoped it would fade completely in the coming days.

Now standing beside the center cameraman, overlooking the living room set, Jane watched Sienna and Reed go through their lines for a key scene. She had to admit, the anger on Reed's face was palpable. It was also an emotion she hadn't ever seen on him in real life.

Jane wondered for a moment what would evoke such emotions in him. She hoped she never found out.

The scene ended for the fifth time, and finally the director called for a break. Sienna's face relaxed, the emotions of the scene dropping away. Reed rolled his shoulders and shook his head as though he needed physical distance from the man he had portrayed moments earlier.

Sienna approached Jane and lowered her voice. "I wanted to let you know I'm going to dinner on base tonight."

"Celebrating?" Jane asked.

"We are," Sienna said. "I can't tell you how relieved I am to know they caught the guy who was stalking me."

"Oh, I have a pretty good idea."

Sienna studied her for a moment. "I guess you do."

"Did you want me to get you something to eat while you're on break?"

"No, I can grab something from the craft table," Sienna said. "Want to join me and Reed for lunch?"

"Yeah, I'd like that." She glanced across the room to where Reed was talking to Toni.

"Maybe you should invite Reed over tonight for a celebration of your own," Sienna suggested.

"I was thinking the same thing." One of the runners passed by them, and Jane lowered her voice. "But maybe I should have you issue the invitation."

Sienna grinned at her. "I can do that."

* * *

Reed straightened his tie and wondered what Jane and Sienna had planned for tonight. A nice dinner. That had been all Jane had said when she had texted him during lunch today.

It was silly, really, that they worked in such close proximity but had resorted to texting and then deleting the messages to each other when they wanted to talk so they could avoid starting rumors. For the past two weeks, he had been careful to seek out Sienna every day to keep up the pretense that they were dating. He looked forward to the day Sienna and Craig married so they could drop the charade. In truth, he wasn't sure they would make it that long.

He knocked on Jane's back door.

When it swung open, his breath caught. The yellow cotton dress she wore accented her waist and fell loosely to her ankles. Her feet were bare. "You look beautiful."

Her smile was instant. "Thanks. You look rather handsome yourself."

"Why, thank you." He motioned to the apartment overhead. "Do you know if Sienna and Craig are ready?"

"Actually, they aren't joining us tonight."

"What?" Reed stared at her in confusion. Everyone knew the only way any of them could date in public was if they went as a foursome.

"Craig is taking Sienna to the officers' club for dinner."

"Jane, you know I would love to take you out, just the two of us, but we both know we can't take the risk that I might be recognized."

"We aren't going out." Jane reached out and took his hand, drawing him inside.

He crossed the threshold and took in the scene before him. The white tablecloth, two taper candles flickering in the dimly lit room, a bottle of sparkling cider in a bucket of ice. The scent of tomato sauce and mozzarella teased his appetite. "What's all this?"

"We can't go out to a nice dinner, so I thought it would be fun to create our own." A timer buzzed, and she moved into the kitchen. Picking up a hot pad, she opened the oven and slid out a pan, replacing it with a cookie sheet that had thick slices of garlic bread on it.

"Is that lasagna?"

She glanced over her shoulder. "It is."

"That's my favorite."

"I know." Jane set it on the stove. "Sienna got your mom's recipe for me. I thought you would enjoy a taste of home."

"Are you serious?"

"I doubt it will be quite the same, but it's the thought that counts, right?" She opened the refrigerator and retrieved the salad.

After she set it on the table, Reed closed the distance between them. "Are we celebrating something in particular? Did I miss an anniversary or something?"

"We've only been dating a few weeks. That's not long enough to have an anniversary." Jane reached up and kissed his cheek. "I just wanted to do something special for you. Do you mind?"

His heart stumbled, and he tried to remember the last time someone had put so much effort into such a kind gesture. "You really are amazing."

"Not me." She motioned to the long-stemmed glasses on the table. "Can you pour us some cider? Everything will be ready in a minute."

Reed did as he was asked. Five minutes later, he sat across from Jane and took his first bite of lasagna. And tasted home.

"Is it okay?" Jane asked.

"It's better than okay," Reed said, not sure what to think about the odd feeling in his chest. "My mother would approve."

"Glad to hear it." She took a bite of her own and nodded. "This is good. I can see why your mom's lasagna is your favorite."

"How did you even know this was my favorite food? We've never eaten Italian together before."

"I asked Sienna. She wasn't sure, so she called your mom and found out for me."

"I have to say, this dinner is better than anything we would have had in a restaurant."

"I'm glad you think so."

"I know so." He reached across the table and squeezed her hand. "Great food without the constant interruption of waiters, but best of all, I get to be with you."

24

FAT RAINDROPS SPLATTERED OUTSIDE JANE'S window as she and Reed finished dinner, and she wondered if she had somehow ended up inside a movie instead of her usual, boring life. Okay, her life wasn't that boring. She did, after all, work for a famous actress. Still, she was the one dating this time, and she couldn't quite get her head around that wonderful fact.

His gratitude over dinner touched her. And his insistence on doing the dishes amused her.

She leaned against her kitchen counter, an unused dish towel in her hand. "Can I at least help put away the dishes?"

"Nope. You cooked. I get to clean."

"Do you realize what a catch you are?" The words popped out of her mouth before she thought to censor them.

"Huh?" Reed reached into the soapy water and unplugged the drain.

She let herself finish her thought. "A guy who is kind, generous, and does dishes—I'm surprised you don't have a dozen girls lined up trying to be Mrs. Reed Forrester."

His grin flashed. "What makes you think I don't?"

One eyebrow lifted. "Are you trying to make me jealous?"

"Hey, you're the one who's talking about other women, not me."

"You're right. What was I thinking?"

"Beats me." Reed dried his hands and crossed to her. When he leaned down and pressed his lips to hers, her brain shut off. She let the kiss overcome her, her heart and mind opening to him until there was nothing left but what the two of them created in this moment.

Remembering that they were truly alone tonight, she pulled back, hoping her cheeks weren't as flushed as they felt.

"Are you up for watching a movie before I go?" Reed asked. "We could Netflix something."

"I'd like that." They debated briefly on what to watch, ultimately settling on a comedy.

When Jane snuggled beside him on the couch, he put his arm around her shoulders, and she found a sense of home that she had rarely experienced since arriving in Virginia.

She angled her head so she could see his face. "Thanks for coming over tonight."

"I'm the one who should be thanking you," Reed said. "You're full of surprises."

"I try."

"Trust me. Tonight, you succeeded."

* * *

They laughed. They talked. An hour after the movie ended, Reed found himself reluctant to say good night. How was it that simply being in the same room as Jane made everything light and fun? The stress of the work week seemed to melt away at the very sound of her voice.

"You know, I was thinking," Reed said.

"About?"

"Maybe Sienna needs to start working on an end date for this fake relationship we've got going on."

"I thought you were going to stretch it out until she gets married."

"That's still three months away. Don't you want to be able to go out and eat in public by ourselves? To not have to worry about pretending we aren't dating in front of our coworkers?"

Jane drew her legs up so she was sitting cross-legged on the couch, facing him, the skirt of her dress now tucked around her knees so that even her feet were hidden. "Actually, it's kind of nice not having to worry about our date getting interrupted by fans asking for your autograph."

"I hardly ever have that happen," Reed said. It was true that since being linked with Sienna, the frequency had increased, but thankfully, the incidents were still in the tolerable range. "I guess being Sienna's assistant, you're pretty used to that."

"I am, but I'm also good at knowing how to avoid it," she said.

"What do you mean?"

"When you aren't where you are expected to be, a hat and a pair of sunglasses can do wonders," Jane said. "I'm sure you've been around the Blake family enough to pick up on a few tricks too."

"True."

"One thing I have learned over the years is that even if you weren't pretending to date Sienna, we wouldn't want everyone at work speculating about us."

"I wouldn't care."

One eyebrow lifted. "I gather you've never dated a coworker before."

"Actually, no," Reed admitted.

"Trust me. I've seen enough on-set romances to know how quickly people can sabotage them. I don't want that to happen to us."

"Our relationship isn't like that," Reed said. The idea that he wouldn't see Jane if *Beachfront* were to cancel sent a streak of panic through him. He reminded himself that the initial response in their test market had been good, but he could understand Jane's concern. He also knew that show or not, he intended to keep Jane in his life. That thought startled him speechless.

"I hope not," Jane said.

Reed saw it now, the flash of vulnerability in her expression. "You've been burned before."

"It was nothing." Jane smoothed the fabric draped over her legs. "Let's just say I'm well-versed in how people will create friendships to get what they want."

"I'm not like that."

"No, you aren't, but we haven't been working this show long enough for everyone else to know that." Jane seemed to debate before she added, "There are already several women at work who are rooting against you and Sienna making it."

"What? Who?"

"It doesn't matter who. The point is these women will treat me differently if they think I'm the latest in the string of your girlfriends."

"Jane, I haven't had a girlfriend for a long time."

She tilted her head, her hair falling over her right shoulder. "Why not?"

"Partially because I was focused on my career and I didn't want an on-set romance for the exact reason you just described," Reed said. "Before that, I think I was leery of the singles scene because a lot of times I felt like the girls I dated were more interested in getting a ring on their finger than they were in me."

"At least no one is asking yet when you're going to put one on Sienna's finger."

"It's only a matter of time." Reed ran his fingers over the back of her hand. "Which is even more reason for me and Sienna to end our fake relationship.

I started to buy tickets to Busch Gardens for us and realized we can't make even the simplest plans without worrying about bad press. I want more than that for us."

He saw the doubt on her face and pressed on. "No one would expect Sienna was with Craig if she just broke up with me."

"True, but right now every time we double date, we're giving them the chance to go out without worrying," Jane reminded him. "If we give us more freedom, we take away theirs."

"You really don't mind keeping our relationship private for the next few months?" Reed asked.

"As long as we can spend time together, it doesn't matter to me where we are or what we're doing."

A flood of emotions rushed through him at the plainness of her words and the knowledge that she meant them. How was it that Jane could be so comfortable around the Hollywood lifestyle and not care whether they lived it or not? The depth of his feelings expanded beyond anything he had ever experienced, and the words "I love you" nearly toppled out.

Before he could weigh the implications of what he had nearly spoken aloud, Jane leaned forward and pressed her lips to his. His heart pounded in his chest, and he breathed in her scent, the mixture of ocean breezes, vanilla, and a hint of tomato sauce. Her fingers teased the back of his neck, goose bumps rising on his skin.

They could have been in the middle of a deserted isle. There was nothing but them in that moment. Every thought, every breath was for Jane.

25

TAP, TAP, TAP. TAP, TAP, tap. The knocking against wood echoed through his head. Reed rolled over and burrowed under his pillow in an attempt to muffle the sound. His alarm hadn't gone off, and until it did, he wasn't budging.

The incessant knocking stopped briefly only to be interrupted by the ringing of his cell phone. The moment the ringing stopped, the knocking started again.

He cracked one eye open. Early-morning sunlight peeked in under the bedroom blinds, enough that he could make out the ball cap he had dropped on the nightstand beside his cell phone. Grumbling, he reached for his phone to check the time: 6:45 a.m.

"Someone wants to die," he muttered, throwing his covers off. His phone still in hand, he stumbled out of the bedroom and shouted, "Coming!"

The knocking stopped a moment before he unlocked the door and jerked it open. Blue eyes that mirrored his stared back at him. Reed blinked twice to bring the older version of himself into focus. Barry Forrester. His father.

"It's about time." Barry adjusted the laptop bag hanging from his shoulder.

Reed struggled to find his voice. "Dad? What are you doing here?"

"I'm here to see you." When Reed just stared, his father continued. "Are you going to invite me in?"

"Yeah, sorry." Reed waved him inside and closed the door. "I didn't know you were coming to Virginia."

"I was in New York for a couple days and thought I would pop in for the weekend." His eyes swept the room. "This is where you're staying?"

"I know. This place has the personality of a doorknob."

"Then why are you living here?"

"I already talked to you about this." Reed raked his fingers through his hair. "I don't want to commit to a long-term lease until I'm sure how the show is received."

"Sienna already bought a house. That's a pretty good indication that the producers expect it to last."

"Sienna has also made a lot more money than I have." Reed motioned for his father to sit down on the couch as he lowered himself into an armchair.

"You've made plenty of money, enough that it's silly not to diversify your investments into real estate."

Reed acknowledged the truth of his father's words and leaned back against the stiff leather. "I don't want to buy something until I can get what I want."

"What do you want?"

He lifted his hand and ticked off his list on his fingers. "Single-family home. Beachfront. Something close to work but away from the tourists."

"Something like what Sienna has."

"Yeah, but her place is divided into apartments. It's nice, but I want something all my own."

Barry pulled his laptop free of his briefcase and set it on the coffee table. "What's your Wi-Fi password?"

Reed looked it up for him and rattled off the string of letters and numbers.

"That's a pretty complex password."

"Yeah. Jane reset it for me after Sienna had so many problems with her laptop and phone."

"Who's Jane?"

"My girlfriend."

Barry's fingers froze on his keyboard, and he looked up. "Girlfriend? What about Sienna?"

"Sienna and I are just friends. The stuff online is staged so we don't have to deal with the press snooping into our real private lives."

"Even after twenty-five years, I'm still not used to the craziness of Hollywood." Barry tapped a few more keys before he leaned back against the couch cushions. "Tell me about this girlfriend of yours."

"She's smart, kind, gorgeous." Reed smiled at the thought of her. "She actually works as Sienna's assistant."

"I'd love to meet her. Do you think she would be interested in looking at houses with us today?"

"I wasn't planning on looking at houses today. Jane and I were going to hang out at her place this afternoon and grill some steaks. You're welcome to join us."

"Sounds great. I'll come over for dinner . . . after we go house hunting." Barry motioned to his computer. "I've already found five worth seeing."

Reed's eyes narrowed. "You picked these places out before you even got here, didn't you?"

"Go get dressed. Our first appointment is at nine."

Reed stood. "Dad, I think you're taking this real-estate career of yours a bit too far."

"It can't hurt to look."

"How many times have you told me that looking leads to buying?" Reed asked pointedly.

"Once or twice." Barry looked around the room again. "Besides, if you were set on staying, you would have made this place feel more like home."

His father's words resonated through him, and after several seconds, Reed took a step toward his bedroom. "Okay, you win. I'll text Jane to make sure she knows I'll be over later than planned."

"If you want, she can come with us," Barry suggested. "It never hurts to get a woman's opinion."

"True, but we aren't supposed to be seen in public together right now. Technically, I'm dating Sienna."

"No one is going to care about us walking in and out of houses," Barry countered. "And if they do, they'll see you with your girlfriend's assistant, not your girlfriend."

"True." Reed lifted his phone and tapped the keys on his screen to send the message.

Barry's eyebrows drew together. "How serious are things with this girl anyway?"

"We've only been dating for a month or so."

"That's not what I asked," Barry said.

"I'm in love with her."

Now it was his father who fell silent. Finally, he waved toward the hall. "You'd better get ready, then. We don't want to keep her waiting."

* * *

Jane's hair was still damp when the doorbell rang. She pulled it back into a ponytail and grabbed her purse, her curiosity piqued. She had still been in bed, debating whether she'd wanted to get up or roll over and go back to sleep, when Reed had texted.

Her stomach grumbled. She didn't know what he had planned this morning, but she hoped it included food at some point. She'd had time only to grab a banana after taking a quick shower and dressing for the day.

She slipped on her sandals and opened the door, and her heart experienced the same slippery meltdown it had the night before when he'd kissed her good night. How could just the sight of him have such an effect?

"Hey there. Are you ready?"

"Yeah." She stepped out, pulled her door closed, and locked it. "Where are we going?"

"Shopping." Reed took her hand and led her down the front steps.

"Why are we going shopping at nine o'clock in the morning? I thought you wanted to sleep in today."

"My dad changed those plans."

"Your dad?" Jane asked as they got to the car and the passenger side door opened and a man in his fifties stepped out.

"You must be Jane." He offered a hand. "Barry Forrester. It's good to meet you."

"Nice to meet you too." Jane shook his hand and shot a questioning look at Reed. "You didn't tell me your dad was coming for a visit."

"I didn't know."

Barry held the door open for Jane. "Here, you take the front seat."

"Oh, that's okay. I don't mind sitting in the back."

Barry simply shook his head. "I insist."

Feeling awkward, Jane slid into the passenger seat while Reed rounded the car. Like his son normally did, Barry waited until she was safely inside to close the door for her.

A moment later, Reed started the car. "Okay, Dad. Where to first?"

He rattled off an address. "It's about two miles past where you work."

"Where are we going?"

"House hunting." Reed pulled onto the street.

"You're buying a house?"

"He is if I have anything to do with it," Barry said.

"Dad, I only promised to look."

Appreciating the comfortable banter between Reed and his father, Jane twisted around in her seat so she could see Barry. "So, you aren't a fan of Reed's apartment either?"

"Not really."

Apparently recognizing her as an ally, he handed her a piece of paper. "This is the first one we're looking at. What do you think?"

"It's nice. I like the yard."

"How come you're showing the listings to her, but I didn't get to see them?" Reed asked.

"Son, trust me. It's always wise to get a woman's opinion." He looked up from the other papers he held in his hand. "Besides, if I'd given you too much information, you would have tried to tell me what was wrong with all of them before we'd even walked out of your apartment."

Reed looked at his father in the rearview mirror. "Okay, that's probably true."

"Take the next left. It's the blue house on the corner."

"How many houses are we looking at today?" Jane asked.

"Only five."

Jane's eyes widened. "Only?"

"I thought I would take it easy on him today." He lowered his voice. "Don't tell him this, but I came into town yesterday and checked out a couple dozen places. These are the top choices."

Reed pulled up to the curb. "You know I'm sitting right here."

Barry ignored him and pushed the car door open. "Let's take a look inside." He rubbed his hands together. "This is going to be fun."

26

REED HAD NEVER THOUGHT HE would agree with his father that house hunting could be fun, but walking through one house after another with Jane, he discovered he was enjoying himself. He supposed it was the possibilities that drew him in.

The first two places had great locations, but the interiors lacked the openness he hoped to find in a floor plan. The third house was nearly perfect, except that it was several miles from the beach and located near a major intersection. When they pulled up to the fourth house, Reed turned off the engine and stared. The house itself was modest in size, but it was located on a small knoll above where the beach curved. Two Adirondack chairs on the lawn faced the stunning view of the ocean.

Behind him, his father studied the listing. "This can't be right. The info sheet says this place is over four thousand square feet, but it doesn't look that big."

"Shall we take a look?" Jane asked.

"Yeah," Reed said as they started up the walk. "What else does the listing say?"

"The house is currently vacant, so it's possible to have a quick closing."

After his father accessed the key in the lock box and opened the door, Reed stepped inside and stared across the open living room to the bank of windows overlooking the water.

Walls the color of melted butter framed the view, along with gauzy white curtains.

Reed continued forward until he reached a set of french doors that led to a wide deck. He stepped through those doors, easily able to imagine standing in this exact spot for years to come.

Jane's voice sounded behind him. "This view is incredible. It's like the neighbors don't exist."

His gaze swept to the north and then to the south. She was right. The houses on either side of them were built far enough back that they weren't visible from here.

He moved to the railing and noticed a second deck below him and a patio on the ground floor. Though the house appeared to be a modest one-story structure from the road, in reality, it was three stories built into the side of the hill.

Delight fluttered inside him. Turning, he took Jane's hand and pulled her back inside. "Come on. Let's check out the rest."

It boasted an open-style kitchen and two bedrooms, including the master, on the top floor and a second master and two smaller bedrooms on the second level, all of which opened into a modest living room. The ground level included an in-home movie theater; a game room, complete with a wet bar and second refrigerator; yet another bedroom and bath; and an additional bathroom that led from the game room to the beach.

"These lower levels explain why the square footage looked off," Barry said.

Reed opened the sliding glass door that led to the patio. He could see it now, the inlet that ran along the north side of the house and prevented anyone from building too close on that side. When Jane followed him outside, he asked, "What do you think?"

"I love it." She put her hand on his arm. "What about you? Can you visualize yourself living here?"

"It's like it's already mine." He looked down to see her grinning at him.

"I know what you mean."

Barry opened the door wider and passed by them to sit at the patio table. He opened his briefcase and drew out a folder. "Do you want to make an offer?"

Reed pulled out a chair for Jane before lowering himself into the seat between them. "You're the expert, Dad. Tell me what I need to do."

"Oh, those magic words." He pulled out a pen. "I was hoping I would hear them from you this weekend."

"You're sneaky. You know that, right?"

"Only when it comes to making sure you're happy."

Reed looked up and took in his surroundings before focusing on his father again. "Thanks, Dad."

"You're welcome."

* * *

"I can't believe I just did that."

Jane watched Reed pace across her kitchen while she prepared the baked potatoes they planned to have with their steak tonight.

"It's a great house." Jane couldn't begin to imagine having the resources to buy her own home, much less one with so much space and such a great location. Reed paced across the room again. "Why are you so nervous?"

"What if they accept my offer and the show gets canceled?"

"It's not going to get canceled." Jane poked the last potato and washed her hands.

"Or I could get dropped from the cast if the response for me isn't good enough."

Drying her hands on a dish towel, she turned to face him, grabbing his hand before he could start another journey around her kitchen. "Reed, if you decide you don't want the house after all, you can always withdraw your offer."

He took a deep breath as though trying to settle his emotions. "I do want the house."

"Are you scared the owners will accept your offer, or are you scared they won't?"

"Both." He pressed a hand to his stomach. "I'm sorry. I'm a nervous wreck."

"What's the best-case scenario?"

"I don't know."

"Okay, let me take a stab at it." Jane kept his hand in hers. "Let's assume *Beachfront* is going to run for many years and your offer is accepted."

"Jane, this house has six bedrooms."

"Okay, so we'll draw a map so you won't get lost."

Reed chuckled. "You're bringing positive energy to a whole new level."

She squeezed his hand. "Maybe you should pray about it."

"I already did, but I can't seem to get my mind to stop racing." He looked down at her, and Jane could have sworn she saw a lightbulb go on in his head. "Would you pray with me?"

Surprise came first, followed by an overwhelming warmth that could only be the Spirit. "I'd be happy to pray with you."

With her hand still in his, they made their way into her living room and knelt down together.

When Reed began his heartfelt prayer, Jane could feel his uncertainty, his doubts, and his desires. The warmth of the Spirit magnified, and Reed paused for a long moment before closing his prayer.

Rather than stand, he leaned back on his heels. His face was a shade paler than normal. "I think I just bought a house."

"Yeah?"

"I hope they accept my offer." He pushed to a stand and offered her his hand. "I never thought about it before—how nerve-racking it is to wait on a contract."

"I'm praying you won't have to wait long." She took his hand. "Let's go for a walk. It will be good to get your mind off of everything."

"Good idea."

They were a quarter mile down the beach when Reed's phone rang. He looked at the screen, excitement showing on his face. "Hey, Dad. Any news?"

Reed fell silent, and a sense of wonder spread across his face. "Thanks a lot." He paused again. "Yeah, she's right here." Another pause. "Okay, I'll talk to you later."

"Well?" Jane asked as soon as he hung up.

He scooped her into his arms. "We bought a house."

Jane let out a squeak of surprise when his embrace lifted her from the ground and he spun around. As soon as her feet hit the sand, she looked up at him. "They accepted the offer?"

"They did. I close in two weeks."

"Congratulations, Reed." Jane gave his hand a squeeze since she didn't dare kiss him outside. "I'm so happy for you."

"I'm happy for us."

His words settled over her and sent a flutter of hope and anticipation through her. "Us?"

"Yes, us." Reed gazed down at her as though he too recognized a change between them. "I hope to build a future in this new house. I want you to be part of that future."

Jane gave his hand another squeeze. "I want that too."

* * *

Reed headed toward his apartment, stunned by how quickly his life had changed. He still couldn't wrap his mind around this new reality. He was buying a house. And he was doing it with the approval of the woman he loved.

Reed hadn't completely come out and said it to Jane, but this purchase wasn't simply somewhere he would sleep between workdays. This new house was where he hoped to build a home, and he could no longer imagine doing that without her.

Any doubts he'd had about their future had disappeared when they had prayed together. He had offered a silent prayer before he had told his father to write up the contract. He had prayed again before letting him send it. Yet it wasn't until he'd knelt with Jane that he'd found peace of mind and a knowledge that this decision was the right one for him.

He knew they hadn't been dating long enough to take things to the next level. In truth, he wasn't sure he was ready to, but in his mind's eye, he could see how things would play out, how he hoped they would play out.

Marriage. Children. Career.

She could choose, of course, whether she would want to keep working. Even if this role didn't last as long as he hoped, he had enough connections in Hollywood to always have work. And as much as he loved his new house, having Jane with him was what would always create a sense of home.

As though he needed to make sure it was still there, he took the long way home and drove by the house that would soon be his. Security lights illuminated the front door, the lock box still hanging from the doorknob, the For Sale sign still in the yard. He imagined the Under Contract sign would be added within the next day or two.

He slowed his car, wishing he could go inside again to start planning for the future.

Earlier today, making a move in only two weeks seemed crazy. Since praying with Jane, his anxiety had been replaced with anticipation. He simply couldn't wait.

27

THE NAGGING WORRY WOULDN'T LEAVE. Craig wanted to pretend that everything was okay now that Sienna was once again safe, but knowing a chemical weapon might very well be unleashed on American soil kept eating at him. Storm clouds swirled in the distance. Rain splattered on his windshield as he made his way to the office.

In reality, Virginia Beach wasn't likely to be affected directly. No, Jamal's group would go after a bigger target: New York, Washington, Los Angeles, Chicago. That didn't lessen Craig's anxiety. And he wasn't the only one feeling it.

Every day during his squad's morning prayer, regardless of who was speaking, they pled for guidance in finding the weapons. The latest intelligence report indicated the men they had marked with tracking spray had not left Abolstan, and so far, no one had managed to find Jamal Elazar's current location.

Craig parked his truck and headed inside, the heavens opening up seconds before he reached shelter. He didn't bother increasing his pace. He held the door open for the woman behind him before following her inside. A quick shake of his head sent droplets of water showering down around him.

"Hey, Craig."

Craig looked back. Jay had walked in behind him. Like Craig, he didn't look like he had made any effort to dash through the rain, instead accepting the reality that he was going to get wet. "Hi, Jay." Craig motioned to the glass doors. "Looks like our jump may be postponed with this weather."

"That's my guess." The two men fell into step and headed through the maze of corridors leading to their offices. "Looks like today will either be a sit-at-a-desk day or an obstacle-course-in-the-rain day."

"Believe it or not, I think I'd rather have the desk for a change."

"Me too," Jay admitted. "I don't like not knowing what's going on with Jamal's group."

They entered Brent's office for morning prayer, and the rest of their squad was already inside.

"I'm sure it's no surprise that the powers that be are postponing today's training exercise," Brent said. "After PT this morning, I suggested we spend some time working with intelligence on Jamal's group."

"We were hoping you would say that," Tristan said.

"Then you got your wish. The FBI has a lead they want us to follow." Brent moved to the front of his desk, the men shuffling to form a circle. "I think it's my turn to pray."

They all bowed their heads, and Craig listened to the familiar words asking for inspiration, guidance, and protection. His own silent prayers repeated Brent's sentiments. As soon as the amens were offered, everyone headed for their offices, but Brent stopped Craig.

"Craig, I need to talk to you for a minute," Brent said. Craig stopped as the rest of the squad departed. "I have some news."

"What's wrong?"

"I'm not sure if something's wrong, per se, but I wanted you to be aware that the FBI sent me a report on Xavier Guadalupe, the man stalking Sienna."

"And?" Craig prompted.

"They're concerned that they may not have the right man."

The words hit him harder than a punch in the gut. "What?"

"The evidence was solid enough to make the arrest, but the prosecuting attorney doesn't know if they have enough for a conviction."

"What does this mean?"

"It means that I think you should give the lead agent a call. Maybe if the two of you put your heads together, you'll be able to see if this guy really is the culprit or if someone threw us a bone so we would stop our search." Brent handed him a paper with a name and phone number scribbled on it. "Good luck."

"Thanks. I'm going to need it."

* * *

Jamal rushed into the room, a backpack in hand. "We've got to clear out of here."

"What?" Abdul asked.

"Now!" Jamal shoved his laptop into his pack and crossed to the bulletin board. "Someone's tracking us."

Disbelief transformed into fury in an instant. "How? We moved here so no one would be able to find us."

Jamal didn't answer. Instead, he ripped their mission plans off the board, not bothering to take the thumbtacks out first.

Spurred into action by Jamal's obvious sense of urgency, Abdul called out to Munjid. "Start loading everything into the van!"

Abdul rushed into the bedroom and retrieved one of the packed explosives from the closet. He hauled it into the living area. "How much time do you think we have?"

"I don't know. Minutes. An hour." Jamal finished with the mission board and spoke with authority. "We need to leave now."

"Our fingerprints . . ."

"We'll load everything up. Then you can stand watch while Munjid and I wipe everything down."

"It'll be faster with all of us." Abdul set the first bomb by the door and returned to retrieve the second. After he had everything ready to go, he hurried to the kitchen and loaded the few dishes they had used that morning into the dishwasher. Though it was less than half full, he started the wash cycle. He then retrieved the cleaning kit he had stored beneath the kitchen sink and started wiping down the counters, handles, and doorknobs.

Jamal entered and grabbed two wipes. "We need to leave."

"Five minutes," Abdul responded. "Then we'll load the car, and one of us can stand watch."

"You're playing with fire."

"No," Abdul countered. "I'm playing with bombs."

Satisfied that the kitchen surfaces were sanitized, he retrieved a garbage bag and opened the refrigerator. He swept the refrigerator contents into the bag and repeated the process with the freezer.

Munjid rushed into the room. "I wiped down the living room. What next?"

Abdul tied off the bag. "Wipe down the refrigerator."

While Munjid went about his task, Abdul and Jamal emptied the trash in the kitchen and bathroom and hauled all three bags outside. After a quick look around to make sure they were alone, they stored their garbage in the back of the van.

When they entered the apartment, Munjid called out to him from the bedroom. "I'm almost done in here. I only have the bathroom left."

"I'm going to start the car to cool it off." Abdul slipped his pack onto his back and lifted one of the explosives.

"I'll get the computer gear," Jamal said.

"Munjid, grab the last pack on your way out." Abdul didn't wait for a response before heading out the door, Jamal right behind him.

Abdul rushed to the van and turned on the engine to get the air conditioning started. He waited two full minutes before he deemed the temperature cool enough to store the explosive inside. Not happy about moving in broad daylight, he donned his sunglasses and a ball cap. Anxiety brewed within him until he saw his brother emerge from the building.

Abdul climbed behind the wheel, Jamal taking the front passenger seat.

Not two seconds later, three black SUVs pulled into the parking lot.

Munjid saw them too. Abdul saw the slight hitch in his step and the brief internal debate illuminated on his face. If he ran, he might make it to the van . . .

Munjid ran. In the other direction.

"No!" Abdul whispered under his breath.

The SUVs picked up speed briefly before the squeal of tires filled the parking lot. Doors opened, and agents poured out, each with "FBI" lettered in white across their black vests.

"FBI! Stop right there," one agent shouted.

Beside him, Jamal spoke softly. "There's nothing we can do."

Abdul couldn't look. He forced himself to put the van in drive. With the agents' focus on Munjid, Abdul made his way onto the road.

A moment later, gunfire filled the air and he couldn't help but look back. A figure lay sprawled in the center of the parking lot, a black duffel lying beside him.

* * *

Craig entered the weight room and ignored Damian's attempt to engage him in conversation. His pent-up frustrations were threatening to explode if they didn't find a release soon. His teammates must have sensed his mood because no one else spoke to him as he moved to the corner of the room to stretch. He had tried to call Agent Rinzler three times yesterday and still hadn't heard back. If he didn't get a response soon, he would have to take some time off and drive to the FBI office this afternoon. He was thinking about how to broach that subject with his commanding officer when Brent walked in.

Brent motioned to the squad. "Everyone in my office. Now."

"Is everything okay?" Damian asked.

Brent looked around the room at the handful of other military personnel using the equipment. "Let's go."

Ten minutes later, they all walked into Brent's office. Seth closed the door behind him. "Okay, we're all here."

"What's going on?" Craig asked.

"I got a call from Charlie this morning. The FBI traced the virus planted in Jane's phone to an apartment in Maryland."

"And?" Quinn asked.

"A shoot-out resulted in the death of a suspect."

"Do they know who he is?"

"Munjid Maleb."

"Any relation to Abdul Maleb?"

"Younger brother. But that's not all." Brent picked up a manila envelope and slid a photo from inside. He held it up to reveal a duffel bag that had been cut open to reveal the contents: a toxic bomb.

"Is that what I think it is?"

"If you think it's a chemical weapon, then, yes. They've confirmed the toxins contained inside match the signature of what was stolen from the facility in Syria."

"What aren't you telling us?" Seth asked.

"They believe our analysis was right," Brent said. "This is one bomb. Based on the amount of toxins missing and what is in this device, the analysts believe there is one more out there."

"You said this one was recovered in Maryland?"

"That's right."

Silence enveloped the room. Seth was the first to speak. "Then they did get the chemical weapons across the border."

"Yes," Brent said gravely. "They did."

* * *

Abdul drove for nearly two hours before their lack of fuel forced him to pull into a gas station.

"I am sorry about your brother," Jamal said from the seat beside him.

"He died protecting our cause."

"We won't let him down," Jamal promised. "We will avenge both of our brothers' deaths."

Abdul swallowed hard. "Our plans must change. We have only one weapon left."

"Then I suggest we use it wisely," Jamal said calmly. "The Americans will expect us to strike in one of their big cities."

"We will strike in one of their big cities," Abdul responded.

"Which one?"

"I don't know how the women caused this to happen, but they must pay for their actions and for their arrogance."

"What women?"

"The actress and her friend." Abdul's jaw clenched briefly before he continued. "You said they are living in Virginia Beach."

"That's correct."

"I want them eliminated." Abdul fought against his rising emotions. He swallowed hard. "And after they are dead, we will make it our mission to send their friends and neighbors to join them."

Jamal retrieved a map from his backpack and studied it. "There are several naval bases in the Virginia Beach area."

"We can use the same plan we developed for Baltimore's inner harbor."

"If we study the wind patterns, the damage could be extensive," Jamal added. "The death toll could rival that of 9/11."

"When we are done, the Americans will never be the same."

Jamal bowed his head slightly. "And neither will we."

28

Reed could hardly believe the day had come. In an hour, he would own his first home.

"Are you ready?" his dad asked as they approached the office doors of the settlement company.

"As ready as I'll ever be."

"You picked out a good house, son. I only wish it were in California."

"I know." Reed looked at the scatter of trees surrounding the brick office building. "I have to say, though, I really like Virginia."

"Bloom where you're planted. That's what your grandmother always used to say."

"I remember."

His father rubbed at his left arm as though massaging some dull ache there.

"Are you okay?" Reed asked.

"I'm fine." He pulled open the door and waited for Reed to enter before following him inside.

Ten minutes later, Reed sat beside his father and signed one document after another until the magic moment came when the settlement agent stood and shook Reed's hand. "Congratulations on your new home."

"That's it?"

"That's it." The agent handed Reed a key ring with two keys on it, along with three garage-door openers.

"Thank you." Reed pocketed the keys and retrieved the inch-thick folder that now held all of his paperwork.

"Ready to go check out your new house?" his dad asked.

"Let's go." Reed led the way to the car.

"Did you think to pack anything to take over with you?"

"I packed a few things, but my bed won't be delivered until Thursday," Reed said. "I didn't want to schedule it too early in case the closing got pushed back."

"That's three days," his dad said. "Of course, if you want to spend the night sooner than that, you can always go pick up a mattress at one of the furniture stores."

"Every place I've looked takes forever to get stuff delivered."

"Not if you shop in the clearance room."

"What clearance room?"

"Most furniture stores have an area for discontinued and discounted items."

Reed's eyebrows lifted. "Dad, I think I can afford to pay full price."

"Maybe so, but there's a big advantage with the clearance stuff. You can take it home the same day."

"In case you haven't noticed, I drive a Mustang. I don't think I'm going to be able to transport a mattress in my car."

"No, but we can rent a truck for a couple hours."

"True." Even though three days didn't seem like a long time, he was anxious to leave his apartment behind and start settling into his new home. "I guess it can't hurt to look."

* * *

For only the second time since arriving in Virginia, Jane left work early. With Reed gone all afternoon, Sienna had been busy shooting. Thankfully, Toni had been willing to cover for the extra couple hours.

Jane made her way to Reed's new house, along with a basket filled with sparkling cider, a set of champagne glasses, and an assortment of his favorite snacks. Excitement filled her when she parked in front of his house and hurried up the front walk.

She rang the bell and waited. And waited. She rang the bell a second time, leaning closer to the door to make sure the chime was working. It echoed inside, but again the door went unanswered.

Uncertain why Reed wouldn't be here yet, she reached for her phone. The rumble of a truck engine sounded behind her, and she turned as a box truck with the local hardware store logo displayed on the side came to a stop. To her surprise, Reed sat behind the wheel, and his father was in the passenger seat.

Reed maneuvered the truck and backed into the driveway, hopping out and moving to the back to open it.

"Hey, have you been waiting here long?" he called out to her.

"Only a couple minutes."

"Hi, Jane," Barry said.

"Hi, Mr. Forrester."

"I think you should be calling me Barry by now."

"Okay, Barry." She smiled and waved at the rental vehicle. "What's in the truck?"

"I picked up a few things so I can stay here tonight." He unlatched the back and rolled it open to reveal a mattress and box springs leaning against the side. Next to them, several boxes occupied the area nearest the cab and a love seat in soft yellow dominated the front section.

"I thought you already bought a bed."

"I did, but Dad pointed out that I'll want to set up at least one of the guest rooms. I can sleep on this mattress until mine gets here."

"Smart. What's in the boxes?"

"A patio table and chairs." Reed pulled at the end of the love seat. "I saw them when we went to rent the truck."

"I can't wait to see what you picked out." Jane edged closer. "What can I help with first?"

Reed dug his keys out of his pocket. "Can you unlock the door? Dad and I can carry this stuff in."

"Sure." Jane accepted the key and went to the front door while the two men pulled the love seat out of the back. Jane picked up the basket she had left on the porch, unlocked the door, and pushed it open wide.

She waited for them to pass by before she continued inside and set the basket on the hearth of the fireplace.

"Let's set it down here for now." Reed lowered his end of the love seat when he reached the living room.

"I thought you were going to put this in the master bedroom," Barry said.

"I haven't decided yet, but I might as well leave it here until I get some living room furniture." Reed turned to Jane, his eyes landing on the basket. "What's that?"

"A little house-warming gift."

Reed crossed to her and looked at the contents, a smile illuminating his face. "This is great. Thanks."

"You're welcome."

"Come on, you two," Barry interrupted. "Let's get this truck unloaded. We have to have it back in an hour."

Jane and Reed followed him outside. The men retrieved the first half of the box springs. Once they passed by her again, Jane climbed into the back of the truck and unloaded one of the smaller boxes, a photo of a patio chair affixed to the outside.

Reed came out the door as she reached the porch. "Jane, I can get that stuff."

"It's not that heavy." She maneuvered past him. "Where do you want it?"

"Back porch."

"Okay." A few minutes later, Jane carried the last chair through the house, followed by Reed and his father carrying the box containing the patio table. She had barely set her package down when she heard a loud thud and then a grunt of pain.

Jane whirled around. Reed was struggling to hold the large box upright, his father now sprawled on the floor just inside the door.

Concerned the table was going to fall on Barry, Jane sprinted forward and grabbed one end of the box. "Are you okay? What happened?"

"I'm all right. I tripped on the threshold," Barry said.

"Let's lean this over here." Reed nodded to his right. Together he and Jane set the box down and tipped it against the entryway wall. He offered a hand to his father. "Are you sure you're okay?"

"Yeah." Barry accepted Reed's hand and pulled himself up to a stand, immediately wincing when he put weight on his left foot.

"You don't look okay to me." Reed waited until his father was able to balance on his right foot before he leaned down to examine his left. Even from a distance, Jane could see the disfiguration. "Um, hate to break it to you, Dad, but I think we need to go to the hospital."

"I'll be fine."

"Maybe," Reed said, "but neither of us will be fine if Mom finds out you broke your ankle and I didn't take you in to get it checked out."

"There's no need to bring your mother into this."

"Then humor me and let me take you in to get it X-rayed."

"We still need to return the truck."

It had been a while since Jane had driven anything as large as the monstrosity in the driveway, but away from LA traffic, she was pretty sure she could manage it. "Reed, take my car. I'll return the truck for you."

Hope illuminated his face. "Are you sure?"

"I'm sure."

Ten minutes later, with Reed's car keys in her purse, Jane climbed into the cab of the truck and reacquainted herself with a standard transmission.

* * *

Reed expected their visit to the emergency room to consist of X-rays and either a splint or an ace bandage. When the triage nurse noticed the way his dad kept rubbing his left arm, he ended up hooked to a bunch of monitors to check his heart.

Reed stood helplessly by and watched the nurse input his latest vitals into the computer in the corner of the room.

"I'm fine," Barry insisted. He looked pointedly at the nurse. "I'm not having a heart attack."

"I'll believe you as soon as the doctor comes in and agrees with you," she countered. "She should be here any minute."

"Thank you," Reed said. He leaned against the wall and debated whether to let his mother know what was going on.

"Don't even think about calling your mom until we talk to the doctor."

"Are you reading my mind now?" Reed asked.

"I'm reading your expression," Barry said. "I'm fine. Really. My arm is sore because I did too much lifting yesterday."

His words were still hanging in the air when a doctor in her thirties walked in.

"Mr. Forrester? I'm Dr. Aullet."

"Can you get me out of here?"

"I'll do my best." She looked at Reed. "You're his son?"

"That's right."

"Well, let's have a listen." She slid her stethoscope to her ears and moved to Barry's bedside.

Reed held his breath as though the sound of his breathing might interfere with the doctor's diagnosis. After a moment, he forced himself to exhale.

After listening to his dad's heart, the doctor looked at the monitor. She tapped a few keys on the keyboard.

"Well, Mr. Forrester, I'm forced to agree with you. Your heartbeat is regular, and other than the pain in your arm, I'm not seeing any other signs of a heart attack," she said. "You said you were lifting weights recently?"

"Yesterday afternoon."

"That would explain the soreness." She moved farther down the bed. "Now, what's the problem with your ankle?"

"Good question." Barry pointed at Reed. "He thinks it's broken. My vote is for a sprain."

She pressed a finger against the swollen skin, and Reed heard his father's quick intake of air. The doctor continued to examine his ankle and foot. "Well, I'm afraid I have to agree with your son on this one. We'll have an X-ray taken to confirm it's a fracture, but you're likely going to be off the dance floor for a few weeks."

"I liked you better when you were telling me good news," Barry said.

"And yet, somehow, I'll find a way to survive," Dr. Aullet said.

Barry chuckled.

"Someone will be in to take the X-ray in a few minutes."

"Thank you, Doctor."

She nodded before slipping out of the room.

"You could still be wrong, you know," Barry said.

"I hope I am," Reed said.

A knock sounded at the door. When Reed pushed it open, Jane stood on the other side. "I came to see if you or your dad need anything."

"An escape plan," Barry called from behind him.

"Come on in." Reed motioned her into the room.

Her eyebrows lifted when she saw the lines running from Barry to the monitor positioned beside him. "Did something happen? I thought you brought him in for an X-ray."

"The nurse was worried Dad might be having a heart attack."

"What?" Jane's face paled.

"Don't worry. He's fine." Reed looked at his father before adding, "Except for his broken ankle."

Relief and concern both appeared on her face. "Glad to hear your heart is okay. Sorry about the ankle."

"Reed, can you go find a nurse to unhook me? I need to go to the bathroom," Barry said.

"Sure." Reed stepped out of the room, but the nurses' station was empty. Noticing two paramedics several rooms down, he guessed someone was having a more serious emergency than his father. Two wheelchairs were parked between his dad's room and the one beside his. He wheeled one inside.

"No one is out there right now, but I can help you if you want. The bathroom is across the hall."

"What about all this stuff?" Barry lifted his arm that had the blood pressure cuff attached to it and a line running to the monitor.

"Oh, I can take care of that." Jane crossed the room, pressed a button on the monitor, and in less than twenty seconds, disconnected the various monitor cords trapping Reed's father.

Reed stared at her. "How did you know how to do that?"

"I spent a lot of time in emergency rooms with my mom when she was going through treatments." Jane motioned to the monitors. "If you run into any of the nurses, you can tell them I paused the alarms."

"You are full of surprises."

Her cheeks flushed. "I'll wait here in case the tech returns before you get back."

"Thanks, Jane."

As soon as Reed helped his dad into the wheelchair, Barry looked up at Jane. "While we're gone, you can work on my escape plan."

Jane chuckled. "I'll do what I can."

29

JANE PULLED INTO THE PARKING lot of Reed's apartment building and noticed him outside loading his car. She pulled into the spot beside him and climbed out. "Good morning."

"Morning." He loaded a suitcase into the trunk and closed the distance between them. His intention was clear when he started to lean in for a kiss, but she shook her head, dropping her voice to a whisper. "We're in public."

"Oh yeah."

"How's your dad doing?" Jane asked.

"Hanging in there. He's not happy that he isn't able to help me move into my new place, but he's going to meet me there in a little while."

"Can he even drive?"

"He said he has a ride," Reed said. "My guess is that he'll call a cab so he won't have to ask me to pick him up."

"I can always go get him if you need me to."

"Thanks." Reed loaded another suitcase into his car before closing the trunk.

"What can I help you with?"

"Actually, I think I have everything loaded."

Jane's eyebrows lifted. "Everything?"

"Yeah. Besides the stuff I dropped off last night, I got up early this morning and took a load over." He pulled open his car door. "Do you want to follow me over?"

"Sure. I'll see you in a few minutes." A half hour later, Jane stood in the middle of Reed's kitchen and peered into the single box he had set on the counter for her to unpack. Two plates, one bowl, three plastic cups from his favorite smoothie bar, a dozen assorted pieces of silverware, and a pair of chopsticks.

She knew Reed had said he needed to do some shopping, but she hadn't expected his kitchen to be so understocked.

"How's it going?" Reed asked when he walked in holding a case of water bottles.

"Is this all you have for the kitchen?"

"Yeah. My apartment came furnished, so I didn't have to worry about buying much. I guess I need to do some shopping."

"Do you want to pick up some things tonight?"

"No, I already ordered Chinese to be delivered." He glanced at his watch. "It should be here in a half hour."

"What about plates and forks?"

"There's a bag around here somewhere with paper plates and plastic utensils."

"I haven't seen it."

Reed pulled his keys out of his pocket and held them out. "Would you mind checking my car? It's probably in the back seat."

"No problem." Accepting the keys, she headed outside. She was nearly to the car when a silver sedan turned the corner. The memory of being followed a couple weeks ago sent a ripple of fear through her. She took a retreating step toward the house before she saw Reed's father in the passenger seat. Willing her heartbeat to steady, she unlocked Reed's car and retrieved the bag of paper plates tucked behind the driver's seat.

The sedan parked beside Reed's car, and for the first time, Jane took notice of the driver, a dark-haired woman around her mom's age. Both doors opened, and Jane headed for the passenger side when she saw Barry struggling to angle his crutches out the door.

"Can I help you with that?" she asked.

"These darn things. I never have been any good at using them."

"Then maybe you should stop breaking bones," the woman, now standing outside the car, said.

Jane recognized the underlying sarcasm in the woman's voice. "I take it this kind of thing has happened before."

"A couple of skiing accidents and she won't let me live them down."

"The first was on our honeymoon. The second day." She circled the car and offered her hand. "You must be Jane. I'm Deanne, Reed's mother."

"So nice to meet you," Jane said. "I didn't know you were in town."

"It was a last-minute trip," she said. "Reed doesn't even know I'm here."

"She didn't trust me to fly home by myself."

"That, and I really wanted to be here when Reed moved into his first house."

"Come on in. Reed was in the kitchen a minute ago." Jane waited for Barry to settle his crutches under him and then led the way inside through the front door. As soon as she crossed the threshold, she called out, "Hey, Reed. You have company."

"I thought Sienna and Craig were coming over later." Reed emerged from the kitchen, his eyes widening with delight. "Mom! When did you get here?"

"Late last night." Her last word was muffled against her son's shoulder when he scooped her into a hug. As soon as Reed released her, she craned her neck to look up at him. "I thought it would be fun to surprise you."

"This is the best surprise." Reed motioned to Jane. "I see you met Jane."

"I did." Deanne took a look around the entryway and main-level living room. "This place is great."

"Want a tour?"

"I would love one."

Barry leaned on his crutches. "I think I'll stay up here."

"I was going to finish putting some things away in the kitchen. I think there's a folding chair in there with your name on it," Jane said.

"Sold."

"Hon, could you call the Chinese food place and add on to our order? It's the same place we ordered from last week," Reed said before Jane could head into the kitchen.

"Sure."

Deanne motioned to Barry. "Dad knows what I like."

Jane led the way into the kitchen and opened the pantry door to retrieve one of the two folding chairs Reed had stored there. She set one up for his dad.

As soon as he settled into his seat, she pulled out her phone. "What would you like me to order for you? I'm assuming Reed already ordered orange chicken and shrimp with lobster sauce."

"Tell you what. You dial. I'll order."

"That I can do."

* * *

"I like her."

Reed glanced over his shoulder when he reached the bottom of the stairs. "What?"

"Your girlfriend," his mom said. "She seems very sweet."

"She is." He didn't try to stop the goofy grin forming on his lips. "I'm glad you came out. I wanted you to meet her."

His mother fell silent as she wandered through the second-level bedrooms and living area. When they reached the ground floor, she spoke again. "From what your dad was saying, he thinks she's going to be our future daughter-in-law."

Reed stared at her, open mouthed. "What?"

"You heard me."

"Isn't it usually the parents' job to advise their kids not to jump into anything too fast?"

"I think so." Again, she fell silent as she went from room to room, exploring Reed's new house. Finally, she returned to the rec room. "Reed, you did good. You picked a great house."

"Thanks."

"It's the kind of place you can build a home in."

Leave it to his mother to hit the nail on the head. Since she already suspected where his intentions were headed with Jane, he didn't filter his feelings. "I don't think I would have jumped into this if I hadn't already started dating Jane."

"I suspected as much." She walked to the sliding doors and looked out through the glass. "Of course, if your show does do as well as expected, I think your dad is going to be looking for more property in Virginia Beach."

"What do you mean?"

"A nice condo on the beach would make a great rental property."

"If you think we ever won't have room for you to visit, you must not have been counting the number of bedrooms. I could have four kids and still have space."

"Maybe I'm hoping for more grandkids than that."

"Now you really are getting ahead of yourself."

"Yeah, moms do that sometimes."

Reed chuckled and reached out to hug her. "I'm really glad you're here."

"Me too, son." Her arms wrapped around him and held tight. "Me too."

30

Tables, chairs, sofas, end tables, bed frames, dressers, lamps. Reed hadn't truly understood how overwhelming the task of furnishing an entire house could be.

Jane sank into the soft cushions of an oversized leather chair and looked up at Reed. "How about this one?"

He sat on the matching sofa. "It's not bad." Recognizing a possible missed opportunity, he stood and nudged her over so he could sit beside her. He stretched his arm across the back of the chair, pleased with himself when his movement caused Jane to fall against him. "Yeah, I like the chair better than the couch."

Jane rolled her eyes. "The idea is to pick furniture you like even if I'm not right beside you."

Reed leaned back more fully, testing the give in the cushions. "I actually do like this one."

Craig and Sienna wandered in their direction. "Hey, guys, come check this one out."

Sienna sat in the middle of the couch and arched an eyebrow in approval. "I like it. The leather would be great for any of the living rooms."

"I'm thinking four of these chairs in the rec room downstairs," Reed said.

"Smart. It's a lot easier to clean sand off of leather than fabric."

"So true." Reed thought through his mental list of purchases. Even though he had bought something for half of the rooms in his house, not one of them was complete. "Help me find some good end tables to go with these. I'd like to have at least one room fully furnished before we quit for the day."

"I saw some cool end tables in the back room." Craig offered Sienna his hand, pulling her up to stand beside him. "It's this way."

Reed and Jane both stood and fell into step behind Craig and Sienna. An hour later, Reed had managed to furnish two guest rooms and select several other items. Craig pulled his truck up to the loading dock, and Reed watched two store employees load two bed frames and a new mattress set into the truck.

"We'll be back in about thirty minutes to pick up the rest of the stuff," Craig said.

"Do you want us to wait here or come with you to help unload?" Jane asked.

"Why don't you and Sienna go pick up bedding for me, and I'll go with Craig to unload," Reed said. "We can meet back at my house when we're done."

"Don't you want to be involved in those kind of decisions? I thought you wanted to pick out the decorations yourself."

"I trust you." Reed dug his car keys out of his pocket and handed them to Jane along with a credit card. "Here."

"Okay." Jane looked at him skeptically. "If you're sure."

"I'm sure," Reed said. "I'll see you in a little while."

Beside Jane, Sienna rubbed her hands together in anticipation. "This is going to be fun."

"Jane, don't let her get out of control," Reed said. "No pink fuzzy cushions."

"I was thinking zebra stripes," Sienna said. "Maybe a leopard print."

Reed was starting to reconsider his decision, but before he could voice any further objections, Jane said. "See you later."

Reed stood rooted to his spot staring after the two women as they disappeared back into the store. Craig slapped a hand on his back. "Reed, you must really be in love with that girl."

"What?"

"You just gave her your car keys and your credit card and then deliberately sent her shopping with Sienna." Craig lifted a hand. "Only way I can figure is you're either in love or insane."

"I'm not crazy," Reed countered instinctively.

"That's what I thought."

* * *

"The guys must still be picking up the second load," Jane said as she approached Reed's house with its empty driveway.

"I'm sure they'll be here any minute." Sienna pushed the garage-door opener clipped onto the passenger-side visor.

Jane pulled into the side of the garage farthest from the door leading to the house to make sure she left a clear path for Reed and whatever furniture he still had to unload. She climbed out of the car and looked at the back seat. The very full back seat.

"I'm not sure Reed is going to be happy when he sees all the stuff we bought."

"Are you kidding?" Sienna asked. "He'll be thrilled. We totally scored on bedding."

"And throw pillows and dishes and silverware and pots and pans," Jane added, listing off only a few of their purchases.

"If you leave it up to him, he will live off of paper plates and plastic forks for the next three months, not because he wants to but because he won't get around to buying what he needs."

"Maybe, but I don't want to open anything until he gets home so I can return whatever he decides not to keep."

"Fair enough." Sienna opened the back door and started unloading.

Jane gathered several items and led the way inside. With no furniture to speak of in the kitchen yet, she leaned one of the bedding sets against a cabinet and laid out the purchases on the counter. Sienna followed her lead, displaying everything so Reed could see it all before they began washing and putting things away.

"I'm going to put the laundry detergent in the laundry room. We know he'll use it eventually."

"Okay." Jane retrieved the last load from the trunk. She stored the dishwasher detergent and dish soap in the cabinet beneath the sink and then began putting away the few basic groceries they had picked up.

When she heard Craig's truck pull up outside, her stomach fluttered with anticipation. Would Reed appreciate them buying so many extra necessities, or would he be annoyed that he had been denied the opportunity of choosing things for himself? She opened the door leading to the garage as Reed approached carrying two bar stools.

Craig entered and set the remaining two stools down. "Looks like you girls were busy."

"Yeah," Jane said.

Craig started toward the front of the house. "I'm going to unlock the front door so we can bring the tables in through there."

"Okay, thanks." Reed scanned the display on the counter, both eyebrows lifting.

"I saved the receipts, so I can return anything you don't want," Jane began hastily. "We just thought you might want us to pick up some of the basics for you since you don't have much time during the week."

"Show me what you've got." Reed moved closer and picked up the box of silverware, looked at it, and set it back down. Slowly, he moved down the line of items, studying each one without saying a word.

Razor sharp butterfly wings fluttered in her stomach. "I'm sorry, Reed. I should have stopped with the bedding, but when I was thinking about all the things you needed, I got carried away." She picked up one of the shopping bags she had set aside. "I can take it all back."

"Don't do that." He put down the cutting board he had been holding. "This is great." He turned to her. "You did great."

"Really?" His words quieted the butterflies, but she was still skeptical.

"Really." He closed the distance between them and lowered his lips to hers. "Thank you. Everything here is exactly what I would have picked out for myself."

"I doubt that."

"Don't doubt it." He kissed her again. "You have excellent taste."

"I tried to pick out things that I thought you would like."

"Apparently you know me even better than I thought."

As compliments went, she couldn't think of one she would prefer to hear more. She smiled. "I'm glad to hear it."

An odd expression crossed his face before he took both of her hands in his. "So am I."

31

REED SHIFTED THE NIGHTSTAND IN the second-floor guest room a few inches and stepped back to admire the results. Jane and Sienna had already made the bed, the white comforter offset by light-blue and green throw pillows. A blue glass bowl filled with seashells sat atop the dresser, and an afghan in the same blue lay across the foot of the bed.

A woman's touch. He hadn't before realized what a difference such a thing could make, but he couldn't deny the sense of home that washed over him as he stood in the room Jane had helped him put together.

He walked into the second-level living area and listened for a minute to try to gauge where everyone else had disappeared to. He heard voices downstairs and headed to the lower level.

The rec room was still noticeably bare, but the delivery of the chairs he had ordered today would solve that problem. The sliding-glass door was open, letting in the evening breeze and the scent of the ocean.

He opened the screen and joined Craig and Sienna on the back patio. "What's up?"

"Sienna and Jane bought some steak to grill tonight, but I'm afraid you're out of propane."

"I can go get some," Reed said, not looking forward to the prospect of braving Saturday beach traffic.

"Why don't we cook at my place tonight?" Sienna suggested. "The stores are such a nightmare on weekends."

"Good idea. I can't say I really want to stand in line with all the tourists who need things for their beach rentals."

"That's what I was thinking."

"Where's Jane?"

"She's upstairs in the kitchen," Sienna said.

"I'll let her know the plan."

Craig motioned to the propane tank. "Do you want me to unhook this and take it with us? By the time you head home, the lines will have died down and you can fill it on your way back."

"That'd be great. Thanks."

"We'll be up in a minute," Craig said.

Reed made his way inside and up the two flights of stairs to the kitchen. A rush of warmth poured over him at the mere sight of Jane. She had pulled her hair back in a ponytail, the delicate curve of her neck exposed as she loaded dishes into the dishwasher.

The countertops were now bare, and the evidence of Jane's purchases had disappeared, except for the box of dishes she was currently washing. "You got a lot done."

Jane's cheeks flushed under the intensity of his gaze. "I put the boxes for everything on the shelves in your garage."

"Did you already get it all put away?"

"Except for these." She slid two more plates into the dishwasher and filled the soap dispenser with detergent. After she closed the door and pressed the button to start the wash cycle, she waved her hand to encompass the kitchen cabinets. "If you don't like where I put things, I can help you move everything around, but I didn't want to leave it all lying out."

Reed opened the cabinet beside the refrigerator where his new glassware sat neatly on the top shelf above the plastic cups he had been using.

Reed looked back at Jane and took her hand in his. "You're amazing. You know that?"

"I just wanted to help." She gave his hand a squeeze. "You're too busy to live out of boxes for long."

Touched by her kindness, he leaned down and pressed his lips to hers. His free hand lifted to run down the length of her ponytail before cupping the back of her neck. He changed the angle of the kiss and let himself fall.

Pure and simple, his feelings rose up inside him until he couldn't help but let them spill out in his words. He pulled back and waited for her eyes to flutter open and meet his. "I love you."

Surprise melted into acceptance in an instant, and she blinked back tears. She reached up on her toes and gave him a gentle kiss before offering him the most priceless thing he could have ever asked for. "I love you too."

* * *

Footsteps approached on the stairs, and Jane wished her time alone with Reed could stretch out a little longer. As though he read her mind, he kissed her once more, drawing out the sensations that continued to overwhelm her. He loved her.

His words played through her mind, and she couldn't resist drawing out the kiss with him until Sienna rounded the corner.

"Oops. Didn't mean to interrupt," Sienna said with a smile.

Reed kept his arms around Jane. "Are you guys ready to go?"

"Yeah. Craig is loading the propane tank in the back of his truck."

"Let me get the steaks out of the fridge." Reluctantly, Jane stepped out of Reed's embrace and retrieved a plastic grocery bag from where she had stored it beneath the kitchen sink.

"Jane, why don't you leave those here, and we can have them tomorrow night," Sienna suggested. "I have that salmon at my house that we were going to fix. We can eat that tonight."

"That's a good idea." She replaced the grocery bag. "Did you want to text George to see if he wants to join us?"

"I doubt he's back yet. He went to Richmond for the day."

"I forgot about that." Jane glanced around. "Is there anything else we need from here?"

"I don't think so." Sienna headed for the door.

"We'll follow you over," Reed said. He led Jane into the garage and opened her car door. Before she could slide into her seat, he leaned down and kissed her again. When he pulled back, he was grinning. "Today was a very good day."

Her lips curved in response. "I agree. It was one I'll always remember."

Reed kissed her once more. "Me too."

* * *

Craig helped Sienna out of his car and waited for Reed and Jane to join them in Sienna's driveway. "You know, Reed, once you get your kitchen fully stocked, we're going to end up at your place as much as we're here."

"I don't mind." Reed put his hand on Jane's back and guided her forward. "One of the things I love about my new place is that it'll be great for entertaining."

"I'm sure the squad will be more than happy to help you break it in," Sienna said.

"That's not a bad idea," Reed said.

"Go for potluck," Craig suggested as they all started toward the deck. "We have some pretty amazing cooks between the guys and their wives."

"That's the truth," Sienna agreed.

"A couple more weeks and all of the furniture should be in place," Reed said.

"Except for your main living room," Jane reminded him.

Reed gave a casual shrug. "Yeah, except that."

"Hey, as long as you have a grill and some beach chairs, no one will care if you have a couch," Craig said.

They all climbed the steps onto the deck and started toward the back of the house. Craig's foot came down in unison with Sienna's, and he heard the click, the telltale sound of a mine arming itself. His hand went up immediately, signaling everyone to stop as he would do with his teammates. "Nobody move."

Sienna froze. Seeming to sense the gravity of the situation, she snapped at the others. "Reed, Jane, stop!"

Craig let out the breath he hadn't realized he'd been holding.

"What's wrong?" Reed asked.

"I think I heard a mine arm." Craig prayed he was wrong, but the ripple of danger coursed over him, through him.

"A mine?" Sienna asked. Her mouth opened and closed twice before she managed to add, "As in a bomb?"

"Yeah." Craig pulled his phone free of his pocket. He quickly calculated the distance between his teammates' homes and Sienna's house. He called Tristan.

A child giggling erupted through the line before Tristan responded with a smile and a hint of Texas. "Hey, Craig. What's up?"

"I need you at Sienna's ASAP. I think I have a bomb problem."

"Be right there."

"What now?" Reed asked after Craig hung up.

Craig barely kept his voice steady. "Now we stand still while we wait."

* * *

Reed never realized how hard it was to stand still until now, when he knew his life might depend on it. And not only his life but Jane's, Sienna's, and Craig's lives too.

He tried to pretend he was on set waiting on his mark while the director fiddled with details before calling out "Action." Today, Reed hoped the action was nothing more than a false alarm.

The absurdity of the situation and the unlikelihood that someone would plant a bomb at Sienna and Jane's house caught up with him. "How sure are you that there's really a bomb?"

Craig craned his head enough for their eyes to meet. "I hope I'm wrong, but we can't take the chance that I might be right."

When Craig reached out and put a comforting hand on Sienna's arm, Reed turned his attention to Jane.

Her face had gone white, her eyes wide with fear. "It's going to be okay," Reed said, not sure if he was trying to convince her or himself.

Jane blew out an unsteady breath. "How . . . how far away does your friend live?" she managed to ask.

"Five minutes."

"How long has it been?" Sienna asked.

"Three minutes and thirty-two seconds."

The oddity of Craig giving the time down to the second nearly made Reed smile.

The squeal of tires rounding a corner sounded in the distance, followed by the rev of an engine as a car increased speed and headed toward them. Less than a minute later, rubber marked pavement when the vehicle came to a screeching halt.

A tall, sandy-haired man jumped out of the vehicle with a speed Reed couldn't help but admire. It took him a moment to recognize Craig's teammate Tristan. Though he was dressed casually in a plain white T-shirt and a pair of cargo shorts, the combat vest he wore left no doubt as to what this man did for a living.

"Sit rep?" Tristan called out as he raced toward them, his eyes scanning the yard.

"Under the deck," Craig replied. "Sounded like a pressure trigger."

A second car rounded the corner and came to a stop by the truck. This time it was Quinn who shot out of the driver's seat and raced to help. By the time he reached them, Tristan was already sprawled on the ground, a small flashlight in his hand pointing at the underside of the deck.

"Quinn, do you have your tools?" Tristan asked.

"Yeah." As Tristan had done a moment before, Quinn pulled a flashlight free of the vest he wore.

"Can you see anything?" Craig asked, his tone surprisingly calm.

"Yeah. I can see two devices, but I can't tell which one is armed." Tristan knelt and pulled at a piece of the wooden lattice that lined the porch.

"Careful. Looks like a tripwire running the length of the deck," Quinn warned.

"ETA on the rest of the squad?" Tristan asked, now studying the structure of the deck from a new angle.

"Three to five minutes."

Tristan's eyes swept over the four on the deck, his eyes lingering on Reed before he looked at Jane and then back at Reed.

The intensity of his stare held a message, but Reed struggled to find the meaning. When he glanced at Jane and saw the shock on her face, he understood. These men needed him to keep Jane calm.

Reed gave a barely perceptible nod and gave Jane's hand a squeeze. Together they had to hang on a little longer.

32

JANE GASPED IN AIR, HER head spinning as she struggled to breathe. Reed's hand squeezed hers again as various members of the Saint Squad positioned themselves along the deck, under the deck, and in the yard. They moved so fast she had a hard time keeping track of where they were, their abbreviated conversations hard to follow.

The six men worked as one, three currently working beneath the deck and two others kneeling by the back corner where they had apparently found another bomb of some sort.

Bombs. The word kept playing through her head until her own brain felt like it too might explode from the possibilities. For the first time in her life, she had found someone she could envision spending her future with, and now she didn't know if their future would last years or mere minutes.

She breathed in the scent of roses and seawater, but the smell of fear overshadowed everything else.

Reed's voice pierced her rambling thoughts. "It's going to be okay." He squeezed her hand yet again. "Jane, look at me."

Paralyzed by the what-ifs, she couldn't get her head to comply.

"Jane." Reed repeated her name and slid his hand up to her chin. Using two fingers, he tilted her face toward him until their eyes met. "We're going to be okay. These guys do this for a living."

"My knees are shaking," Jane managed to say, surprised both by the words that came out of her mouth and the fact that she was able to string together a complete sentence.

"Mine probably are too." Reed motioned to the surf. "Look out at the water and pretend we're standing on the beach, watching the waves. I've seen the way you can stand in one spot for hours when you like the view."

She looked out and tried to focus on the water. The roar of the waves carried on the wind, and she tried to let it soothe her, but her heartbeat continued to pound in her head. She closed her eyes for a moment, took a deep breath, and opened them again. A wave of foam rolled onto the sand, followed by another spray of water running onto the beach. Seconds continued to tick by, and slowly she could feel her breathing slow enough that she no longer felt she was going to hyperventilate.

Tristan and Quinn crossed into her view. Reed's words repeated in her mind. *These men do this for a living.* She watched them speak briefly before going back to work. She sure hoped they were good at their jobs.

* * *

Craig hated this. It was bad enough that the woman he loved was in danger, but standing around helplessly wasn't his style. He itched to regain his freedom, to see what exactly had been planted beneath him.

"Got it," Quinn announced from his spot at the edge of the deck. "The booby trap is disarmed."

"Check to make sure we didn't miss any more devices," Brent ordered Jay. "Quinn, Tristan, disarm the two we've found."

The two men bent down to scoot under the deck.

"You see this?" Tristan asked Quinn.

Quinn's response was to call out to Brent. "We've got a dead man's switch on these. We have to disarm them simultaneously."

"Tell me when you're ready. I'll give you a countdown," Brent said.

"In position," Quinn called out.

Tristan repeated the same words a moment later.

Craig's impatience simmered as Brent began the countdown. If his teammates didn't disarm the devices at precisely the same time, the next few seconds could very well be his last.

Been there before, he reminded himself. So had Sienna, though not in quite the same way. He gave her shoulder an encouraging squeeze. If any two members of his squad could be completely in sync, they were Quinn and Tristan. The two were practically brothers.

"On three," Brent commanded.

Craig focused on Sienna, the woman who had become his whole life. The whisper of the breeze teased the ends of her hair, the world fading, except for Brent's voice. "One, two, *three.*"

Two sets of wire cutters snipped in unison. The silence continued, and Craig let out the breath he had been holding. "Are we clear?" he managed to ask after several seconds passed.

"Clear," Tristan confirmed from where he lay beneath the deck.

Quinn scooted out first and looked up at the four people still standing motionless. "You can move now."

Craig rolled his shoulders and took a step forward. "Come on, Sienna."

Sienna didn't budge until he put an arm around her shoulders and guided her back the way they had come. The lack of color in Jane's face made him wonder if he would need to come back to carry her off the deck. Reed must have had the same thought. As Craig and Sienna passed them, Reed scooped Jane into his arms.

She squeaked in alarm, her arms gripping Reed's neck.

"I've got you," Reed said and followed Craig onto the lawn.

Craig felt the tremor that worked through Sienna. She drew a deep breath, followed quickly by another.

"Craig, over here," Brent called. "You need to see this."

Torn between the desire to comfort Sienna and the need to understand the newly disarmed threat, he looked from Sienna to Brent and back to Sienna.

Reed came to stand beside him and lowered Jane gently to the ground. "Craig, go ahead. I'll stay with Sienna and Jane."

Sienna gave him a shaky nod in agreement. "I think I'll just sit here for a minute."

"I'll be right back. I want to make sure we don't have any more surprises before we leave." Craig gave Sienna's hand a squeeze before starting across the lawn. He was appalled and embarrassed that his own legs weren't steady. In an attempt to disguise his weakness, he broke into a jog.

The moment he came to a stop beside Brent, his commander lowered his voice. "We have three more mines to disarm."

"What?" Craig asked even though he'd heard him perfectly. Working through the unwanted news, he asked a more important question. "Where?"

"One is attached to the underside of the grill. It looks like it has a heat trigger that would go off as soon as the grill reached three hundred degrees."

"Attached to the gas line?"

"Yeah. If that one went off, it would take the whole house with it."

Craig fought back a shudder. "And the other two?"

"Similar placement to the first two but on the back side of the deck. One is right outside the back door and the other at the top of the stairs leading to the beach."

"And they're connected like the first two?"

"Yeah, but there's something else."

Craig glanced over to where Reed, Jane, and Sienna now sat on the grass beside the driveway. "I don't know if I can handle anything else."

"Tristan noticed something about the booby trap that ran between the devices."

"What?"

"It was the same design as the ones we found in Abolstan."

"At Elazar's hideout?"

"Yeah." Brent led him to the corner of the deck and squatted down.

The moment Craig saw the wiring, he was transported back in time. The device was identical to the one he had disarmed in the woods as his squad had made their way to the abandoned structure.

"You said when the house blew up that you thought they had wired it to a propane tank."

"Yeah. I think the one on Sienna's grill gives us a glimpse of what it would have looked like before we set it off."

Craig straightened and held his hands out to his sides before letting them drop. "I give up. What's the connection?"

"I don't know. What in the world would Jamal Elazar want with Sienna?" Brent asked. "The intel reports indicate he's been seeking blood vengeance since the death of his brother a few years ago, but Sienna didn't have anything to do with that."

"I can't imagine it's Elazar. His group goes after impact. Large groups, high-population targets. It doesn't make sense they would go after one person," Craig said, still trying to wrap his brain around someone going to any lengths to kill Sienna, much less setting six complicated explosives. "Maybe the connection is the bomb maker."

"Maybe . . ." Brent said, though his doubt was evident.

Craig faced Brent's reservation head on. "Why do you think it's Elazar?"

"Because intel indicates the group is very isolated. They don't open up to outsiders. That's why no one has managed to infiltrate this cell."

"Yes, but if they didn't have anyone with that skill, they could have contracted out without including the bomb maker in their plans."

"True."

The light dawned in Brent's eyes at the same time Craig felt that familiar sense of heightened awareness. "If we can find the bomb maker, intel might be able to trace the money back to Elazar."

"And figure out who's backing them financially," Brent finished for him. "In the meantime, I suggest you talk to Sienna about relocating for the foreseeable future."

Seth approached. "The bomb squad is on the way."

"Have Damian and Jay sweep the beach in case there's anything else hiding out there."

"Already did," Seth said. "Tristan and Quinn are in position to keep the perimeter secure."

"Thanks." Brent glanced at where Sienna and Jane stood with Reed. "Seth, do me a favor and call base housing. See if you can find a place for Sienna, Jane, and George to stay."

"Will do." Seth pulled his cell phone from his pocket and stepped away to make the call.

"Go make sure Sienna is okay," Brent told Craig. "We've got this."

33

JANE COULDN'T WRAP HER BRAIN around this new reality. Someone had tried to kill them.

This little piece of land with the amazing views had come to feel like home, yet now she didn't know if she would ever be able to stay here with any sense of security.

Her heartbeat had slowed somewhat, although she doubted it would get back to its normal rhythm anytime soon. Reed's arm remained firmly around her shoulders, a source of comfort as they waited on the lawn.

After what appeared to be an intense discussion with his commanding officer, Craig crossed to them. He immediately drew Sienna into his arms before speaking. "How are you guys holding up?"

"I don't think I've ever been that scared before," Jane admitted.

"I'll second that," Reed said. "That wasn't the kind of firsthand research I would have ever volunteered for."

"I don't blame you." Craig looked down at Sienna. "Seth is calling to see if we can house you, Jane, and George on base for the next little while."

"What about our clothes and stuff?" Jane asked. "I'm sorry, but I'm not sure I'm ready to walk on that deck again quite yet."

"I'm with her," Sienna said.

"Call George and see if he can meet us at the mall," Craig suggested. "We can pick up whatever you need for the next day or two."

* * *

Craig paced across Reed's nearly empty living room, certain Brent had to be wrong. "What do you mean they don't have any rooms on base?" He moved his cell phone from one ear to the other. "How can they be full?"

"It's that time of year," Brent reminded him.

Craig bit back his impatience. Summer was that annoying vortex when new arrivals were living in temporary quarters while waiting to see if they could get on-base housing. "I can't let her go back to her place."

"I agree," Brent said. "She's welcome to crash at our house."

"Thanks for offering, but you don't have room for her, Jane, and George, and I'd rather keep them all together until we get on the other side of this threat."

"Understood," Brent said. "What about Jay's place?"

"I don't know . . ." Jay was the only teammate who had a house large enough to take in Sienna and her two newly homeless friends, but he also lived with his parents and his sister-in-law. "I think it would be too hard to maintain security with so many people coming and going."

"You'd have the same problem with a hotel." Brent fell silent as both men thought.

"Maybe I can find a vacation rental for a few weeks."

Reed's voice sounded behind him. "What about my house? It's plenty big enough."

Craig looked at Reed, who now stood in the doorway.

"Brent, hold on a second." Craig lowered his phone. "Reed, I'm not sure you understand what you're offering. We can't guarantee someone won't be able to find Sienna here, especially since you've been linked with her publicly."

"You had all of us swap out our cell phones, and my house was purchased under my company's name, not mine."

"You have a company?"

"Yeah. It's pretty common for people who have unpredictable incomes in jobs like mine," Reed said. "It lets me balance out the income I take each year and keeps the taxes under control."

Craig lifted the phone again. "Brent, can you meet me at Reed's place? He's offering to let everyone stay here. I want to do a security assessment before we move anyone in."

"I'll be there in fifteen minutes."

"Thanks. I owe you."

"I've heard that before."

* * *

"Are you sure about this?" Jane asked Reed as Craig and Brent passed into view. The two men walked along the beach, finally stopping to stare at the house.

The news that she, Sienna, and George were going to be staying with Reed had come on the heels of their arrival at Reed's house.

A stop at the local Walmart had given them the chance to pick up the basics of what they would need over the next few days, but she hadn't thought about what would happen once those few days were over. Her legs were still shaking, her mind not able to completely comprehend what had happened to them only hours earlier.

Reed took one of her hands in his, as though he could calm her through the simple touch. "I have plenty of room, and you all need a place to stay."

"You're still settling in. I wouldn't think you would want all of these houseguests," Jane said.

"If I didn't want everyone here, I wouldn't have offered." Reed leaned on the deck railing. "Besides, we spend most evenings together anyway. Having you all here will prevent me from possibly leading someone to you."

"Reed, I hate to break it to you, but if someone tries to follow you in search of Sienna, having us at your house isn't going to help anything. They'll still find us all here."

"Craig and George will make sure nothing happens," Reed said. "Speaking of which, did I mention Craig is staying here too?"

"What? Where are you going to put everyone?"

"George is staying in the upstairs guest room, and Craig is going to crash on the first floor," Reed said. "He was pretty set on being near the basement doors."

"You don't have any furniture on the first floor."

"I mentioned that. Craig didn't seem to care." His shoulders lifted. "I guess SEALs don't worry about things like that."

"Sienna and I can share a room if we need to."

"I'm sure Craig will let us know if he decides he wants a bed." Reed took a step toward the house. "Come on. Let's go fix something for dinner. I have a feeling everyone is going to be hungry after they finish working on the security systems."

Jane watched Craig make a sweeping motion toward the house. "I don't know how much they'll be able to do before dark."

"Craig is highly motivated." Reed led her inside, releasing her hand when he held the door open for her.

"I don't know how you can be so calm. My heart is still racing."

"I guess I'm a better actor than I thought." Reed took both her hands in his. "I've never been so scared in my life."

"That makes two of us," Jane reached up on her toes and pressed her lips to his. "Thank you for letting us stay here."

"You're welcome." Reed smiled. "Of course, if you really want to show me how grateful you are, you'll make that cherry cobbler for dessert tomorrow night."

"Why not tonight?"

"I didn't want to press my luck," Reed said. "You've had a pretty full day."

"That's an understatement."

34

"I STILL DON'T KNOW HOW this is possible." Craig finished syncing the external camera feeds to the laptop he had purchased two hours earlier. One look at Brent told him his commanding officer shared his bewilderment.

"The only connection between Elazar's men and Sienna that I can see is you."

"I can't see how Elazar or any of his people would have been able to identify anyone on our squad, much less our names, where we live, and the identity of the woman I'm secretly engaged to." Craig tapped another screen to load the next image.

"You're right. It's a huge stretch." Brent raked his fingers through his hair. "We were all wearing night-vision goggles for our mission in Abolstan, so surveillance equipment wouldn't have been able to identify us."

"Our support personnel was limited," Craig added. "Not that I think anyone in the navy would be involved with Elazar's group."

The words were barely out of his mouth before a worm of doubt burrowed into his thoughts.

"First things first," Brent said. "Make sure you do a complete electronic sweep of everything Jane, George, and Sienna brought into the house. Reed too."

"That's going to be fun."

"I know Jane and Reed have never dealt with this level of security before, but George is former military, and Sienna grew up in a fishbowl. They get it."

"Not at this level." Craig finished syncing the cameras, his screen now showing eight boxes, each feeding live images from the perimeter of Reed's house. "I'm starting to think we should go into business as security consultants when we all retire."

"You're twenty-six. I think you're a bit young to think of retirement."

"Right." Craig pushed the laptop farther onto the new folding table he had purchased at the same time as the laptop.

"I know it's not ideal, but we can do the same thing we did last time Sienna was having security issues."

"Run drills here on the beach?" Craig asked.

"That was my thought. Our squad can look for blind spots, and we can see if George can identify various problems we throw at him."

"I'm starting to think I should let Sienna's dad send George some help," Craig said.

"Sienna won't be happy."

"I know, but one person can't keep surveillance going twenty-four hours a day."

"If you want to do that, talk to George and Sienna about hiring someone directly. Bringing Sterling Blake into the equation opens up too many possibilities for an intelligence breach."

"True," Craig said. "Any suggestions on where to hire on some temporary help?"

"Actually, I might have an idea." Brent pulled his phone out of his pocket. "A couple of guys who used to swim for my mom are training to become SEALs. What better way to see what the teams are all about than to come learn how we do things?"

"I have to think these guys would already have jobs while they wait to get into BUDs," Craig said, referring to the SEAL training program.

"Yeah, but Sienna has the means to pay them well enough to make it worth their while. Besides, I think at least one of them already has his acceptance. He's just waiting for his report date."

"In that case, can you see if they're interested?"

"I can make it happen, but are you sure Sienna will go for it?" Brent asked. "You'd need to check with Reed too. The only way for this to be effective is for them to stay here."

"True." Craig started toward the stairs. "See if they're interested and available. I'll work on the logistics."

"Will do."

* * *

Sienna sat in the center of the bed that wasn't hers, in a room without a single personal touch, and wept. How could this be happening? Again.

She had managed to keep up a calm facade when they'd waited for Craig's squad to disarm the bombs. Bombs. Plural. Six bombs. She drew a ragged breath, surprised her heart didn't jump out of her chest with how hard it continued to pound.

The tears had burned in the back of her eyes when they had driven to Walmart to pick up some necessities for her and Jane. Every step on her rubbery legs had been a challenge, but she had put on a mask of control like putting on her makeup before a scene. She had held on through the brief discussion of which rooms she, Jane, and George would stay in at Reed's house.

But as soon as that decision had been made and Brent had arrived to help Craig enhance security, she had disappeared into her new living space and let the emotions take over. Memories of last winter, of the threats against her life, of the multiple times she could have died and miraculously hadn't came rushing back. That terror was supposed to be behind her, never to be experienced firsthand again. So why was it back, and who wanted her dead now?

She heard the knock on her door and swiped at the tears on her cheeks. "Who is it?"

"It's me," Craig answered.

Sienna wiped at her cheeks again and pushed herself to a sitting position on the edge of the bed. "Come in."

Craig's eyes swept over her, and whatever awkwardness he felt about entering her bedroom dissipated in an instant. He crossed to her, took her hands, and pulled her to a stand. Enveloping her in a comforting embrace, he held on for a long moment before he spoke. "We're going to get through this."

"How?" She buried her face in his shoulder, both of them falling silent.

"I need to talk to you about security," Craig said.

Sienna pulled back, horrified. "Please tell me you didn't call my dad."

"I didn't call your dad." She relaxed briefly until he added, "But I do want to hire some extra help to work with George."

Though Sienna typically balked at the idea of utilizing a large security team, after today, she found herself open to the idea. "What did you have in mind?"

"Brent thinks we can hire a couple of guys who are waiting to get into the teams. They're basically Navy SEAL wannabes."

"And you think these guys can help?"

"I know it's not the same as having my squad around all the time, but with me staying here, we can make it work." Craig rubbed her back, still holding her in his embrace. "Brent said he would run some training exercises here too. It will help us find weak spots and also give the new hires some real-life experience before they go into BUDs."

"Okay."

"Okay?" He pulled back so he could see her face clearly. "No arguments?"

"No arguments." A shaky sigh escaped her. "Let Jane know who we need to put on the payroll."

"Do you think Reed will be okay with having a couple extra houseguests?"

"If it keeps all of us safe, I think he'll agree to whatever you suggest."

"Let's go talk to him." Craig took her hand in his. "When is the basement furniture getting delivered, again?"

Sienna managed a smile. "Not soon enough."

35

CRAIG STOOD ON THE PORCH and watched Brent's Suburban pull into Reed's driveway. When Brent said he thought he could find some people to help with security, he hadn't expected him to work so fast, and he certainly hadn't expected the help to show up at eight o'clock on a Sunday morning.

All four doors of the vehicle opened in unison. A dark-skinned man seated in the front stepped out. He appeared to be in his early twenties and carried himself with the confidence of an officer. Broad shouldered and standing around five nine, he reminded Craig of a wrestler ready to analyze every weakness before pouncing.

Behind him, a man around twenty or twenty-one took in his surroundings with a combination of curiosity and cockiness. The latter trait would serve him well in the teams if he learned to harness it.

The third passenger, a redhead who was caught somewhere between boy and man, stood shy of six feet and looked to Brent for instructions. As soon as Brent motioned him forward, he fell in step and approached the house with the rest of them.

"Craig, meet your new team." Brent motioned to the two younger men. "Tim and Landon swam for my mom in high school. They've both been accepted into BUDs but won't report until late October."

"Thanks for helping us out." Craig shook hands with both of them.

Brent continued the introductions. "And this is Lieutenant Josh Harlen. He's been working at Norfolk while waiting for his training date. I was able to get him reassigned to work with us for the next few weeks."

"Lieutenant." Craig shook the man's hand in turn.

"Josh," he corrected. "I've heard the Saint Squad isn't big on formality when it comes to getting the job done."

"Very true." Craig headed for the side of the house. "Let me show you where you can store your gear."

Brent opened the back of the Suburban, and the men each collected their luggage. When they were ready, Craig continued. "I'm afraid our living quarters are pretty basic, but bunking on a mat instead of a bed is good training for working in the teams."

"Sleeping on the floor is a small price to pay to have such easy access to the beach," Landon said. "In Stafford, the best we have is the Potomac River, and the waves aren't anything like the ocean."

"I remember," Brent said, coming up behind them. "I told them all they could hang out here and keep an eye on the house while we go to church. Then they can go to the late ward in our building."

Craig looked at the three men, surprised. "Wait. You're all LDS?"

All three men nodded.

"What are the chances?"

"Pretty crazy, huh?" Brent said. "The navy may have to consider making another Saint Squad."

"That would be a tall order, trying to follow in your squad's shadow," Josh said.

Craig remembered well the rumors he had heard about the Saint Squad when he was in BUDs. He had been both excited and terrified when he had received his orders to join the elite group.

Brent gave the three prospective SEALs the same advice he had given Craig when he was the new guy. "Focus on doing your best, and rely on each teammate's strength. And never ignore a prompting from the Holy Ghost."

"Words to live by," Craig said. He crossed the patio to the sliding-glass door and led the way inside. "We're all sharing this level of the house."

He didn't miss the way they looked around the empty room. "This room will be our security base of operations." Craig's hand waved to encompass the flat-screen on the wall and the two laptops set up on the makeshift desk. "I borrowed a couple of futon mats and put them in the bedroom through there, and there are a few sleeping bags if you'd prefer."

"What would you like us to do for now?" Josh asked.

Brent moved to the computers. "Craig, I can show them the basics. Can you have George come down to meet them? I thought he could run things while we're at church."

"I'll take over upstairs and have him come down." Craig started up the interior staircase, making it only four steps before turning back. "Thanks again for coming."

* * *

Jane barely slept. The prospect of going to church today evoked mixed emotions. She wanted the peace she hoped taking the sacrament would bring. Going out anywhere, though, terrified her.

Dressed in a long knit skirt and a scoop-neck white shirt, she emerged from her bedroom tentatively. Across the living area, Sienna's door opened. Jane's apprehension was mirrored on Sienna's face.

Jane drew a deep breath and slowly let it out. "Are you up for this?"

"I'm not sure," Sienna said. "Part of me never wants to go outside again, and another part of me is going stir crazy."

"I know what you mean." They headed up the stairs and found Reed and Craig in the kitchen, dressed and ready to go.

"You both look nice," Reed said, crossing to greet Jane with a kiss on her cheek.

"Thanks."

Craig greeted Sienna in a similar fashion, but he didn't settle for her cheek. "Brent is going to drive us to church today."

"He is?" Sienna asked.

Footsteps pounded on the stairs, and Brent emerged, followed by George. "Okay, the new guys are all set. Ready?"

"Let's go." Craig took Sienna's hand and headed for the door.

Jane and Reed followed, and Jane couldn't help but hesitate when they reached the threshold. She took in the empty cul-de-sac before she let herself move forward.

Reed pulled the door closed behind them and locked it before sliding an arm around her. "We'll get through this."

"I only wish we knew what 'this' was."

"I know what you mean."

* * *

Three weeks ago, Reed had thought buying a six-bedroom house was excessive. He had justified the purchase because of the great location. Now he was wondering if his new home was large enough.

Technically, he still had a spare bedroom in the basement, but his plan to use it as an office/library combination had prevented him from furnishing it yet. Craig and the three men he had brought in had stored their clothing in it, along with some futon mats.

The large area that would someday be his rec room now looked like a low-budget, high-tech security room.

Tim, one of the three new arrivals, walked into the kitchen. He couldn't be more than twenty years old. "Sir, Craig asked me to find out what time you will be leaving for work this morning."

"About seven thirty," Reed said. "And you don't have to call me sir. Just call me Reed."

"Yes, sir."

"Feel free to raid the kitchen up here for something to eat. We'll look into stocking the downstairs kitchen tonight."

"Thank you, but Commander Miller took care of that last night," he said, referring to Brent.

"Is Craig still here?"

Tim nodded. "His squad is planning to run through some training exercises here today."

"No doubt to give you and your buddies some experience."

Tim offered a slight smile. "That is my assumption, sir."

Reed popped the last bite of toast into his mouth. "I'm going to finish getting ready. Tell Craig and his friends not to break anything."

"I'll pass along the message." Tim turned toward the stairs.

"Hey, Tim?"

"Yes, sir?"

"Was your dad in the military?"

"Yes . . . Why?"

"Wild guess." Reed skirted around the counter. "I might get used to you calling me sir, but I mean it when I say you can call me Reed. You and your friends are doing us a huge favor by being here."

Tim fell silent before he nodded again. "Reed, it's our honor to be here."

"I understand the sacrifices people in the military make, especially those in special forces," Reed said. "Believe me when I say the honor is mine."

36

"BRENT, YOU WANTED TO SEE me?" Craig asked from his commanding officer's doorway.

"Yeah. Come on in, and close the door."

Craig stepped inside. Seth was leaning against the back wall of the office, and his presence caused a spurt of hope to shoot through Craig. Seth's wife was often their connection to the flow of information from the intelligence world. "Did the CIA find something?"

"They tried to identify the bomb maker, but the only one who was even close was Qadir El-Baz," Brent said. "He built the explosives that killed thirty-two in Brussels six years ago."

"Where is he now?"

"Dead," Seth said. "He died in prison two months after his arrest."

"Could he have any associates who learned from him?"

"That's our guess," Brent said.

"Vanessa sent over the background on El-Baz. He was an extremist in every sense. Paranoid, very few known associates. Interrogators never did get much information from him about the people he worked with or what else they had planned."

"This guy wasn't a hired hand?" Craig asked.

Seth shook his head. "From everything I've seen in the intel reports, it appears he used his skills to further his cause."

"Which was what?" Craig asked.

"I know we get tired of hearing this, but it appears he was working with a group of Jihadist extremists," Seth said.

"Jihadists?" Brent asked now. "They attack for political gain or to undermine the western world. Going after one person doesn't make sense."

"I don't care what their normal motivations are," Craig interrupted. "The more important thing is identifying the connection. How in the world did the same type of explosive device end up at Elazar's compound and Sienna's house?"

"The FBI's counterterrorism unit is working with the CIA to figure out the answer to that," Seth said.

"I can't sit around and wait for them to find the connection."

The other two men studied him before Seth spoke in his calm way. "You think you're the common denominator."

"Don't you?" Craig asked. "I doubt Sienna has ever heard of Elazar, and I can't think of any reason he would go after her unless it was to get to me for some reason."

"All right," Brent said. "Let's go back to the beginning. After PT today, we'll have a research session. You two can dive into the time line of our strike at Elazar's compound and when Sienna's electronics were first infiltrated."

Brent picked up a pen and started making notes on the pad of paper on his desk. "Tristan and Quinn can search for any electronic signals that originated from the camp the night we were there to see if there's any way we could have been identified."

"The CIA didn't find any money transfers to pay for a bomb," Seth said, "but I can have Vanessa ask them to look into funding strings. They have to be getting money from somewhere."

"I'll have Jay and Damian search for their travel and living arrangements while Amy and I try to narrow down potential targets," Brent said.

"These days, anyplace that has a crowd could be a target," Craig muttered.

"I know. I'll have Amy and Vanessa see if they have any chatter that might help us narrow it down."

"What about the missing toxins?"

"The whole intelligence community is looking for that. We'll leave it to them. Our goal is to find anything that connects these guys to Sienna. That puts our focus on the US."

Seth pushed against the wall and straightened to his full height of enormous. "I'll let the guys know what's going on."

As soon as Seth left, Brent put his hand on Craig's shoulder. "Come on. Let's go get the others for morning prayer. Today, especially, we need all the help we can get."

* * *

"How are the new guys working out?" Brent asked.

"Better than I expected, actually," Craig said. "They're quick and eager to learn. Landon has enough experience with electronics that he's a natural on surveillance."

"I thought we might include them on our next training exercise," Brent said. "Tristan is nursing a sore hamstring, so I'll have him monitor everything and make sure we don't have any unexpected visitors."

"When do you want to do it?" Craig asked.

"Tomorrow night. I want to give the new kids time to prepare."

"I'll let Sienna know so she doesn't have a panic attack when she sees people sneaking around the yard."

"Good idea, but George is the one you need to tell."

Craig chuckled. "Yeah, he can be scary if you get on his bad side."

"You got on his good side quick enough."

"Only because he adores Sienna and she didn't give him a choice."

"Sienna is always a good person to have on your side," Brent said.

"I couldn't agree more."

* * *

For three nights, the Saint Squad had attacked Reed's house from every angle. Their three temporary recruits had worked both sides of the equation, monitoring activity on the perimeter and joining the pretend attack force. Tonight, two of those men had been entrusted to Craig as part of tonight's invasion team.

Craig recognized their hesitation. He remembered feeling that combination of excitement and terror the first time he had tried to free climb.

Tim had proven he was willing to try anything, but the idea of climbing up the side of Reed's house didn't appear to be in his comfort zone.

Landon simply stared, mouth open, eyes wide.

"It's not as hard as it sounds," Craig assured them. He reached out and tugged on one of the two lines he had rigged to the deck above to ensure their safety. "Hook your harness to one of the lines. Then together we'll climb up to the deck."

"What about you?" Tim managed to ask. "Why aren't you wearing a harness?"

"I don't need one." Craig waited for both men to clip in before he put one hand between two bricks on the side of the house.

Brent approached. "Are you ready?"

"We are," Craig answered for all of them.

Brent gave him a wry stare. "They don't look ready to me."

Not sure why Brent was questioning him, Craig glanced back at the commander. "Only way to learn is to try."

"True," Brent said. "But telling them they get peach cobbler when they get inside might give them an extra incentive."

"Peach cobbler?" Landon asked. "With ice cream?"

"With ice cream," Brent confirmed. He smothered most of the grin trying to break free. "Craig, you lead the way. I'll coach them from down here."

"Sounds good. That means I'll get the first piece." Craig pulled his body off the ground and found his first toehold. "Follow me."

Trusting Brent to give the two young recruits additional instructions, he continued upward, listening for their movements to make sure he didn't get too far ahead.

Rapid breathing below him caused him to pause. Apparently the promise of dessert hadn't completely erased the young men's nerves. "Relax. Visualize your next upward movement. Don't think about where you've been. Focus on where you're going."

"Okay," Tim answered.

The scrape of a shoe against brick caught his attention. Immediately, one of the lines went taut.

"You're okay," Brent called from below. Craig held his position while Brent helped direct Landon until the young recruit started upward once more.

Though the climb took three times as long as it normally would, finally, Craig climbed over the railing and waited for Tim and Landon to join him.

The moment they reached the deck, their faces looked illuminated with exhilaration and a sense of accomplishment.

"Not bad," Craig said. "Give you a few more times and you'll be ready to get rid of the ropes."

"Now what?" Landon asked.

Craig reached into one of the pockets of the vest he wore and retrieved a thin tool. "It's time to learn how to pick a lock."

"Now I see why the navy does such an intensive background check before admitting recruits to SEAL training," Tim said. "You're teaching us how to be criminals."

"Sometimes the only way to beat the criminals is to know how to act like them."

"I'm glad you're on our side," Landon said.

"Trust me," Craig said. "It won't be long before I'll be saying the same thing about you."

* * *

The smell of something baking drew Reed out of his bedroom and into the kitchen. He sniffed the air. Peach cobbler. His favorite.

He had to admit, he hadn't expected to find himself enjoying his new routine with so many people in the house. Most weekdays, he drove into work with Sienna, Jane, and George. Most nights, Craig and his buddies laid siege to his house or hung out and took turns playing games or watching security footage.

Best of all, each evening, Reed and Jane were able to spend time together without worrying about being seen by the outside world. Board games, movies, shared meals, running lines. The evening activities had repeated themselves over the past two weeks, but he rather liked the predictability.

Reed entered the kitchen and found Jane sitting on a stool, her laptop open in front of her on the counter.

"What are you up to?" he asked, moving to sit beside her.

"Messaging with my mom." She finished typing something and hit the enter key before looking at him. "Are you done prepping for tomorrow?"

"Almost. It smelled like it was time for a break." He heard movement outside. "The Saint Squad is at it again?"

"Yeah." Her eyebrows drew together. "Should I be worried that the sound of men climbing up the side of the house doesn't scare me anymore?"

"Maybe it's a sign that you feel safe again."

"It's hard not to with a bunch of armed men running around all the time," Jane said. "I still can't believe you've been okay with all of this."

"All of what?"

Voices sounded outside the door leading to the deck. Jane pointed. "This. You've been invaded. Literally. And we don't have an end in sight."

"It's only been two weeks. Craig said the FBI is supposed to give them an update on Wednesday. Maybe we'll know more by then." He put his hand on her knee and leaned forward to press his lips to hers. The familiar ripple of pleasure pulsed through him. "Besides, I kind of like having you so close."

"There are certainly advantages," Jane agreed. She leaned in for another kiss. Her lips had barely brushed against his when Reed heard the door creak open. She gave him a dry smile. "And disadvantages."

"Yeah. I guess we have some of those too."

Three men entered through the previously locked door. The oven timer buzzed.

"Is the cobbler ready?" Craig asked.

Reed exchanged a glance with Jane. "I'll get the ice cream."

37

CRAIG LEANED BACK AND BLEW out a satisfied breath. A quiet, uneventful Sunday meal was precisely what he'd needed to help his mind and body recharge. Tim, Landon, Josh, and George had opted to eat their meal in the basement, where they were taking turns watching the surveillance cameras and challenging each other to games of pool. The pool table had arrived on Friday, and everyone had enjoyed breaking it in after last night's training exercise. Craig was half tempted to challenge some of the young guys to a match himself. Given the alternative of spending time with Sienna, though, he opted for the latter.

From where they sat on Reed's deck, they could enjoy the breeze coming off the water as well as their privacy.

"Thanks for dinner, Jane." Craig stood and picked up his plate.

"You're welcome."

Sienna rose. "I'll help clean up."

"You don't have to do that," Reed said.

"It's the least I can do since we all know I'm not going to take a turn cooking dinner."

"True." Reed chuckled.

Craig helped Sienna clear the table, leaving Jane and Reed to enjoy the cool evening breeze. His squad had already conducted multiple training exercises over the past two weeks, and so far, the new guys had done well. Despite his confidence that the security at Reed's house would hold up against nearly any threat, he was ready to solve the question of why Sienna and Jane had been targeted.

"What are you thinking?" Sienna asked as she began rinsing dishes.

"I'm still wondering how a bomb that looks like one we encountered while on a mission ended up at your house," Craig said. "We've had everyone searching for a connection, but no one has been able to answer that question."

"Do you think we'll ever solve this mystery?" Sienna asked. "I have to admit I'd really like to be able to settle into my own place again."

"I know what you mean."

They worked together to load the dishes in the dishwasher, then they went into the living room. The couches Reed had ordered had been delivered earlier in the week; the house was beginning to look like a home. Matching lamps atop the two end tables both glowed to combat the loss of daylight, and a scatter of framed photos was arranged on the table closest to him.

"Looks like Reed has been busy," Craig said.

"Jane's been helping every night after we get home from work," Sienna said. "I think getting him organized keeps her from thinking about why we're all staying here."

"I can understand that." Craig took her hand and led her to the couch. He waited for her to sit before moving beside her. His gaze landed on the photos, and he noticed for the first time that Sienna was prominent in one of them. "When was this picture taken?" Craig lifted it for a closer study. "I've never seen it before."

"Oh, that was at the airport in LA the day Jane moved out here," Sienna said.

Craig started to put it down, but something in the background caught his attention. He lifted it again, and his eyes narrowed. "Who took this?"

"Jane's mom." Sienna tilted her head and looked at him quizzically. "Why?"

"Does she have more photos from that day?"

"Actually, she took it with Jane's phone."

"Jane's phone that was hacked and everything was erased?"

"Yeah." Awareness lit Sienna's features. "I know that look. What's going on?"

"I think I know why someone has been messing with you and Jane."

"Why?"

Craig didn't respond. Instead, he pulled his phone free and dialed Brent. The moment he answered, Craig said, "I think I've got something."

"What?"

"I need to show you in person."

"I'll be right there."

Twenty minutes later, Craig opened the door to let Brent inside.

"What's going on?" Brent asked the moment the door closed behind him.

"I think the prosecutor might be right about Xavier Guadalupe being framed." Craig led him into the living room so they could speak privately and handed him the photo. "Take a look at this."

"Sienna and Jane." Brent looked up at him and shook his head. "What am I missing?"

"Right there." Craig tapped the dark-haired man visible over Sienna's left shoulder.

"Is that . . . ?"

"Jamal Elazar? Yeah." Craig pointed to another dark head, the face turned toward the camera. "My question is, who is this guy? They appear to be together."

Brent's jaw clenched. "Abdul Maleb."

"Wait. Didn't he help execute the attack in London?" Craig asked. "I thought he was dead."

"Wishful thinking." Brent shook his head. "If these two are together, we've got much bigger problems than just keeping Sienna and Jane safe." Brent tapped the photo. "When was this taken?"

"Mid- to late July," Craig said. "It was right before we returned from our summer deployment."

"That's more than two months ago," Brent said. "They could have something going down at any time."

"Yeah, and this was taken at LAX. Who knows if that was their end destination or if they were heading somewhere else."

"Get the exact date for that photo. Let's see if Homeland can figure out what flight these guys were on."

Craig went into the kitchen, where Sienna, Reed, and Jane were washing the dessert dishes. "Jane, what day did you move out here?"

"July 15."

Brent retrieved his phone from his pocket. "I'll call it in."

"Call what in?" Sienna asked. "Can you please tell us what's going on?"

Craig looked at Brent, who gave him a subtle nod of permission. "You might want to sit down for this."

"We're about done in here." Reed dried his hands on a dish towel, then put one hand on Jane's back. "Let's go sit in the living room."

They made their way out of the kitchen and sat on the two new couches, Craig beside Sienna and Reed beside Jane.

"Brent and I don't think it was a stalker coming after Sienna," Craig said.

Sienna faced him more fully. "That should make me feel better, but your expression is scaring me."

"If not a stalker, then who?" Reed asked.

"A terrorist."

"What?" Reed and Jane asked in unison.

At the same time, Sienna's eyebrows rose. "Excuse me? What would a terrorist want with me?"

"They didn't want you. They wanted the photo Jane's mom took in LA. Two known Jihadists got caught in the background."

Reed looked at him, confused. "Why would they care? It was a photo on a cell phone."

"One of these men was believed to be dead. The proof that he isn't would raise alarms, but when added to the evidence of who he was traveling with, it makes his presence a top threat concern within the US."

"Even if that's true," Reed said, "I would think that once they realized the photos weren't posted online, they would have left Sienna and Jane alone."

Sienna and Jane exchanged looks.

"What?" Craig asked.

"I asked Jane to hold the photo to use during our promos," Sienna said. "If these guys were standing close enough to get caught in the background, they probably heard us talking."

"The guy who ran into Jane," George said from the doorway. "He must have been one of the men you're talking about."

"Wait." Craig focused on Sienna as the world of possibilities narrowed in an instant. "What did you say about releasing the photos?"

Sienna thought for a moment. "I told Jane she would have to use that one for our promos."

"Did you say when?"

"I don't remember."

Jane scooted forward in her seat. "She did. I commented about how she had plenty of press lined up for the next couple weeks, and she said to hold it until the first of October."

"Oh, that's right." Sienna nodded. "Jane has been putting together a whole segment on my adventure of moving to Virginia, the change from filming movies to filming a television series. That kind of thing."

Brent walked back in. "We've put the wheels in motion. Amy is sending a report forward to the intelligence community."

"Good, because if I'm right, this is happening in the next couple weeks."

"How do you figure?" Brent asked.

Craig explained the timing. "If they were going to strike before October first, they wouldn't have cared about Jane's photo."

"We'll pass that along to intel. Hopefully, they'll be able to narrow down the target and the time line," Brent said. "Sometimes they put these strikes in place months, if not years, in advance."

"This all sounds terrifying, but I have to ask: Is there anything we can do to get these guys to believe Sienna and Jane are no longer a threat to them and their plans?" Reed asked.

"I don't know," Craig said. "If I'm right, Jane's cell phone was hacked by these guys going after those photos, but that happened before the bomb scare. I'm not sure why they wanted to kill Sienna and Jane at that point."

"Regardless," Brent said, "I have to believe that by now, they're focusing on their mission instead of finding Sienna and Jane."

"I hope so, although I don't want to know what could happen if their 'mission' is successful," Sienna said.

"You and me both," Craig said. He turned to Brent. "In the meantime, I think we need to enlarge these photos so everyone is familiar with what they look like, including Sienna, Jane, and Reed."

"Good idea. If they do show up in the area, we need to make sure everyone can recognize the threat." Brent held up his phone. "I'll talk to Amy about having her put together some composites to keep here at the house for the security team and Reed, Sienna, and Jane."

"Thanks."

"As for now," Brent continued. "We have work to do."

* * *

Jane stared at the framed photo, still struggling to understand how such a simple moment in time had turned her world upside down. The frenzied excitement it had caused in Craig and Brent made her feel like she was watching a spy movie instead of standing in the middle of a real-life threat.

Footsteps sounded behind her, and she whirled to see Reed enter the living room.

"Hey. I didn't know you were still up," he said.

"Couldn't sleep." She glanced at her watch. "I thought you went to bed an hour ago."

"I tried, but I couldn't stop thinking about what Brent and Craig were saying." He lowered himself onto the couch beside her and tapped the glass. "Who would have thought a single photo could cause so much damage?"

"If you hadn't printed it out, we still wouldn't know why those guys tried to kill us."

Reed reached his arm out and rested it on her shoulders. He tugged her closer until she nestled into his side. "Everything is going to be okay."

Jane drew a shaky breath and let it out. The warmth of him beside her helped chase away the worst of the demons that plagued her every time the sun went down. "You really have been amazing through all of this."

"I haven't done anything."

She tilted her chin to see him more clearly. "You weren't even moved into your house yet when you opened your doors to seven other people," Jane reminded him.

"It's not that big a deal." Reed lifted his free hand and waved it to encompass the room. "In case you haven't noticed, we have plenty of space here."

Jane reached up and kissed him. "You're still pretty amazing."

"Glad you think so."

Jane let his earlier comment play over in her mind. When Reed spoke of his home, he spoke as though it was something they were creating together instead of a place he had bought solely for himself.

A seed of hesitant anticipation grew in her chest. Did he really see her in his long-term future? Was the love they shared the kind that could last into the eternities? They sat in silence as a minute stretched into two and then three. Her gaze wandered around the room to where boxes were stacked in the corner and two pieces of artwork leaned against the wall.

The sense of home washed over her again, and she let herself dream about many more moments like this one. "I think we need to finish putting your house in order this weekend," Jane finally said.

"There's no rush." His fingers rubbed back and forth on her shoulder and sent goose bumps shivering over her skin. "I figure anything I don't get to before our winter break, I can unpack then."

"It's not even October yet. Winter break is almost two months away."

"I know, but we'll have a few days to work on stuff here before we fly home for Thanksgiving."

"What?" She straightened. "You never mentioned plans for Thanksgiving."

Reed shrugged. "I figured we would both want to go to California and visit our families."

"Well, yeah. I'd planned on it. I don't want my mother to be alone for the holiday."

"I don't know what you normally do, but I'd love it if you would both join us for Thanksgiving dinner."

The prospect of making plans that were two months away both delighted and terrified her. She wanted Reed in her future, but she was also afraid to hope for that future to continue indefinitely. "Are you sure?"

"I'm sure. My mom and dad both really like you."

"I like them too. And I would love for you to meet my mom."

"Great. Next time you talk to your mom, see if she's cool with it."

"Were you planning to stay in California for the whole break?"

"I haven't decided yet. It may sound weird, but I kind of want to be here to finish settling in." He waved toward the stairwell. "Assuming all of this craziness is over by then."

"It had better be. I am so ready to find out what normal feels like here in Virginia."

Reed leaned forward for a kiss that caused her heartbeat to quicken. "I think I'm going to like our new normal."

She smiled. "Me too."

38

JANE LOOKED OUT AT THE ocean, the water filled with boats of all kinds, many navigating their way toward the large marina. The trees lining the road were beginning to turn, the October breeze bringing the red, orange, and yellow leaves drifting to the ground.

For nearly a month now, she had lived under the same roof as Reed and six other people. She didn't know how they had all managed to get along so well with the frequent training exercises and the security sessions George insisted on twice a week. She was beginning to think she could work in law enforcement after all of the briefings he had put her through. And she looked forward to the day when she would no longer have to look at photos of suspected terrorists every day.

This outing with Reed had been a welcome surprise, but as she looked around, she wasn't sure why Reed had brought her to the harbor. She had read about the new marina in Virginia Beach, but she couldn't think of any reason Reed would want to bring her to such a public venue. She glanced to her left where a banner stretched across the lawn on the edge of the parking lot. Today's event announcement was written in large black letters.

"A boat show?" Jane asked. "That's your surprise?"

"We live on the water. I think we need to take advantage of it."

"By buying a boat?"

"We do have our own pier," Reed reminded her.

"True." Jane didn't correct him that she didn't have her own pier. "With the promos starting up, you may need a way to put some distance between you and your adoring fans."

"Yeah right." Reed climbed out of the car and circled to open her door. "I don't know that I'm ready to buy yet, but I thought it would be worth looking. Prices are always lower in the fall."

"Do you have an idea of what you want?" Jane asked when she stepped out beside him.

"Nothing fancy. I'd like something that can hold at least four to six people and would be good for waterskiing."

Her expression brightened. "I love to water ski."

"Do you know how to drive a boat?"

"I've only done it a couple of times, but I bet you could teach me."

"I bet I could." He put his hand on her shoulder to guide her forward but immediately dropped it, a reminder that they weren't supposed to look like anything beyond simple friends while in public. They made their way to the path leading to the dock, and Jane let her gaze linger on the boats making their way into the marina.

"It looks crazy out there. Maybe we should have waited until this afternoon to come," Jane said.

"I think it's going to be busy all day. This boat show is supposedly one of the largest on the eastern seaboard." He pointed to several speedboats motoring past. "Something about that size would be great. What do you think?"

"It's hard to tell from here."

"I have something that might help." He moved off to the side of the lawn where a coin-operated telescope stood. He pulled some quarters out of his pocket and fed them into the slot. He looked through first, angling the lens toward the boats he had been watching.

"I like the one with the red stripe. Take a look." Reed stepped back to give her a turn.

The one he had been looking at had already passed out of view, so she adjusted the metal tube to compensate.

"It looks like you could fit five or six, depending on how many people can fit on the back bench." She held the telescope steady as another one came into view, a blue two-seater. "The blue one looks too small."

"I can tell that without the telescope," Reed said.

She started to step back as another boat crossed in front of her. This one had two rows of seats in addition to the back bench. "How much more would one like that be?" She pointed.

"Which one?"

"The white cabin cruiser." She studied it, approving of the streamlined design that incorporated a small below-deck area under the bow. "It might be nice to have the ability to get out of the sun."

"True."

The driver leaned slightly to his right to adjust his speed, and Jane's breath caught in her chest. "No." The word came out in a whisper, the man's face visible for several seconds. The same face that had been captured in the photo in LA, the one she'd been looking at in their drills for weeks now.

"What? What's wrong?"

Jane pointed. "The driver. That's him!"

"Who?"

"Abdul Maleb. One of the guys in the picture." Jane stepped back and waved for Reed to look through the scope. "From the airport in LA."

"What?" Reed quickly moved forward to look, but the man's body was already angled away from them again. "I can't see his face."

"Reed, it was him."

"Are you sure?"

"I . . ." Was she sure? Doubts began to surface, but fear overrode them. "I've looked at his photo so many times—maybe it's someone who just looks like him, but I don't think we can take the chance that I might be wrong."

"Good point." Reed pulled his cell from his pocket and dialed Craig's number. A moment later, he spoke into the phone. "Craig, I know it sounds crazy, but Jane thinks she saw that Abdul guy here at the boat show."

Reed nodded once and held the phone out to Jane. "He wants to talk to you."

"What exactly did you see?" Craig asked.

Jane described the boat and the man piloting it.

"Where is the boat now?" Craig asked.

"It's heading for the marina."

"I'll call in some help. Keep your distance, but I want you to watch where it docks and let me know. Then get out of there."

"Okay." Jane hung up the phone and turned to Reed. "He wants us to let him know where it docks."

"Are you sure you're okay with this?" Reed asked. "If Craig is right, this could be the man who tried to kill all of us."

"And if we don't help now, who knows what kind of damage he'll do." Jane kept her gaze on the white boat as it continued forward. "We don't have to go down there. We can see better from up here anyway." The words were barely out of her mouth when a yacht passed in front of the boat in question. "So much for that idea."

"Come on." Reed took her hand. "We should be able to see him enter the harbor from over there."

They jogged to the knoll overlooking the harbor. The constant activity on the water was dizzying. "Do you see it?"

"Not yet." Reed continued leading her, both of them searching.

"Is that it?" Jane asked, seeing one with the same design.

Reed stood on his toes, trying to see over another vessel that was in front of it.

"The driver isn't wearing a hat." Reed motioned again to a spot behind the one Jane had pointed out. "It should still be behind that yacht."

Several other boats crossed in front of the yacht they were watching. When their target's hiding place turned to angle into a slip in the harbor, Jane's heartbeat quickened. "It's gone!" Her gaze swept over the area. "Do you see it anywhere?"

"No." He was clearly frustrated. "He must have changed direction when all of those other boats were entering the marina."

"How are we going to find it now?" Jane asked, trying to keep the rising panic out of her voice. "Most of these boats are white."

"I know."

Jane drew a deep breath and mustered her courage. "I hate to say it, but we may need to go down there."

"I was thinking the same thing." Reed tugged off his baseball cap and handed it to her. "Here. Wear this. It'll make it harder for him to recognize you with that and your sunglasses on."

"Thanks." Jane used her fingers to pull her hair back into a ponytail and then fed it through the back of Reed's beloved Dodgers cap.

"Let's look from up here first." They continued along the knoll above the pier and angled toward a path leading to the water almost a quarter mile away. "Maybe we'll get lucky and find it again before the cops get here."

"I hope they get here soon."

"That makes two of us."

39

CRAIG SPRINTED FROM THE TOP of the dock on base to where Brent, Jay, and Damian were loading gear into their boat for their upcoming dive.

"Brent, we've got a problem." Craig held up his phone. "Jane thinks she saw Abdul at the boat show."

"The one here in Virginia Beach?" Quinn asked.

"Yeah."

Jay suddenly dropped the pack he held and straightened. "Carina and Sienna are there today."

Craig whipped his head around to face Jay. "What?"

"Some surprise Sienna was planning," Jay said tensely.

Brent motioned them all into the vessel. "Let's go."

Craig texted Sienna as he moved to the boat. *Take cover! Leave the boat show now! Tell Carina too.* Beside him, Jay had his phone in hand and was also texting frantically.

Brent moved behind the wheel. "Craig, call Charlie and have him bring in the FBI. Damian, notify the Coast Guard. Jay, let the rest of the squad know what's going on, and have them coordinate with the FBI."

As soon as their orders were given, Brent started the engine. They all scrambled on board, and Jay called out, "All bodies in!"

An instant later, Brent put the vessel in gear and started forward. When they were clear of the dock, he increased speed. Not sure he would be heard over the roar of the engine, Craig used his cell phone to text Charlie. *Abdul Maleb spotted, Virginia Beach boat show, white speedboat with cabin, twenty-two footer. ETA ten minutes.*

The response came an instant later. *Sending agents your way. Keep me updated.*

Roger.

Craig took position beside Brent. "FBI is on the way."

"So is the Coast Guard," Damian added.

Brent glanced over his shoulder. "Jay?"

"Amy is trying to get a helicopter, but without a positive ID from law enforcement, she doesn't know if she can pull it off."

"Have Tristan stay behind in case we get approval, and tell the others to meet us at the boat show."

Damian relayed the message.

Concerned that he had yet to get a response from Sienna, Craig retrieved his phone to text her a second time. Beside him, Jay also had his cell in his hand.

They rounded a jut of land, and all of them fell silent. Boats. Everywhere. Speedboats, yachts, sailboats, cruisers. Nearly every slip at the harbor was full, and at least fifty other vessels were out on the water. The dominant color: white.

* * *

"Is this too much?" Sienna asked. "I'm afraid Craig will be annoyed if I give him something this expensive for his birthday."

"I thought the same thing last year when I bought Jay his boat," Carina said. "The way his eyes lit up when he saw it was priceless."

"Really?"

Carina nodded. "Of course, that was before he started with the 'You shouldn't have; it's too expensive' talk."

"That's the talk I worry about."

"It's bound to happen no matter what you do, but that's because we both have great guys who are interested in more than our money," Carina said. "Besides, didn't you tell me Craig's grandfather has a boat they use when they go out on the lake?"

"Yeah. Why?"

"If someone in his family already owns one, it's not like you're giving him something that's out of this world. I mean, if you were buying him a Ferrari, he would probably feel weird about it, but owning a boat in Virginia Beach is pretty common."

"That's true." Sienna studied the sleek speedboat in front of her. Two seats, a bench running along the back. It was big enough for them and another couple or for Craig to take a few friends out. "And this one isn't too extravagant."

"Yeah."

Sienna's phone chimed for the second time in less than ten minutes, but her focus remained on the vessel. Carina's phone sounded an instant later.

"I really do like this one," Sienna said.

"If he gives you a hard time, you can remind him that Jay already has a boat. Between the two of them, they would be able to take the whole squad out."

"Very true."

Carina retrieved her phone from her purse to check her most recent text message and gasped.

"What's wrong?" Sienna asked.

"We've got to go." Carina grabbed Sienna's arm. "Now."

The urgency in Carina's voice unsettled Sienna enough to let herself get pulled away from the pier. "What's wrong?"

"I don't know, but Jay just texted me and said we need to leave."

"Maybe he's worried Craig decided to come with Jane and Reed. I know they were talking about coming."

"No, it's something else. His message started with 'Take cover.' That means there's danger." Carina broke into an easy jog, and Sienna forced herself to keep up as they made their way through the crowds on the dock.

Questions flooded through her mind. What in the world could make Jay worry so much that he would insist they leave?

They reached the parking lot, and Sienna came to a screeching halt.

Carina looked back at her, confused. "Sienna, what are you doing? We need to get out of here."

Two cars away from where Carina now stood, the door of a plain white van opened and a dark-haired man stepped out, the man Sienna knew primarily from pictures, the man who had tried to have her killed.

Her gaze quickly shifted from his face to the weapon in his hand.

"Carina!" That was the only word she managed to utter before Jamal rushed forward and grabbed Carina by the arm.

"Keep it down, and stay calm," he said, his English perfect, his Middle-Eastern accent evident. "No one has to get hurt."

Carina's face paled.

Sienna's eyes darted around in search of anyone who could help, but despite the crowds on the dock, this part of the parking lot was eerily quiet.

"Come with me." He waved the gun toward the van.

Both Carina and Sienna stood rooted to their spots.

"Let me rephrase: you can get in the van, where I'll be sure you won't cause us any trouble, or I can shoot you right now. Your choice."

Die now, or die later. Neither option held any appeal, but if Jay knew they could be in danger, later might hold a different outcome than this man intended.

Stall. That word flashed into her mind, and she grasped for inspiration on how to do that.

"Why? Why do you want to hurt people you don't even know?" Sienna finally managed to ask.

"It doesn't matter."

"It does matter." Sienna nodded toward the dock. "What did these people ever do to you?"

"They killed my brother."

A blood vengeance. Sienna tried to wrap her mind around how to combat such deep hatred, but she couldn't begin to understand his motive.

Luckily, Carina jumped in. "Who killed your brother? Was it someone here?"

"Your people killed him." Hatred erupted on his face. "It doesn't matter who pulled the trigger. You are all infidels. You threaten my way of life, the life my brother should have continued to live."

"How did he die?"

"It doesn't matter."

"Of course it matters," Sienna said now. "If it didn't, why would you do this?"

"Because your people bomb our cities, you monitor our borders, and you keep us from getting food and supplies," he said.

"Whatever you're planning today won't change that," Carina said. "If anything, you'll make it worse."

"Nothing can be worse. It's time you know you can't hide within your borders." He tugged on Carina's arm and shoved her toward the van. She let out a cry of alarm. "If you scream, I will shoot you."

"Don't shoot," Sienna said desperately. "Please. Don't shoot."

"Then do as I say."

40

REED DIDN'T WANT TO THINK about the danger, despite his constant prayers that they would be able to avoid it. Drawing deeply on his acting abilities, he tried to pretend he was one of the Navy SEALs, someone who had learned to put his fear on a shelf until he was past the moment of danger. Jane's presence beside him made the task impossible.

Their walk along the bluff overlooking the marina had given them too many possibilities. Jane had pointed out eight boats that appeared to be very similar, but the type was common enough that there could be more farther down the pier where they wouldn't be visible behind the other vessels moored there.

Only walking along the entire pier would give them the vantage point they needed. Though he hated the idea of putting Jane in danger, they both knew they might make the difference between a quiet arrest by the FBI and a terrorist attack that could kill hundreds. He couldn't stand by and watch that happen. He had to at least wait until he could pass the torch to the authorities.

"Where should we start?" Jane asked.

"Let's start on the south side." Reed led her toward a ramp. "We saw four boats down there that looked like they could be the right one."

They were nearly to the dock before Jane said, "I think we should look at the two in the middle first. I would think this guy would want to be as close to the main action as possible."

"Good point." Reed looked in the direction of the parking lot, not seeing anything out of place, except for the lack of activity. He kept expecting to hear sirens heading their way or for his phone to ring. So far, nothing.

"It's been fifteen minutes," Reed said in a low voice as they approached the nearest suspect. "I thought the place would be swarming with cops by now."

"Me too. I never realized how many boats are white."

"I never cared before what color people painted them," Reed said.

They reached the first speedboat to find a man in his fifties standing beside it.

"Want to take a look?" he asked when he saw Reed studying his vessel.

"No, thanks." Reed increased his pace to avoid the inevitable sales pitch. Sure enough, the man started talking about speed and handling as they walked by.

They both slowed their steps when they approached the second boat with similar color and style. This time a woman in her thirties stood on board.

Reed and Jane continued past to make sure they didn't see anyone else in the area who looked familiar. Once they were satisfied Abdul wasn't there, Reed turned and headed back the way they had come.

"Which way next?" Reed asked.

"Where do you think the biggest crowds will be?"

Reed looked around, this time searching for any main concentration of patrons. He didn't have to look far. Fifty yards to his left, a strip of food vendors had set up near the clubhouse. Dozens of people milled about, including several in their dress uniforms.

"Do you know what's going on over there?" Reed asked.

"I think I heard something about some navy hero cutting the ribbon for the grand opening of the clubhouse today."

"That would be the perfect time to strike," Reed said, seeing the possible outcomes unfolding in his mind.

"What time is the groundbreaking?"

"I think it's at ten."

"That's in less than an hour."

Jane started toward the clubhouse. "If that's when they strike, the boat should be somewhere over there."

Reed took a deep breath and uttered another silent prayer that they would remain safe and that disaster would be averted. Something in his chest sprouted and spread outward. With a new resolve, he straightened his shoulders. "Let's go."

* * *

Craig's phone rang, but he couldn't read the screen beneath the glare of the sun. He put one hand up to his ear to block out the sound of the engine. "Simmons."

"Craig, it's Charlie. We've got a problem."

"What?"

"Big accident on I-64. The FBI agents are stuck in traffic with nowhere to go," Charlie said. "I can call in the cops, but I'm worried about alerting these guys that we're on to them."

"I don't think we have a choice." Craig's mind raced. "Also, any chance you can talk to Amy to see if the FBI can help us get approval for the use of a helicopter? Tristan is ready to pilot, and that would give us a better view."

"That's a good idea," Charlie said. "I thought about sending in one of ours, but an FBI helicopter overhead could cause a panic."

"And a naval helicopter is something everyone sees all the time around here."

"Exactly," Charlie agreed. "I'll make the call."

After they hung up, Craig relayed the information.

"Call or text Tristan. Tell him to gear up and get over to the helicopter pad," Brent told him. "We don't know how much more time we've got."

Damian leaned forward so he could be heard. "Is this a good time to mention that we're all crazy for racing toward what could be a chemical weapon attack?"

Brent shook his head. "No, not really."

"Okay." Damian shrugged. "I'll wait until tomorrow to tell you."

* * *

Sienna moved slowly forward, her eyes darting around the parking lot again in the hope that someone would see them. Normally, she hoped she wouldn't be noticed when in public venues such as this, but right now, having a fan spot her might very well save her life and Carina's.

"Come on." Jamal pulled open the side panel of the box van. "Inside."

Jamal shoved Carina toward the door, and she yelped with pain when her knee connected with the bottom of the van. None too gently, he gave her another shove, and Carina stumbled into the van.

He lifted the gun and aimed it at Sienna. "Get in. Now."

The realization that both she and Carina had their cell phones gave Sienna a brief glimmer of hope. And if someone did notice they were missing, surely the Saint Squad would come find them.

Bits of overheard conversations played through her mind. The past crimes of the man in front of her. The recent missions for the Saint Squad. Craig and Brent talking about types of chemical weapons. Reality crashed over her and dragged her deep into a sea of despair. If this man was planting a chemical weapon, anyone searching for them could be walking right into the kill zone.

Carina sat up on the metal flooring of the work van. The moment Sienna took position beside her, Jamal stood in the doorway. "Now hand over your cell phones."

Mixed emotions settled in the pit of her stomach, creating a constant ache. Carina moved slowly, her eyes remaining on their captor the whole time as she handed over her cell.

Sienna didn't know how Carina could stand to look this man in the eye. She lowered her gaze to the phone she pulled out of her pocket. The unread text message from Craig flashed, and her emotions took another turn.

Take cover! Leave the boat show now! Tell Carina too. He knew they were in danger.

"Hand it over," Jamal insisted again, breaking into her thoughts.

Sienna pressed the button on the side to darken the screen and passed it to him. She looked around the inside of the vehicle, instinctively searching for possible means of escape. When Jamal retrieved a thick roll of duct tape from beneath the passenger seat, her mood plummeted even further.

A tear escaped. How would any of them survive the day?

* * *

Jane nearly stumbled when they turned toward the fourth boat in question. No one was on board, but the slender man heading toward them was most certainly the person they were seeking. She looked down to avoid his eyes and squeezed Reed's hand.

"What?"

She lowered her voice. "The guy heading toward us. That's him."

To her surprise, Reed's response was delivered at normal volume. "Wait a minute, hon. I want to get a picture of this one to show my dad."

Jane looked at him like he was crazy. Then she saw the way he held his cell phone up, the angle he chose. While to anyone around them it would appear he was taking a picture of the boat in front of him, in reality, he had reversed the camera and was angling to photograph Abdul as he passed by.

Jane didn't speak. She didn't dare. She kept her eyes trained on the boat Reed had expressed interest in and willed her pulse to drop back below two hundred. The footsteps drew closer. Make that three hundred.

Undoubtedly, she was going to die any minute. If Abdul didn't kill her, her heart would explode and take care of the job. Footsteps grew louder, and Jane heard Reed click several pictures. Then he leaned down and whispered in her ear. "Breathe."

Jane let out the breath she hadn't realized she'd been holding and sucked in air. Two deep breaths later, she managed to speak again. "What now?"

"I'm texting these photos to Craig and Charlie."

"At least now we know which boat might be a problem." Jane moved to the side to get a better view of the craft . . . and saw two more just like it in the slips beyond. "Kind of."

Reed sent his message and followed her gaze. "Great."

41

BRENT NAVIGATED THROUGH THE HARBOR, weaving in and out of the boat show traffic on the water.

"If these guys see us coming, they're going to know we're onto them," Craig said. "We stick out like a sore thumb."

"Don't worry about that for now. Check in with Reed and Jane to see if they can narrow down where we should look."

Craig sent a text to Reed a second before Jay's phone rang. He listened briefly before his tension shot up. "What do you mean they won't let you have the helicopter?"

"What's going on?" Brent asked.

"Apparently Commander Elso had a jump scheduled, and he's having a fit about getting bumped," Jay told him.

"Tell Tristan to get the commander on the phone." Brent moved to his right. "Damian take the wheel."

As soon as Damian took over the controls, Brent got completely out of his way. Craig wondered briefly how Brent was going to deal with the red tape of overriding the base's flight schedule. When his cell phone vibrated, he looked down and clicked on the image Reed had sent him.

Brent's voice carried authority when he spoke into Jay's phone. "Commander Elso, this is Commander Miller."

"Brent," Craig interrupted, sticking his phone into his view. "You've got to see this."

His eyes shifted to look at the screen, and Brent nodded his understanding. "Commander, you know how after every terrorist attack, news comes out about how someone could have done something different to stop it?" Brent paused briefly, presumably allowing the other man to answer. "You're about to become that something. We have a positive ID of a terrorist and suspect an attack is about to happen. Now, you are going to get out of my man's way and give him whatever he needs to provide support. Do I make myself clear?" He fell silent for a moment before adding, "Thank you. I appreciate your seeing things my way."

Brent waited a few seconds before he handed Jay's phone back to him and focused his attention more fully on the image Reed had sent. "Jay, tell Tristan I want him to concentrate on the parking lot. If Abdul is already off the boat, he's trying to get out of here."

Jay relayed the information.

Craig forwarded the image to the rest of his team before checking his messages again. Reed had sent him details on the location where they suspected Abdul's boat was located. His eyebrows drew together. "Did Carina text you back? I haven't heard from Sienna," Craig asked as soon as Jay hung up.

"She texted me to say she got my message," Jay said.

Craig lifted his phone and called Sienna's phone. His heart dropped. "It went straight to voice mail."

Jay immediately hit speed dial. "So did Carina's."

"How long has it been since you last heard from her?" Brent asked.

Jay pulled up his text messages, and Craig craned his neck to see the screen. Jay used his free hand to shade it, and both men did the mental math based on the time stamp of the last text.

"Seven minutes," Jay said.

"The Coast Guard should be here any minute," Brent said. "Damian, tell them to send a message to the boats that aren't docked and start clearing them out of the marina."

"What if Sienna and Carina are on one of those vessels?" Craig asked, clearly panicked. "If neither of them answered . . ."

"They may not be able to," Jay finished for him.

"How many cutters are they sending?"

"Two." Damian pointed. "Here comes one now."

Brent waved at the radio. "Get them on a secure channel."

Damian called into the command center and switched the channel on the radio. After making contact with the Coast Guard cutter, he handed the microphone to Brent and put it on speaker. "Here you go."

"This is US Naval Commander Brent Miller. We need to clear as many vessels out of the area as quickly as possible, but we have a possible hostage situation."

"How do you want to proceed?" the voice on the other end of the radio asked.

"I suggest we set up a barricade and search each vessel before it passes." Brent pointed at Craig in the way of an order. "I'll have my men coordinate with the police to have them do the same thing in the parking area and surrounding streets."

"If we're trying to evacuate, do we really want to hold people here?"

"Our suspect was seen less than ten minutes ago. He's not setting anything off until he's well clear," Brent said. "We've also narrowed down the location of the problem. I'm going to drop a couple of my men off at the dock. Then we'll help you clear vessels."

"Roger that."

Brent signed off and looked at the three men facing him. "Two of us need to deal with the explosive, and two of us will help the Coast Guard. Jay, Craig, where do you want to be?"

Craig's first instinct was to stay on the water in case Sienna and Carina were being held on one of the many boats nearby. Logic fought through his tumultuous emotions. If Abdul had been seen walking on the docks, he must be leaving by land.

Jay spoke first. "If that explosive goes off, we're all dead. Of the four of us, Brent, you have the most experience with defusing bombs."

"I want to go with you," Craig managed to say over the lump in his throat.

Jay's eyes met his. "I'll stay on top of the search."

Craig managed a nod but didn't trust himself to speak further.

"Did Reed send you the location of Abdul's boat?"

Craig swallowed hard. "Yeah. Head for the dock nearest the clubhouse."

Damian adjusted his course. Ninety seconds later, he pulled up alongside a speedboat with a deck level that wasn't much higher than their own. Brent and Craig hopped on board, using the vessel as a pathway to the dock.

"Hey!" a man on board yelled at them. "You can't come through here."

"US Navy," Brent announced. "We have a potential situation. Clear out of here. Now."

Brent and Craig didn't wait to see if the man heeded their warning. They were already sprinting forward, praying they could find the bomb in time.

* * *

Reed's phone rang, and he answered it after seeing Craig was on the other end.

"Reed, where's Abdul now? Can you still see him?"

"Hold on." Reed shifted his gaze to search the crowd. It took him a minute before he finally located the man they had seen walking away minutes before. "It looks like he's leaving."

"I need a huge favor," Craig said with a hint of panic. "Tristan and Quinn will be there in less than a minute. I need you to follow Abdul and tell Seth where he goes."

"I was afraid you were going to say that."

"Please, Reed. We know Sienna and Carina were at the boat show, but we can't get in touch with them. If Sienna was seen . . ."

Concern overshadowed the possible danger to himself. "Text me Seth's number."

"Thanks, Reed."

"What was all that about?" Jane asked as soon as he hung up.

"Sienna might be in trouble." Reed took two steps toward Abdul. "Wait here for Craig." He dug his keys out of his pocket and tossed them to her. Walking backward, he added, "As soon as he shows up, get out of here."

"What about you?"

"Text me when you go to the car. If I can, I'll meet you there." Reed turned and jogged toward the crowd and the ramp to the parking lot beyond.

"Be careful," Jane called after him.

He lifted his hand to signal he had heard her. He scanned the crowd, and he suffered a moment of panic when he realized he had lost visual contact with Abdul. He was almost to the clubhouse when he caught sight of him again.

He picked up his pace, myriad prayers racing through his mind, all of them focused on safety for all, especially his friends and loved ones.

* * *

Jane took an automatic step back when she saw Brent and Craig racing toward her, both of them outfitted with communication headsets and assault rifles in their hands. The way their eyes continually scanned the area made her think she had just fallen into the middle of an action movie right before the climax. She prayed this one would have a happily ever after.

Craig reached her first. "Which boat?"

"I don't know." She motioned to the two on her left that were nearly identical and another one two slips down on her right. "We think it's one of these three. We saw Abdul coming from this direction."

"Wait here, and tell us if you see him," Brent commanded, already heading for the one on the right.

Craig boarded the boat on the left nearest the clubhouse. Jane watched as both men conducted an initial search of the deck and storage areas before entering the cabin at the front of the boats.

As though her body had a mind of its own, she headed for the third boat. She boarded, conducting her own search as she had seen Craig and Brent do moments before. She lifted the seat of the back bench, and her breath caught. "Craig! Brent! Over here."

Brent came topside first, and instantly, he was on the pier, his footsteps pounding as he sprinted toward her. Craig arrived only a step behind him.

"What are you doing?" Craig demanded.

She straightened, her hand still holding the lid of the bench up so they could see inside. "I think I found what you're looking for."

Immediately, Brent's hand went to his ear, and he spoke into the little microphone on his headset. "We found it." He looked down at the deck. "Slip seventeen." Brent repeated the words. "Slip seventeen."

42

SURREAL. THAT WAS THE ONLY word Reed could use to describe the situation he had landed himself in. Here he was, leaving the woman he loved behind as he chased after a terrorist who might possibly lead him to his childhood friend. And in the middle of everything, a chemical weapon was hidden somewhere nearby. He couldn't write it better if he wanted to.

He reached the edge of the parking lot and looked for a blue ball cap and gray shirt. A ribbon of dread rose up inside him when he didn't see Abdul anywhere.

A screech of tires caught his attention, and he whipped his head toward the entrance, where a car skidded around the corner into the parking lot. Behind it, two police cars with their lights flashing approached at high speed.

At first, Reed thought they were chasing the approaching car, but when the police vehicles stopped at the entrance and used their cars to create a barricade, his attention was drawn to the driver. Seth.

Reed rushed to the curb and waved both arms over his head to get Seth's attention. It worked.

Seth sped past the rows of parked cars to where he stood.

Quinn flung the passenger door open and jumped out. "Where are they?"

"I don't know. I was following Abdul, but I lost him less than a minute ago," Reed said. "He's wearing a blue ball cap and a gray shirt."

From behind the wheel, Seth barked out orders. "Reed, go over with the cops in case they try to drive out of here. I'm going to drive the perimeter."

"I'll work the middle, starting from this side," Quinn said.

"What happens when we find these guys?" Reed managed to ask.

"You're a civilian," Seth reminded him. "All you do is make sure one of us knows where they are, and then you take cover."

Reed swallowed the lump in his throat. "I can do that."

* * *

Abdul forced himself to move forward at a steady pace. The knowledge of what this marina would look like after the chemical explosion both delighted and terrified him. Forty-three minutes and counting.

He had chosen this venue because of its easy access and close proximity to the naval base. With the weather conditions, the wind would carry the chemical toxin right into the heart of the base and kill an estimated 70 percent of the inhabitants. Those who did survive would suffer the aftereffects for many years to come.

He reached the van where Jamal was waiting behind the wheel, the engine already running, the windows rolled up.

Abdul yanked the passenger door open and climbed in. "It's done."

"We have a problem." Jamal nodded toward the back.

Abdul twisted to look behind him, his jaw dropping when he saw two women huddled behind him with gags in their mouths, their hands bound.

"What happened?" he asked, deliberately speaking in Arabic so he wouldn't be understood. "Who are they?"

"Sienna Blake and one of her friends." Apology lit Jamal's eyes. "Sienna recognized me. I didn't have a choice."

"Get us out of here. We'll take care of them later when no one will be around to hear the gunshots."

Jamal put the car in reverse and glanced in his side mirror. But instead of moving, he put the car back in park.

"What are you doing? We need to get out of here."

"We have another problem." He motioned to the passenger-side window. "Check your mirror."

He did and instantly saw the issue. "What are the cops doing here?"

"I have no idea."

"Check your phone. See if there's anything on the local news feed."

Jamal pulled his cell out and didn't even push a button before his face paled. "There's an alert, something about a missing kid."

Abdul watched a car exiting the parking lot slow down at the police barricade. The police opened each door and checked the trunk before allowing the driver to continue on his way. He motioned to the women in the back. "We'll never make it out of here with them."

"What do we do? We won't be able to get out of the target area in time without a vehicle."

"Leave them here," Abdul said. "If the heat doesn't kill them, the blast will."

"What about us?"

"We walk out of here. As soon as we get past the police barricade, we'll steal a car and put some distance between us and this place."

"Steal a car? We're going to get caught," Jamal said.

"No, we won't." Abdul motioned toward the street. "The police are about to be too busy dealing with everyone's panic when this van blows up."

"You planted a bomb on our own vehicle?"

"I plan for every contingency." He climbed out of the van and opened the back door. He used his body to shield the women inside from anyone who might pass by and retrieved a hard-plastic briefcase from behind the passenger seat. He opened the case and activated the detonator. The whimper from one of the women was an irritant he ignored, like a buzzing fly.

"How much time until detonation?" he asked, focused on his task at hand.

"Thirty-four minutes."

Abdul programmed fourteen minutes. Just enough time to draw the police's attention and drive the crowd toward the real threat. As soon as he completed his task, he closed the case and placed it on the floor of the front passenger seat so it was out of reach of the women and out of sight of anyone passing by.

"Let's go."

"Are you sure about this?" Jamal asked.

"It's our only option."

Jamal's jaw clenched, but he reached for the door handle and climbed out of the van. When they were both outside, Abdul locked the doors. Walking quickly, they angled upwind, away from the police cars.

* * *

Jane had thought her last experience with bombs would be her one and only. She now prayed she would survive what would hopefully be her last.

"Jane, trade places with me." Brent put his hand up to hold the storage seat open while she circled behind him. The moment she did, she saw the backside of the device for the first time. An old-fashioned digital display revealed numbers in red. 0:34:27. 0:34:26. 0:34:25. She watched, horrified, as the seconds continued to count down.

Shifting his position to her left, Craig took a picture of the device and appeared to text it to someone. She looked down at the single large container that could have passed for a five-gallon water jug, except for the nasty-looking bomb strapped to its side. A second, smaller container was affixed to the other side of the explosive, and two one-inch tubes connected the two containers, wires running through both. Brent spoke into his headset again. "Tristan, get over here. Damian, contact the base and tell them we need a containment field set up."

Beside him, Craig pulled cushions off the top of the seat and threw them aside so he could open it further. "It's booby-trapped. If we try to take the charge out, it will immediately puncture both containers and mix the toxins."

"We're going to need the robot."

"The robot?" Jane asked.

Brent and Craig ignored her.

Brent pulled a flashlight from his vest and used it to further examine the device. Finally, he said, "It's clean."

Craig stepped inside the bench. "Jane, move to the end and hold this open while we remove it."

"You're going to what?"

"We can't disarm it here," Craig said.

"It looks like they used this board under it to lower it down." Brent took position opposite Craig.

The roar of an approaching helicopter filled the air, making further communication impossible. Yet somehow, the two men managed to work together seamlessly. Using hand signals, they positioned themselves on opposite sides and gently lifted the chemical weapon out of the storage bench and lowered it onto the deck.

Though she couldn't hear the words, Brent spoke into his headset again, and a moment later, a large fiberglass box lowered from the helicopter.

43

SIENNA HEARD THE HELICOPTER OVERHEAD and prayed it was someone looking for them. She hadn't been able to understand the two men's conversation, but their sense of urgency made her think that whatever terror they planned to unleash was happening soon.

Beside her, Carina scooted toward the center of the van. Positioned back to back with their hands bound together, the movement caused Sienna to topple to the right, taking Carina with her. They both hit the bottom of the van with a thud.

Her right shoulder throbbed from the impact, and she tried to understand Carina's reason for her movement.

"What are you doing?" The words sounded in Sienna's head but came out in a mumble against the tape over her mouth.

Now on her side, Carina continued scooting. Not seeing any way to help herself, Sienna followed her friend's lead, moving along with her.

It wasn't until her fingers grazed leather that Sienna realized Carina was trying to get to her purse. The zipper sounded, and Sienna curled her fingers inward to keep them from getting caught. When Carina reached into her bag, taking Sienna's hands with her, Sienna's fingers brushed against something metallic.

A lightbulb went on in her head. Carina's gun. Jamal had taken their cell phones but hadn't bothered to check the content of their purses.

Sienna's stomach jumped into her throat. She didn't know what Carina intended, but trying to shoot without being able to see where she was aiming sent a wave of panic through her. What would happen if she accidentally shot the bomb in the front seat? Then again, the bomb was going to kill them if they didn't do anything.

She closed her eyes for a brief moment, a silent prayer running through her head once more, only now she added the extra request that Carina's plan, whatever it was, would work and that no one would get hurt.

* * *

Craig secured the chemical bomb in the container that would protect against any minimal leaks. Unfortunately, if the explosive trigger detonated, the container would shatter and hundreds . . . or thousands . . . would die. He didn't want to think about wind patterns right now. First things first.

Twenty-six minutes, twelve seconds. And counting.

"Take it up," Brent said.

Craig couldn't see who was in the helicopter with Tristan, but when he saw his teammate lean out of the open hatch beside another man, he realized one of the base pilots must be at the controls.

The many possible things that could go wrong marched through his mind as the container elevated from the deck and hung suspended in midair.

"Go find Sienna," Brent said. "I've got this."

Craig looked up briefly before turning and sprinting toward the parking lot.

* * *

Time was running out. Reed didn't need anyone to tell him that. He could read it in the body language of the police he was helping and the Navy SEALs currently searching the parking lot.

A line of twenty cars stretched out from where he stood at the marina exit, two more heading their way. Impatient, he turned to the police officer beside him. "I'm going to see if I recognize anyone in these cars."

"No, you need to stay here."

"We both know we don't have much time left." Reed started forward, letting his defiance hang in the air.

He chose a path a yard away from the vehicles and leaned down as he passed each one so he could see who was inside. Though he got some strange looks, he repeated the process until he reached the end of the line. Not one familiar face.

Straightening, he took another look around. A sea of cars filled the lot before him, at least 80 percent of the parking spaces occupied. Seth had abandoned his car and was searching vehicles on the south side of the lot. Quinn was at the north side, working toward him.

Reed caught a flash of movement near the marina and recognized Craig running in his direction.

Reed moved to the center of the lot to continue the task. When he heard the pop of gunfire, he instinctively ducked behind the black SUV to his right. Another gunshot echoed, followed by a third.

Keeping his body protected by the SUV, he peered to his right to see Quinn with a weapon in hand, he too partially shielded by a vehicle. Reed didn't know that the MG Spitfire the other man had chosen for cover would do much good, but he figured as a trained Navy SEAL, Quinn probably knew what he was doing.

Sure enough, Quinn moved quickly to the next vehicle, continually scanning the lot.

Three more shots sounded, immediately followed by two more.

At first, Reed thought it might have been someone shooting back at whoever had initiated the problem. Then his mind replayed the scene, and he realized each gunshot had sounded from somewhere nearby to his left.

Then he heard the impact again.

Logic told him to stay where he was, safely out of sight. Something else prompted him into action.

The thudding continued, and as he drew closer to it, he could hear muffled moans and cries.

"Reed! Stay down!" Craig called out as he once again sprinted toward him.

"I hear something over here." Reed reached a white work van and could see bullet holes in the side panel. Instantly, he looked around for a potential shooter. Then he heard the muffled cries again.

He pulled on the door handle to find it locked.

Craig reached his side. "You need to stay out of sight until we have this situation under control."

"Listen." Thump. Thump. "It's coming from in there."

Craig peered inside. "Someone's in there." He pulled a thin tool from his vest and slid it between the passenger window and the door panel. A moment later, the lock clicked open. He hit the button to unlock all the doors, and Reed didn't wait before he opened the back panel.

Heat spilled out. Inside, their hands duct taped together, lay Sienna and Carina.

Reed reached out and gently pulled the tape off Sienna's mouth.

"The front seat!" she gasped. "There's a bomb!"

Craig's voice was eerily calm when he responded. "I see it."

* * *

Seeing Sienna gave Craig some comfort in knowing she was okay, but the digital display in front of him kept his heart racing.

He straightened, looked around for the nearest teammate, and shouted, "Seth!" Seth sprinted toward him, and Craig reached into his vest to pull out his utility knife. He handed it to Reed. "Cut them loose and get everyone out of here." Reed didn't have time to respond before Seth arrived at his side. The moment he appeared, Craig said, "We've got a bomb. Single detonator, two circuits."

"Time?" Seth asked.

"Four minutes, thirty-two seconds."

Seth looked around the parking lot. "We have too many civilians around to try to move it. We have to disarm it."

"It's the same design as the ones at Sienna's house. We have to disarm both circuits simultaneously."

Sienna and Carina scrambled out of the back, and Reed edged forward. "What can I do to help?"

"Give me my knife, and get them as far away as you can."

Reed handed it over.

"Be careful," Sienna said beside Craig.

"I will." Craig's focus wandered long enough to make sure Sienna was heading for safety. When her footsteps joined Reed's and Carina's, he forced his attention back to the threat in front of him.

Seth had already circled the vehicle and now leaned in through the driver's side door. Both men fell silent as they studied the deadly device. The blast itself would likely take out only the van and the eight cars within a thirty-foot radius, but the fear it would invoke in those nearby could create havoc in the middle of an already deadly threat. Not to mention the potential ripple effect of gasoline tanks exploding and catching the next-closest vehicle on fire. And the next and the next.

"I've got the blue wire here. You should have one on your side that mirrors it."

Craig identified the correct wire and slid his knife into place.

His chest tightened, and he looked again at the timer. Two minutes thirteen seconds.

"We'll cut when the timer hits two minutes," Seth said.

"Count it down," Craig said. He looked up at his teammate, willing his hands to remain steady. When he caught a flash of metal beside Seth's left elbow, another thought formed. He straightened and looked around once more, the impossible flashing through his mind.

44

SIENNA SCREAMED WHEN THE GROUND rocked beneath her, accompanied by a loud boom. She ducked instinctively before she looked toward the source of the sound and saw flames spearing into the air from the edge of the parking lot. A second explosion erupted seconds later.

"No!" Sienna's heart stumbled as horror crashed over her. Why hadn't she insisted Craig come with her when he had sent her away? Had she bought into his typical attitude that his training made him invincible?

She took a step toward the burning vehicle, but Reed grabbed her arm to hold her back.

She gulped in air, tasting the smoke as well as smelling it. Tears coursed down her face, and her eyes darted around the area near the fire. Craig couldn't have failed. She couldn't live with what that would mean. The thought repeated in her mind, and doubts overwhelmed her.

If Craig had still been trying to disarm the bomb when it had gone off, she didn't know how he would have been able to survive.

Reed tugged on her arm to keep her moving away from the source of the explosion. She tripped, her gaze landing on Quinn, who was walking quickly through the parking lot as though looking for something or someone. How could he appear so normal? Didn't he know Craig and Seth had been in the explosion? Or had they?

"Quinn!" Sienna broke free of Reed's grasp and rushed forward. "Where is he? Where's Craig?"

Apparently understanding her panic, Quinn put his hand on her shoulder and leaned down to speak into her ear. "He's fine. The explosion was deliberate."

"What?"

"If it hadn't gone off, Abdul would have known we were onto them. We need to make sure we get these guys, and letting them think they succeeded gives us an edge."

"And gave me a heart attack."

"Sorry." Quinn's eyes scanned the area before he looked back at her. "Did you see or hear anything that would help us find them?"

"They were speaking in another language. I couldn't understand them."

"How many of them were there?"

"Two." Sienna drew a deep breath and tried to settle her emotions.

"What were they wearing?"

"The driver was Jamal. He had on a blue polo, and he was wearing sunglasses."

"Was the other one Abdul?"

"I don't know. He was wearing a hat," Sienna said, trying to recall the moment when he had opened the back of the van. "I only saw him for a minute when he got the bomb out of the back of the van and armed it."

Quinn seemed to key into something she said. "Did they act like everything was going according to plan, or did they seem flustered?"

Sienna forced herself to see the events of the past thirty minutes. "The driver was really calm, even when he tied us up."

"And the other man?"

"He was annoyed when he saw us, but . . ." Sienna trailed off.

"What?" Quinn prompted.

"He was fine at first, but then they got all tense." She looked at the police cars barricading the entrance. "I caught a glimpse of emergency lights through the window. It must have been the police showing up that freaked them out."

Quinn spoke into his communications headset. "I think our boys are on foot. Second suspect wearing sunglasses and a blue polo."

Sienna's gaze shifted again to the source of the smoke. For the first time, she realized the fire was originating from a car on the very far corner of the parking lot, near a copse of trees.

How was that possible? The van had been parked near the center of the south side area.

Carina and Reed approached behind her, Carina's hand settling on her arm in a gesture of comfort. Sienna's heart lurched with relief when she saw Craig and Seth both working their way toward the southwest corner of the parking lot. Her hair caught in the breeze, and again, Quinn's eyes sharpened.

"Did you see which way they went?" Quinn asked.

Sienna shook her head.

Carina stepped forward. "I heard them outside the passenger-side door before they walked off."

Quinn eyed the smoke before speaking into his headset again. "Focus the search on the northeast side," he said before adding, "upwind."

* * *

Why hadn't he brought a second vehicle? Abdul thought to himself. Or parked outside the main lot? The answer was simple. The marina was located off a main road, and a car parked anywhere outside the parking lot would have drawn attention.

He briefly considered stealing a boat. His primary concern that they wouldn't clear the kill zone fast enough became a nonissue when he saw the Coast Guard cutters in the marina. Any interference by the Coast Guard or any other craft, for that matter, would ensure they would all die together.

"What now?" Jamal asked, clearly already working through similar thoughts.

Abdul slowed his steps briefly and looked for another vehicle they could use for their escape. The idea that they might die for the cause had been a noble one when they had started this journey, but his instinct to survive now kicked into overdrive. Clearly, he had more to accomplish in his life.

His gaze landed on a large four-story structure with boats stored on each level. A large pickup truck was parked beside it. Barely visible beyond the boat storage, he could see the entrance to a dirt road.

"Over there." Abdul changed direction and picked up speed.

Jamal didn't question his plan until they reached the truck. "How will we get past the cops in time? For all we know, they could be looking for us."

"They're looking for the girls, not us," Abdul countered. He edged around the corner of the building, and a rare smile tugged at his lips. Curving around the back of the boat storage, a dirt road ran down to the edge of the marina and continued along the flat, grassy area near the water. "Besides, I think I found our way out."

* * *

Unspeakable relief flooded through Jane when she saw Reed approaching his car with Sienna and Carina. "Are you all okay?" she asked the moment they were in earshot.

"Unlock the car," Reed said anxiously.

She did so, and immediately, everyone climbed in. Jane took the front seat beside Reed, not worried about keeping up the appearance that Sienna was his girlfriend.

"Did Brent and Craig find the chemical weapon?" Reed asked, sliding the key into the ignition.

"They took it away by helicopter. They're hoping to disarm it at the naval base."

The words were barely out of her mouth when Brent emerged at the edge of the lot, his weapon drawn. He motioned two civilians toward the water before continuing forward.

At the entrance, the police were quickly clearing out their line and assuring the people that the explosion they'd heard was nothing to be concerned about, their focus now on making sure Abdul and Jamal weren't inside of any of the vehicles.

As though staging a battle plan, Craig, Seth, and Quinn moved steadily forward, evenly spread out, their eyes constantly scanning. Reed backed out, but instead of heading toward the exit, he angled toward the marina.

"Where are you going?" Sienna asked.

"There's an access road that runs north along the edge of the marina and goes along the beach. We can use it to get out of here instead of waiting in line with everyone else."

"I didn't see another way out."

"It's on the other side of that." Reed pointed at the boat-storage building a short distance away. "I noticed it when Jane and I first got here."

He pulled around the side of the boat storage and onto the dirt road.

In the distance, Jane noticed a pickup truck half a mile ahead of them on the same path. "Looks like someone else had the same idea." Silence fell over the car, but it wasn't until Sienna spoke that Jane understood why.

"Jane, let me borrow your phone."

Concerned by the urgency in Sienna's voice, Jane quickly handed it over.

A moment later, Sienna's side of the conversation explained the source of her concern. "Craig, there's a truck driving on the access road along the beach. We can't see who it is from here, but . . ." She paused before continuing. "It's the only route not blocked off by the authorities. That's what made me think it might be Abdul and Jamal."

Another pause. "Okay, I'll tell him."

She hung up the phone but didn't give it back to Jane. Instead, she spoke to Reed. "Craig wants us to follow that truck, but he said not to get too close."

"So what does he expect us to do?"

"He said to keep them in our sight without putting ourselves in danger."

Reed glanced at Jane and swallowed hard. Then, as though gathering his resolve, he looked forward and accelerated.

45

CRAIG POCKETED HIS PHONE AND spoke into his headset. "We have a possible sighting. Access road past the boat storage."

Brent responded immediately. "Seth, get your car. You and Craig go to intercept."

"Um, Seth doesn't have a car," Craig said, not sure he wanted to explain why.

"Craig blew it up," Seth said.

"You'll have to explain that one later," Brent muttered. "Craig, meet me at the police barricade. We'll borrow a cruiser."

Craig sprinted forward, arriving at the lot entrance two steps behind Brent.

"We need to borrow one of your cruisers," Brent said.

Craig's mind raced with possible explanations if the policeman balked, but to his relief, the man pulled a set of keys from his pocket and tossed them to Brent. "Car on the right."

"Thanks." Brent bolted toward the driver's side, and Craig climbed in opposite him. An instant later, the engine revved to life, and Brent pulled out with a squeal of tires.

He made a quick U-turn and sped forward. "Can you see him?"

"I see Reed's car." Craig slid forward in his seat, a dust trail barely visible in the distance. "He's a mile up, still on the beach access road."

"Jay, where are you?" Brent asked into his headset.

"Already heading your way," Jay responded, the sound of the boat engine audible in the background. "I have the target sighted."

"How much distance does he have before he reaches the main road?"

"Estimate two miles."

"Can you slow him down?" Brent asked.

"With pleasure."

"Keep in mind we don't know for sure if this is our guy."

"If it isn't, I'll apologize later."

* * *

Gunshots sounded in rapid succession. Reed saw the truck in front of him swerve before he noticed the boat heading toward the beach. It appeared to be some sort of inflatable craft, but it was going as fast as any speed boat he'd ever been in.

"That's the Saint Squad," Sienna said from the back seat.

"Look." Jane pointed to the main road above them. "I see a police car."

Reed glanced to his left and saw the police cruiser speeding past them on the main road. He crested over the top of a small bluff and, for the first time, saw the point where the service road accessed the main road. It didn't take a genius to see that the truck would reach the junction before the cops.

More gunfire punctuated the air.

Any doubt that Abdul and Jamal were in the truck disappeared when an arm holding a pistol emerged from the passenger-side window. More shots fired, this time sparking from both the truck and the boat.

The driver of the pickup slammed on his brakes, and Reed instinctively did the same. Reed's heart jumped into his throat when the vehicle in front of him did a sudden U-turn, fishtailed, and headed straight for them.

Reed glanced to both sides. Dunes on his left, beach on his right. Jane to his right. His heart jumped into his throat, and he did the only thing he could think of. He slammed on the brakes and turned the wheel enough to cause the car to skid sideways, effectively blocking the path.

"Everyone out!" Reed shouted, flinging his door open. He jumped out, waving the three women up the dune as the truck barreled toward them. Half a mile and coming fast.

Sienna led the way, ducking down to use the terrain to shield her. "Take cover!"

Carina scrambled behind her, followed by Jane.

Jane stumbled, and Reed reached out to put his hand on her back to keep her moving forward. The gunfire ceased briefly, the rumble of the truck engine competing with the roar of the surf.

Jane faltered again when she reached the top of the dune. When more gunfire sparked, Reed let her fall and dove for the ground beside her.

* * *

Craig's heart jumped into his throat. He had seen Reed's car spin out before the dunes between the main road and the access road shielded his view. He adjusted his weapon in his hand and unclipped his seat belt as they approached the junction.

As though anticipating his intent, Brent said, "Wait until I make the turn."

An instant later, Brent cranked the wheel and skidded onto the access road. The moment the car straightened out, Craig boosted himself out the window, his legs still inside the car, one hand gripping the roof on the inside and the other hand now aiming at the truck in the distance.

More gunfire sounded, and Craig prayed Sienna and her friends had taken cover. The next few seconds passed in slow motion. The truck's brake lights lit up, and the driver slowed briefly before attempting to avoid the blockade Reed's car created and skidding into another U-turn. The back end of the truck fishtailed, and one of the passenger-side wheels went off the dirt road and caught the sand. The vehicle tipped dangerously to the side, and for a moment, Craig thought it was going to flip over.

Instead, the driver's side wheels popped up off the ground, then came crashing back down, the truck now facing Brent and Craig's vehicle.

As Brent continued to close the distance between them, a hand emerged from the passenger side and more bullets flew, this time aimed at Craig. Three bullets impacted the windshield on the passenger side, the bulletproofing keeping them from penetrating the glass.

Craig returned fire. His first shot caused the shooter to pull his hand out of sight, but the temporary reprieve lasted only seconds.

The man reached his hand out the window again, but he didn't manage to get another shot off before Craig squeezed his trigger.

A cry of pain rang out when Craig's bullet tore through the man's forearm. His weapon fell to the ground, but a second gun appeared, this time out of the driver's side window.

Brent swerved when several bullets hit the center of his side of the windshield. Another burst of gunfire sounded, this time originating from the water's edge. Craig didn't have to look to know his teammates were once again in firing range.

Brent hit a rut in the dirt road, and the car jerked to the right. Craig gripped the inside of the car with his left hand to keep his balance. The moment the car regained its momentum, Craig redirected his gunfire at the driver.

The erratic movements of both cars caused his first bullet to miss wide. The second pierced the truck's windshield, the single hole in the glass corresponding with the driver's forehead.

Immediately, the driver's body slumped in his seat, and the truck careened at an even faster speed toward them. Fifty yards. Twenty-five. Fearing a head-on collision, Craig slid back inside the car and fumbled to put on his seat belt.

Gunfire continued to ring from where Jay and Damian had taken position twenty yards off shore.

"Hold your fire!" Brent shouted into his communications headset. He cranked the wheel, sending them to the right as the truck's passenger reached over and grabbed the wheel. A moment later, the truck barreled up the side of a dune and toppled, rolling to its left. Brent increased speed, barely clearing past it before the truck tumbled back onto the access road.

Craig twisted in his seat to see the other vehicle roll a second time and land upside down.

"That was close," Brent muttered.

Craig didn't comment. His focus was already on the dunes ahead where he had seen Sienna head for cover.

"Do you see anyone?" Brent asked, clearly reading his thoughts.

Suddenly, the ground shook from the impact of an explosion.

Again, Craig looked behind him, but now all he could see were flames shooting into the sky from the pile of twisted metal.

* * *

The impact of the blast sent Reed sliding down the sand, his hand pulling free of Jane's. He struggled to catch his breath. Flames sparked over the top of the dune and spread to the beach grass in front of them. His heart pounded in his chest, and he looked up to see that the force of the explosion had knocked Jane several feet to his left. She lay motionless, the burning grass less than three feet from her. "Jane!" He scrambled closer and kicked sand on the fire threatening her. "Jane!"

He put a hand on her shoulder, jostling her gently.

She moaned and rolled her head, her hand immediately reaching for him.

"Are you okay?" Reed asked.

"Yeah. I think so." She motioned to the main source of smoke. "What happened?"

Reed peered over the edge of the bluff at the four Navy SEALs, their guns drawn. Three surrounded the burning heap of metal, and the fourth sprinted toward the dunes.

"Looks like the SEALs got their guys," Reed said.

"Sienna!" Craig shouted as he closed the distance between them. "Sienna!"

Sienna straightened, relief evident on her face. "Over here."

"Are you all okay?" Craig asked when he reached them.

"I think so," Sienna answered for all of them.

An instant later, Craig scooped her into his arms and held on.

Reed turned to Jane and blinked against the sting of smoke lingering in the air. He squeezed her hand. "Are you sure you're all right?"

Jane drew a ragged breath and nodded. After taking a second breath, this one steadier than the first, she said, "I think I should pick where we go on our next date."

Of all her possible responses, he hadn't expected humor from her. His brow furrowed, and he looked at her with confusion. "What?"

"Every time you pick where we go, something threatens to explode."

Reed didn't want to think about the chemical weapon or the reality that they might still be very much in danger. Instead, he asked, "Did you have something in mind?"

"Someplace with a little less excitement." She appeared to think for a minute. "You did say you like roller coasters, right?"

A grin spread across his face despite the impending danger. "Yes, I did."

46

The relief of finding Sienna unharmed lasted only a moment. Time was running out. If the bomb techs on base didn't succeed, all of them would be dead if they didn't clear out of the area.

He glanced at his watch. Three minutes and counting. "We need to get out of here."

Craig grabbed Sienna's hand and led her down the dune, grateful when she broke into a jog beside him.

He looked at their transportation options. The boat Jay and Damian arrived in was beached a few hundred yards away. Brent motioned with his arm. "Everyone in the cruiser!"

Brent arrived at the vehicle first and jumped into the driver's seat. With only four other seats available and seven people still racing forward, Brent barked out orders. "Jay and Carina, take the front seat. Everyone else, pile in the back."

Craig reached the car, jumped in the rear passenger seat, and pulled Sienna onto his lap.

Clearly understanding his urgency, Sienna closed the door for him as Reed and Jane climbed in on the other side, Damian right behind them.

Rather than wait for Jane to scoot onto Reed's lap to make room for him, Damian put one foot in the car, grabbed onto the top of the door frame, and banged on the top to signal Brent.

Instantly, Brent hit the accelerator.

As soon as Jane made room for him, Craig shouted. "Damian, you're clear."

Damian swung himself inside and pulled the door closed in one fluid motion, dust from the road spilling in with him, along with lingering smoke.

Behind them, the pickup truck continued to burn, flames still licking up the residual fuel.

"How much time?" Craig asked, tapping on the front of his seat.

Jay craned his head to see past Carina to the clock on the dashboard. "Two minutes, ten seconds."

Silence fell over the car. They were at least ten miles from the safe zone. Despite all their efforts, they had run out of time.

Brent's cell phone rang, but he didn't answer. A moment later, Craig's phone sounded. He fished it out of his pocket. "Simmons."

"Craig, it's Tristan."

"Status?"

"We're safe," Tristan said, giving the most important information first. "The techs secured the bomb in time, and the toxins have been contained."

The sigh of relief was instant. "Thanks, Tristan. I'll let everyone know." Craig ended the call and shared the good news.

Brent's shoulders visibly relaxed. "Call in emergency services to deal with the truck fire."

"I will."

Brent turned the car onto the main road and headed back toward the marina. He glanced in the rearview mirror. "Now, who's going to tell me what happened to Seth's car?"

Craig and Sienna exchanged glances before Craig said, "Sir, I'm not sure you want to know."

* * *

Jane's body continued to tremble as Reed led her into his house, Craig and Sienna following behind them. One of the local police officers had driven them home because of the damage the truck fire had caused to Reed's car. The police had also confirmed that the two men chasing them were both dead. It was really over.

"I know you probably don't want to hear this," Craig said as soon as he closed the front door, "but you may be better off getting a new car instead of fixing yours."

"I don't think I want the insurance company to agree with you." Reed led the way into the living room. "I'm still attached to that car. I've had it since college."

Jane collapsed onto the couch and settled against Reed as soon as he took the seat beside her. "Exactly how are you going to explain the damage?" she asked. "Do insurance companies even cover things like this?"

"Good question."

"Hey, your conversation with the insurance company won't be nearly as bad as Seth's." Craig and Sienna sat on the couch opposite them, and Jane noticed the grimace on Craig's face.

"What did happen to Seth's car?" Jane asked.

"Craig put a bomb in it," Sienna said.

"Wait, what?" Jane stared at Craig in disbelief. "You blew up Seth's car on purpose?"

"We had to blow something up . . ."

"I know I'm new to all this military strategy stuff," Jane said, "but why would you do that?"

"If we had simply disarmed the bomb in the van, Abdul and Jamal would have known Sienna and Carina were safe," Craig explained.

"So you blew up Seth's car," Jane said.

"Seth's car was the only one we could move away from all the others to make sure we wouldn't cause a chain reaction." Craig shrugged. "He's been talking about getting a new one."

"I've thought about getting a new car eventually too, but that doesn't mean I plan to blow the old one up," Jane said.

"I'll remember that if your car is around when we're in the middle of a terrorist attack," Craig said.

"That's a comfort," Jane said dryly. Another tremor worked through her. She held out one hand and watched it tremble. "I'm still shaking."

"You're not the only one." Sienna looked up at Craig. "Is this really over now?"

"I think so," Craig said, linking his fingers with Sienna's.

"As in, over and I can move back home?"

"I'd like to wait another week to be safe. I thought I could go stay at your place with one of the new guys to make sure we don't see any sign of trouble," Craig said. "If all is quiet, we'll move you back in next weekend."

"Reed, looks like you're stuck with us for a few more days," Sienna said.

His arm tightened around Jane's shoulders. "I think I can live with that."

47

Thanksgiving weekend couldn't have gone better, in Reed's opinion. A day at Disneyland with Jane. Thanksgiving dinner with their combined families. A holiday concert for Sienna's sister, Kendra, on Saturday night. Public moments, quiet moments. All experienced without the worry of someone trying to blow something up or unleash chemical weapons. Thank goodness, that was behind them.

With Sienna and Craig's wedding next month, Reed and Jane had decided to keep their relationship out of the public eye for a while longer. Not that Reed was in any hurry for the paparazzi to home in on Jane and the importance she held in his life.

Sienna had been right about the media. Almost from the moment the promo ads had started, Reed's name had begun popping up on a variety of search engines. Articles and photos, both of him alone and with Sienna, became hourly events. To everyone's delight, Sienna had also been right about *Beachfront*. Their show was a hit, and all indications were that it would run for many seasons to come.

Not shaving for a few days had allowed Reed to blend in during his long weekend in California, but he had rid himself of the four-day beard as soon as he'd returned home. Tonight, he didn't have to worry about running into anyone except the woman he hoped would agree to be by his side for the rest of his life . . . and eternity.

He glanced at his watch, his stomach jumping in anticipation. In his mind, he had gone through so many ways to set the stage, but every elaborate scheme felt wrong. Instead, he had found himself focusing on the memory of the nice dinner she had made for him several months ago. Tonight, they wouldn't have his favorite meal but rather the apricot-glazed salmon Jane's mother had assured him was her favorite.

A cream tablecloth covered the kitchen table, and he had bought two place settings of china for the occasion. The bread basket rested between two taper candles, and sparkling apple cider chilled in a silver ice bucket.

Reed reached into his pocket and fingered the ring box. His heartbeat quickened at the thought of what he had planned. Would Jane think he was rushing things? After all, they had been together only four months. But the days on the calendar didn't seem to matter that much after all they had been through.

The threats against her and Sienna, the weeks living under the same roof, the loneliness that had followed when she'd moved back to her apartment. He hadn't realized how much he had come to rely on sitting with her each night, sharing everything about their day. When the Saint Squad had deemed it truly safe for her, Sienna, and George to return home, Reed had enjoyed the quiet for the first day. As soon as the sun had gone down, though, he hadn't been able to resist calling Jane on the phone and talking well into the night.

The doorbell rang, and his stomach lurched. Taking a steadying breath, he crossed to the front door and opened it. Jane stood on the other side of the threshold.

"Hey there." Jane waited until she had walked inside and the door closed behind her before leaning in to give him a kiss in greeting. "Did you get some sleep last night?"

"Not much," Reed admitted.

She shrugged out of her coat and hung it in the coat closet by the door. "How come?"

Not ready to confess the source of his nerves, he avoided the question. "Dinner is almost ready."

"Something smells amazing." She continued into the kitchen. When she saw the elegant table, she turned to him. "Wow. What's the occasion?"

"You are."

Her eyebrows drew together. "What?"

So many words whirled inside him, and Reed fought back the worst of his nerves. "You fixed a nice dinner for me when we first started dating. I thought it was time for me to repay the favor."

"That's very sweet, but you didn't have to—"

Reed took her hand in his. "I wanted to."

Her lips curved, and she leaned forward for another kiss. "This is wonderful. Thank you."

"You're welcome." A timer buzzed, and Reed moved to turn the stove off and slide the rice off the burner.

Jane leaned against the counter across from him. "You really picked a great house," she said, "and I think this is my favorite room."

"Really? Why is that?"

"Because this is where we were standing the first time you told me you loved me."

The nerves inside him exploded, a warmth spreading from his center into every ounce of his being. He reached for her hand, and his lips found hers. The depth of his feelings poured into the kiss and left him wanting more. As they had when he'd first professed his love, the words tumbled out before he could stop them. "Marry me."

Her head jerked up, her eyes meeting his with a combination of shock and wonder reflected in the deep green. "What?"

Reed drew a deep breath. His hand disappeared into his pocket to retrieve the ring. "I love you, Jane." With his eyes on hers, he lowered to one knee and forced the words out. "Will you marry me?"

A gasp escaped her, and her free hand lifted to cover her mouth. A tear spilled over as she nodded. "Yes." The moment he straightened, she pressed her lips to his. "Yes, I'll marry you."

Reed drew her close, breathing in a sigh of relief and the scent of her, that unique combination of the ocean and vanilla. Drawing the ring out, he took her hand in his. "I hope you like the ring. If you don't, we can exchange it."

She stared at the teardrop diamond. "It's beautiful." He slid it onto her left hand, and her eyes lifted to meet his. "It's exactly what I would have chosen for myself."

"I may have enlisted my sister's help in picking it out," Reed said, amazed by the satisfaction he experienced from seeing the piece of jewelry in place.

"You both have good taste."

"I'm glad you think so." He linked his fingers around her waist, and his eyes sparked with amusement.

"I do have one question though," Jane said.

"What's that?"

"How am I going to explain this to the people we work with?" Jane asked. "We go back to work on Tuesday."

"Actually, I was meaning to talk to you about that," Reed said. "Sienna and I may need you to help set up a press release to announce our breakup in another week or two."

"Have you decided what you want me to use as the reason?"

"You can tell everyone I broke up with her because she smashed my sand castle."

Jane's laughter rang out. "I'm not sure your adoring public is going to believe that."

"It doesn't matter what they believe," Reed said. "All that matters is that my future is built with you."

"I love you, Reed." She pressed another kiss to his lips. "Welcome to our future."

ABOUT THE AUTHOR

TRACI HUNTER ABRAMSON WAS BORN in Arizona, where she lived until moving to Venezuela for a study-abroad program. After graduating from Brigham Young University, she worked for the Central Intelligence Agency for several years, eventually resigning in order to raise her family. She credits the CIA with giving her a wealth of ideas as well as the skills needed to survive her children's teenage years. She has gone on to write more than twenty best-selling novels that have consistently been nominated as Whitney Award finalists, and she is a three-time Whitney Award winner. When she's not writing, Traci enjoys spending time with her husband and five children, preferably on a nice, quiet beach somewhere. She also enjoys sports, travel, writing, and coaching high school swimming.